Quarantine

Quarantine

Jim Crace

ISIS
LARGE PRINT
Oxford and Orlando

First published in Great Britain 1997
by Viking

Published in Large Print 2000 by ISIS Publishing Ltd,
7 Centremead, Osney Mead, Oxford OX2 0ES, and
ISIS Publishing, PO Box 195758,
Winter Springs, Florida 32719-5758, USA
by arrangement with Penguin Books Ltd

British Library Cataloguing in Publication Data
Crace, Jim, 1946 –
    Quarantine. – Large print ed.
    1. Jesus Christ – Temptation – Fiction 2. Large type books
    I. Title
    823.9'14[F]

ISBN 0-7531-6139-7 (hb)
ISBN 0-7531-6198-2 (pb)

Printed and bound by TJI Digital, Padstow, Cornwall

An ordinary man of average weight and fitness embarking on a total fast — that is, a fast during which he refuses both his food and drink — could not expect to live for more than thirty days, nor to be conscious for more than twenty-five. For him, the forty days of fasting described in religious texts would not be achievable — except with divine help of course. History, however, does not record an intervention of that kind, and medicine opposes it.

Ellis Winward and Professor Michael Soule,
The Limits of Mortality, Ecco Press,
New Jersey (1993)

CHAPTER
ONE

Miri's husband was shouting in his sleep, not words that she could recognize but simple, blurting fanfares of distress. When, at last, she lit a lamp to discover what was tormenting him, she saw his tongue was black — scorched and sooty. Miri smelled the devil's eggy dinner roasting on his breath; she heard the snapping of the devil's kindling in his cough. She put her hand on to his chest; it was soft, damp and hot, like fresh bread. Her husband, Musa, was being baked alive. Good news.

Miri was as dutiful as she could be. She sat cross-legged inside their tent with Musa's neck resting on the pillow of her swollen ankles, his head pushed up against the new distension of her stomach, and tried to lure the fever out with incense and songs. He received the treatment that she — five months pregnant, and in some discomfort — deserved for herself. She wiped her husband's forehead with a dampened cloth. She rubbed his eyelids and his lips with honey water. She kept the flies away. She sang her litanies all night. But the fever was deaf. Or, perhaps, its hearing was so sharp that it had eavesdropped on Miri's deepest prayers and knew that Musa's death would not be unbearable. His death would rescue her.

1

In the morning Musa was as numb and dry as leather, but — cussed to the last — was gripping thinly on to life. His family and the other, older men from the caravan came in to kiss his forehead and mumble their regrets that they had not treated him with greater patience while he was healthy. When they had smelled and tasted the sourness of his skin and seen the ashy blackness of his mouth, they shook their heads and dabbed their eyes and calculated the extra profits they would make from selling Musa's merchandise on the sly. Musa was paying a heavy price, his uncles said, for sleeping on his back without a cloth across his face. An idiotic way to die. A devil had slipped into his open mouth at night and built a fire beneath the rafters of his ribs. Devils were like anybody else; they had to find what warmth they could or perish in the desert cold. Now Musa had provided lodging for the devil's fever. He wouldn't last more than a day or two — if he did, then it would be a miracle. And not a welcome one.

It was Miri's duty to Musa, everybody said, to let the caravan go on through Jerico towards the markets of the north without her. It couldn't travel with fever in its cargo. It couldn't wait while Musa died. Nor could it spare the forty days of mourning which would follow. That would be madness. Musa himself wouldn't expect such waste. He had been a merchant too, and would agree, if only he were conscious, God forbid, that business should not wait for funerals. Or pregnancies. Fortunes would be lost if merchants could not hurry on. Besides, the camels wouldn't last. They needed grazing and watering, and there was no standing water in this wilderness and hardly any hope of rain. No, it was a crippling sadness for them too, make no mistake, the uncles said, but Miri had to stay behind, continue with her singing till the end, and bury Musa on her own.

She'd have to put up stones to mark her husband's passing and tend his grave until the caravan returned for her. She would be safe and comfortable if she took care. There was sufficient water in skins for a week or so, and then she could locate a cistern of some kind; there were also figs and olives and some grain, some salted meat and other food, plus the tent, the family possessions, small amounts of different wools, a knife, some perfume and a little gold. She'd have company as well. They'd leave six goats for her, plus a halting donkey which was too slow and useless for the caravan. Two donkeys then. Both lame, she said, nodding at her husband.

Nobody laughed at Miri's indiscretions. It did not seem appropriate to laugh when there was fever in the tent, though leaving Musa behind, half dead, was a satisfying prospect for everyone. With luck, they said, Musa would only have to endure his suffering for a day or two more. And then? And then, when Miri had done her duty to her husband, they suggested, there would be habitations in the valley where she could, perhaps, seek refuge. She might find a buyer for the gold; take care, they warned, for gold can bring bad luck as well. Or she might employ the goats to buy herself a place to stay for her confinement — until the caravan had a chance to come for her and any child, if it survived. Eventually, she'd have the profits from her husband's merchandise which they would trade on her behalf, the sacks of

3

decorated copperware from Edom, his beloved bolts of woven cloth, his coloured wools. She smiled at that and shook her head and asked if they imagined that she was a halting donkey too. No, no, they said; why couldn't she have more faith in their honesty? Of course there would be profits from the sale. They would not want to say how much. But she might be rich enough to get another husband. A better one than Musa anyhow, they thought. A smaller one. An older one. One that didn't lie or use his fists so frequently, or shout and weep and laugh so much. One who didn't get so drunk, perhaps, then sit up half the night throwing pebbles at the camels and his neighbours' tents, pelting goats' dung at the moon. One that didn't stink so badly as he died.

They promised they would return by the following spring, one year at the latest. But Miri understood there'd be no spring to bring them back, no matter where they went. They'd make certain that their winters didn't end. Why would they come so far to reclaim the widow and the orphan of a man who'd been so troublesome and unpredictable? Besides, they wouldn't want to lose the profits they had made. Not after they had held them for a year. No, Miri was not worth the trip. That was the plain, commercial truth.

So Miri let them go. She spat into the dust as they set off along the crumbling cliff-tops to the landslip where they could begin their descent. Spitting brought good luck for traders. Deals were struck with a drop of spit on a coin or in the palm of the hand or sometimes even on the goods to be exchanged. Spit does better business than a sneeze, they said. So, if anyone had dared to look

4

at Miri, they could have taken her spitting to be a blessing for their journey. But no one dared. They must have known that she did not wish them well. They'd given her the chance to change her life, perhaps. But inadvertently. No, Miri despised them for their haste and cowardice. Her spitting was a prayer that they would lame themselves, or lose their cargoes in the Jordan, or have their throats sliced open by thieves, their eyes pecked out by birds. She felt elated, once the uncles and their animals had gone. Then she was depressed and terrified. And then entirely calm, despite the isolation of their tent and the nearness of her husband's death. She would not concern herself with the practicalities of life. Not yet. Women managed with much less. For the moment she could only concentrate on all the liberties of widowhood — and motherhood — which would be hers as soon as he was dead.

CHAPTER
TWO

It was midday, and Miri opened up the outer awnings of the tent so that she could both clear the air of death's bad breath and inspect the landscape for signs of life. Did she expect the caravan, already troubled by its conscience, to turn around for her? Or was she simply fearful of the leopards, wolves and snakes which were at home amongst these hills? She sat cross-legged in bands of sunlight, next to her husband's wrapped body, her hand resting almost tenderly on his ankles. He had a fading pulse. And he was all but silent now. A whistling throat, that's all. He'd lost the strength to shout. And he was cold. So was the inside of the tent.

Miri stared into the distant tans and greys of Judea, trying to remember what she was required to do for him, what prayers, what body herbs, what disposition of the limbs. She'd done her duty in the night and tried to lure the devil out. But that had failed. Her husband's body was a labyrinthine hiding place, so full of caves and chambers that many devils could make homes inside. What was her duty to him now? To call on all the gods by name and ask for mercy for this man? To combat his illness, like the perfect, patient wife, with oils and salves and kisses? To find a stone and drop it on his skull? No, nothing that she did would make a difference. That was the truth, bleak and comforting. Her husband was unconscious and about to die, and she should leave him to it. Let the devil do its work behind her back.

Anyway, this vigil was exhausting her. She could not sit a single moment more. Her child was strong and vigorous; it had pressed its arms and legs against her hips so unremittingly that within the past few months her pelvic bones had widened and the nerves were trapped. Her buttocks and her thighs were torments. She felt she had to move out of the tent or turn to stone. This was the remedy. She would simply walk away — if, first, she could defy the pain and stand up — and return that afternoon to a corpse. It might be cowardly to leave a man to die alone, but there was no one there to block her path. No one conscious anyway. Musa couldn't use his knuckles or his fingers or his heels against her now. He couldn't pull her hair to make her stay. She laid the dampened cloth across his mouth — to keep the devils in, perhaps? — loosely tethered the ailing donkey, and staked the one billy amongst the female goats. Then, turning her back against the flaking crown of the cliffs, she went off across the level scrub towards the valleys and low hills in search of well-drained ground and her husband's undug grave.

It would be hard, she knew, to bury Musa. Hard on the heart, but harder on the fingers. For he was large. She would have to take great care when lifting heavy rocks or tearing at the ground. There were pans of soft clay along the valley beds where anyone — a child even; a child would not resist the opportunity to make its mark in clay — could crack a hole in the earth simply by stamping. But the higher ground where Musa's body would be safe from floods was biscuity like ash-fired pot. Underneath the biscuit there were stones.

Miri hunted for a burial place with views across the salty valley. It was not long before she'd found the perfect spot, an open scarp, backed by low, coppery cliffs, pock-marked by many caves and — it was spring — discoloured by the opposing red of scrub poppies. The world from there would seem large and borderless, she thought, and that would be appropriate for a traveller like Musa whose excursions had been ceaseless while he lived and who would soon find that death was large and borderless as well.

It was a tender day for widowhood, warm and clear and breathless. There in the sinking distance, two days' walk away at most, was the heavy sea below Jericho, and then the cliffs of sodium and brine, the careworn hills, the bluing heights of Moab, and finally (because she could not think that there was any heaven in this place) the rifting, hard-faced sky. It was clouded only by the arrowed streamers of the spring birds, heading for the Danube from the Nile.

What better place to pass eternity?

But for the living Miri it was hard. She felt large and borderless herself. So far her marriage — a few months old, and to a younger, tougher man — was inflexible and empty, a fired pot, a biscuit underlain with stones. At least, she thought, she could be more eager and more dutiful with her husband's dead body than she had been with his living one. She'd bury him with care, as deep as possible. She wouldn't let him face into the view, throughout eternity, across to Moab and beyond. She'd bury him face down, as was the custom for a man who had no heirs (not yet, at least), so that he'd copulate for ever with the earth and all his sons and daughters would be soil.

She put her fingers on the ground, pulled loose the first of many hundred stones, and tried to open up a grave.

CHAPTER
THREE

The salty scrubland was a lazy and malicious host. Even lizards lifted their legs for fear of touching it too firmly. Why should it, then, disturb itself for human travellers — a pregnant woman and the almost lifeless body of a man — no matter if they were abandoned in the furthest of the hills beyond Jerusalem and with none to turn to for some help and salutation except the land itself? It would not, normally at least, have expended its hospitality on them. It was undiscriminating in its cruelties. The scrub, at best, allowed its brief and passing guests to stub their toes on stones or snag their arms and legs on thorns. It sent these travellers to Jericho in rags. Or it lamed their animals. Or, should they spend the night with this hard scrubland as their inn, it let its snakes and scorpions take refuge underneath the covers of their beds.

Yet the scrubland welcomed Miri there, to its dead hills. It gave its hospitality to her. And should she end up on her own, she need not have much cause to fear the night, or hunger, or the animals. It would use what little skills it had to make her life more comfortable, to keep her bedding free from scorpions, her skin unsnagged by thorns, her sleep unbroken. And if it could, it would direct some rainfall to her tent or save her billy from a fall or drive gazelles towards her traps. It would be the one — hooded in a brown mantle — whose breathing twinned with hers. It would be the one, mistaken for a thorn bush or a breeze, that rustled at her side. It would be her shoulder-blades, and then the one that brushed the sand-flies from her lips and eyes. It was bewitched by her already, if that is possible, if the land can be allowed a heart. The stone had stubbed itself upon the toe. The earth was showing kindness to the flesh. It let her pull its stones quite readily out of the ground, so that her husband's grave grew waist-deep without exhausting her and causing any strains. She only broke her nails, though there were some cuts and bruises on her knees. The torment of her buttocks and her thighs was even eased a little by the exercise.

So this is happiness, she thought. Or this, at least, is what adds up to happiness. Here was the mix that she'd been praying for. There's hardship and bad luck in happiness, for sure. There's broken nails. There's blood. There's solitude. But there was the prospect, too, with Musa dead, of sleeping peacefully without his bruising fingers in her flesh, of never running after men and camels any more, of being Miri without shame or hesitation, of letting drop her headscarf for a change and loosening her hair from its tight knots so that nothing intervened between her and the sky.

Indeed, her headscarf was pulled off. Her coils of hair were left to drop and unravel on their own. She then lay back beside her husband's grave, put her uncovered head on stones and, open-eyed, the sky her comfort sheet, she almost slept. She was exhausted and invincible. Her pregnancy had made her so; exhausted by the digging and the dying; invincible because that pulsing in her womb was doughty, irresistible. What greater triumph could there be than that — to cultivate a second, tiny heart?

She had been told, when she was small, that the sky was a hard dish. She might bruise her fists on it if only she could fly. It was a gently rounded dish, blue when not obscured by clouds or night or shuddered into pinks and greys and whites by the caprices of the sun. But now she raised her hands into the unresisting air above the open grave and wondered if the dish were soft. And she could fly right through it, only slowed and coddled by its softness, like passing through the heavy, goaty curtains of her tent, like squeezing through the tough and cushioned alleys of the flesh, to take a place in heaven if she wanted, or to find that place on earth where she'd be undisturbed.

CHAPTER
FOUR

She'd not be undisturbed for long. It was the first new moon of spring that night, and there were travellers — already heading from the towns and villages, already passing through Muntar, Qumran, and Marsaba — who had some weeks of business in the wilderness. They came to live like hermit bats, the proverbs said, for forty days, a quarantine of daylight fasting, solitude and prayer, in caves. Could hermit bats be said to pray? Certainly they were so pious that rather than avert their eyes from heaven they passed their hours looking upwards, hanging by their toes. Their ceiling was the floor. Their fingered wings were folded like the vestments of a priest. Discomfort was their article of faith. And hermit bats — perhaps this is what the proverbs had in mind — possessed no vanity. No need for colours or display. There was no vanity in caves.

The caves near Musa's grave, for all their remoteness, were known to be hospitable, much prized by those who sought the comfort of dry, soft floors while they were suffering, much prized by desert leopards, too. Inside were the black remains of fires and, on the walls, the charcoal marks where visitors had counted off their quarantines in blocks of ten.

There were other caves in Miri's wilderness as well, less prized, in the sheer and crumbling precipice below the tent, which only goats and lunatics could reach and in which only goats and lunatics — and bats — would choose to pass a night — though at this time of year it might seem that lunatics were just as numerous as goats. This was the season of the lunatics: the first new moon of spring was summoning those men — for lunatics are mostly men. They have the time and opportunity — to exorcize that part of them which sent them mad. Mad with grief, that is. Or shame. Or love. Or illnesses and visions. Mad enough to think that everything they did, no matter how vain or trivial, was of interest to their god. Mad enough to think that forty days of discomfort could put their world in order.

Not all the cavers were insane. That spring there had been fever in Jerusalem and many deaths. Musa wasn't the only one to leave his mouth unguarded. Most of the travellers heading eastwards for the solace of the hills were the newly bereaved who wished to contemplate the memory of a mother or a son in privacy, and for whom the forty days were not remedies but requiems. There was a group of nine or ten of these — all Jews — who, for a modest rent paid to the shepherd, had taken up their grieving residence in natural caves above a stream on the trading route just south of Almog, where their deprivations would be slight. There were produce markets at the waterhead, an undemanding walk away, where they could eat once the daylight fast had ended and take their ritual baths, and the caves were relatively warm. Bereavement's punishment enough, they thought.

Why starve? Why freeze at night? Why hide away? How would that help the dead, or bring them back?

There was another group of twenty-four — all men, and zealots, pursuing the instructions of Isaiah, "Prepare straight to the wilderness a highway for our god" — who were keeping to the Dead Sea valley, looking for the Essene settlements. They'd spend their forty days in artificial, dug-out caves, waiting for the world to end (Please God the world won't end in forty days and *one* . . .) and sharing their possessions and their prayers, with only the palm trees their companions.

But those who made it to the perching valley where Miri — half open-eyed — was sleeping, and where Musa and the fever devil were bargaining the final hours of his life, sought something more remote and testing than requiems and communal prayers. There were five of them — not in a group, but strung out along the road where earlier that morning the caravan of uncles had passed by. Three men, a woman and, too far behind for anyone to guess its gender, a fifth. And this fifth one was bare-footed, and without a staff. No water-skin, or bag of clothes. No food. A slow, painstaking figure, made thin and watery by the rising, mirage heat, as if someone had thrown a stone into the pool of air through which it walked and ripples had diluted it.

The first four — their problems? Madness, madness, cancer, infertility — had started their journeys that morning from the same settlement in the valley. Though they had observed the proprieties of pilgrimage by keeping some distance apart, they had at least endeavoured to keep each other within sight and hearing.

15

There were robbers in the hills, army deserters, lepers, devils, animals, avalanches of dry scree, and a threatening conspiracy of rocks, wind and heat which made the landscape treacherous and unpredictable. It was a comfort to have some help close by. By the time they'd clambered up the shifting landfall to the plateau at the top of the precipice and were walking through the flatter scrub towards the tent, they had become separated by only a few hundred paces. They were more hesitant and slow. Exhausted, obviously; but also uncertain of the way, uncertain even if this quarantine were wise. They were searching for the wayside marks, carved in the largest rocks by some holy traveller years before and now much eroded, which indicated where the caves were found. The marks directed them towards the higher ground. They had to leave the camel tracks and the cliff-top path before they reached or even saw the tent, with its abandoned invalid. They walked along the flood-beds of the little valley, and none of them could miss the opportunity to make their own marks by stamping on the soft clay before they headed for the scarp and for the dry and warmer caves behind the poppies and the grave. So Miri woke, startled by sudden noises. The first of the temporary hermits was scrambling through the loose stones of the scarp to choose his place to sleep. Miri could not see who had disturbed her, but she recognized the sound of human feet, slipping in the scree. She could hear others approaching from below.

Miri curled into a ball, a porcupine without the quills. She was no longer undisturbed. Whose unsteady feet were these? She wished that she could disappear into the ground. That was possible. There was an open and inviting grave for her, within arm's reach. She only had to roll the once. A few stones clattered into the grave with her, but they were not noticed. Four pairs of climbing feet were making greater noises of their own and, anyway, no wild land is ever entirely still and silent. It has its discords and its detonations. Earth collapses with the engineering of the ants; lizards smack the pebbles with their tails; the sun fires seeds in salvos from their pods; pigeons misconnect with dry branches; and stones, left loosely to their own devices, can find the muscle to descend the hill. So Miri settled in to Musa's grave and, for the moment, was not seen or heard.

She had been dreaming about her child, of course. The usual mix: anxiety and joy. Her sleep had shut her husband out. But, in those alarming moments when she woke, became a porcupine, became percussion in the scrub, became the first trembling resident of her husband's grave, she had convinced herself that it was Musa who'd woken her. Who else? He had disturbed her sleep so many times before. So it had been his stiff and bloodless feet which sent the small stones tumbling. He'd died, alone, with no one there to mediate. That was the fate that's worse than death. Now he'd come to find his wife. She wasn't hard to find. There was the recent kicked-up trail which led out from the tent across the flat scrub, into the valley, up to the scarp. There was the abattoir of stones, clawed out for him. There was her mocking headscarf, thrown off, snagged on a thorn, and left to flag him to her. There was the grave, and Miri crouching in it, hardly hidden, the tiny sobbing woman in the fat man's hole. How could he miss her? And, then, how could he let her go unpunished? Musa was no mystery to her. He'd use his fists and feet. He'd pick up rocks and earth to finish her. The living would be buried by the dead. That's what the prophets said. The world would end that way.

But minutes passed. There were no rocks. She was not stifled by his body pressing down on hers. Finally she found the courage to crouch in the corner of the grave and peer out, a rodent peeping from its burrow. Of course she did not recognize the people that she saw, but neither was she frightened of them now. They were, at least, the living. No Musa then. Not even death and its three partisans. She was exposed to nothing worse than strangers.

Miri felt too foolish and too shaken to emerge. Just like a child, trapped underneath the mat when adults come. She would simply have to wait for a natural opportunity to escape. Sunset, perhaps. By sunset, surely, Musa would be safe and cold, and she could slip away unseen and go back to the tent. She'd ululate for him. That — precisely — was the least that she could do. In the morning she would get him on the donkey's back — impossible without some help — and bury him. Here were the stones — where she now crouched, a hen on barren eggs — that would be Musa's bed-mates. There wasn't one she hadn't touched while she was digging. What other widow could make such a boast, or know her husband's grave more intimately? How very dutiful she'd been.

For the moment, Miri had little else to do but study stones and, once in a while, when she grew too stiff for her interment, pop her head above the topsoil and watch these new arrivals select their caves, as far from each other as was possible, though close enough for safety in the night. They were like ravens, not like rooks — neither sociable nor hostile with their neighbours. She watched them set up home, one by one, throughout the afternoon. They kicked out the detritus of animals and other visitors, turned stones to check for snakes and scorpions, pulled thorns across the cave entrances to blunt the wind and keep animals out, threw bones as far away as possible. Then they sat in front of their new habitations, looking out across the valleys and waiting for the darkness and, at last, the arced and glinting goblet of the moon. The start of quarantine.

Of course, for all their birdlike meditation and reserve, they could not help but notice Miri watching them. They were so concentrated on the land which would be their host for the next forty days, and so fearful of it, that hardly a beetle could move without them knowing it. How then could they avoid seeing the newly exposed grave and its occupant, both gaping? But none of them behaved as if it were odd, or even unexpected, that there should be a woman who, seemingly, had dug a pit for herself and was content to squat in it all afternoon. This was the season of the lunatics. If her presence made them fearful and uncomfortable, then so what? That's what they'd come for, after all, to encounter and survive anxieties like this.

Miri wished she had the nerve to stand, waist-high in stones and soil, and call to them. She was a rook. She needed company. She'd ask them what their purpose was, what they were seeking in the caves. She'd ask if they might — later, soon — help to lift her husband on the donkey's back and bring his body here for its interment. She could not manage it alone, she'd say, and tell them she was abandoned, widowed, pregnant, borderless . . . and desperate to urinate. Her child was pressing on her bladder now. Her back and thighs were tormenting her again. But Miri was uncertain of the visitors, their sullenness, their lack of smiles, the absence of any conversation or greetings between them. She was afraid that they might ask, Where is your husband now? Then, Why aren't you sitting by the corpse? Or, Have you run away and left the man to die? So Miri dared not leave her hiding place. Nor dared she urinate. It would be a sacrilege, and dangerous. To wet a husband's grave like that would bring bad lack. So she squatted amongst the stones, her bladder nagging, her nerve-ends trapped, her conscience throbbing like a wound, her untied hair turned brown with dust, and waited for the sun to drop.

CHAPTER
FIVE

There were eleven caves above the poppy line — a decent choice for these four visitors. Enough room even for the fifth when he or she arrived. The caves were not hard to see. Their darkly shadowed entrances made a constellation of black stars against the copper of the cliff. There were two easily accessible caves at the cliff foot, partly obscured by salt bushes and fallen debris, and then a further four above, opening on to a sloping terrace. Higher still, and less inviting, were three more caves, set far apart. And then, a hundred paces to the left, a further two, halfway up a seam of darker, stony soil.

The first of the cave-dwellers to arrive and startle Miri had been the oddest of them all. Was that the word? Not odd, perhaps, but out of place. He was a gentile, blond-haired and narrow-faced; quite beautiful, she thought. And a touch sinister. A Roman or a Greek perhaps, a traveller. But there was nothing Greek or Roman in his quality of clothes. He wore a local tunic and a high, woven cap which made his face seem even thinner than it was. His skin was dry from too much sun. But he seemed strong, like leather thongs are strong. Designed to carry loads. And he was heavily and well equipped — a large goatskin for water, a rush bed-mat, a cloak, a walking staff made from an elongated piece of tarbony with ram-horn curls halfway along its length so that when he rested on its nub his weight had to drop and spiral twice before it reached the ground. He'd taken the smallest and the warmest of the middle rank of caves.

The second chose the middle rank as well; his cave was twenty paces from the Roman or the Greek, the furthest to the right, and in a shallow declivity of the terrace which would protect the entrance from his neighbour's gaze, and from the evening sun. He was an elderly Jew, wearing a felt skull-cap; yellow-eyed and yellow-skinned, frail and timid beyond his years, short-sighted, tired, running short of time. He busied himself, peering nervously amongst the stones and scree, collecting thorn roots and branches for a fire, and carrying small rocks for his hearth. He talked out loud to no one in particular. Himself? The lizards? Not prayers or incantations as you might expect. But remarks on everything he saw and found. A good supply of wood and that's a blessing . . . We'll live like kings, old friend . . .

The third was — surprisingly — a female Jew of Miri's own age, though tall and stout and obviously not used to walking. And obviously not used to cleaning out a cave. She could not bear to touch the bones and carrion inside. She couldn't make a decent broom from any of the bushes. She'd chosen her shelter badly, too — one of the two caves on the lower level of the scarp, the first she'd found, easy to reach, but hard to protect. The bushes at the front would encourage flies, and worse. The entrance was a little higher than the chamber itself.

It wasn't likely there'd be rain — but if there were she'd have to sleep in it.

The fourth? A badu villager from the deserts in the south, with silver bracelets and a hennaed beard and hair. He was more familiar. The caravan had often traded with such men; some silver for a dozen goats, some perfume for a roll of cloth, a tub of dates for unimpeded passage through their land. They'd sell their children too, it was said. And their wives. He stood outside his cave, one of the two set at a distance from the others in the darker seam of rock. He pulled and twisted his hair, so tightly that the skin on his skull came up in peaks, and stared at Miri. Finally she had to reach for her discarded headscarf, cover up her hair, and duck into her grave. Why such a man would choose a cave and not a tent was inexplicable. The badus only went into caves to die, and this man — small and unrelenting — seemed too wild to die.

Miri watched the four of them until she and her bladder were set free by darkness. She did not see the fifth.

CHAPTER
SIX

The fifth, a male, was far younger than he might have seemed from a distance. Not much more than an adolescent, then. Bare feet make old men of us all, on stony paths at least. But even when he reached the softer and more accommodating track above the landfall, he walked not from the shoulders like a seasoned traveller intent on vanquishing the rocks and rises in his path, but cat-like from the hips, his toes extended, pointing forwards, and put down with caution before his heels were committed to the ground. He'd learnt the single lesson of the thorn. His feet were already torn and bruised. So: long legs, long neck, long hands, short leopard steps. And like a leopard he paused frequently, not to rest but to sniff the air as if he could locate — beyond the sulphur rising on the valley's thermals — that a caravan of camels had passed, that there were gazelles feeding in the thorns, that there was someone dying in the wilderness ahead.

He was open-mouthed. He looped his tongue from side to side, circling his lips, tasting the atmosphere for smells. In fact his sense of smell had been so bludgeoned by the heat and by his thirst that he could not detect the sulphur even. He was parched and faint. His lips were cracked. His legs and back — unused to heat and effort such as this — were aching badly. If he paused to sniff so frequently, that was because he could smell nothing. It worried him. He hoped to clear the blockage in his nose, and shift his headache too.

He was a traveller called Jesus, from the cooler, farming valleys in the north, a Galilean, and not one used to deprivations of this kind. He'd spent the night in straw, a shepherd's paying guest, and had that morning left his bag, his water-skin, his sandals and his stick where he'd slept. His quarantine would be achieved without the comforts and temptations of clothing, food and water. He'd put his trust in god, as young men do. He would encounter god or die, that was the nose and tail of it. That's why he'd come. To talk directly to his god. To let his god provide the water and the food. Or let the devil do its work. It would be a test for all three of them.

First he had to find a place where he and god could meet in privacy. He'd say, if asked, that god had told him where to go, the details of this very route. He had been standing at the window of his father's workshop and god had called his name. Every time the mallet hit the wood, his name was called. And every time the mallet hit the wood he took a further step along the road in his mind's eye, down from the living sea in Galilee to the salt-dead waters in the south, and then ascending to the desert hills and caves.

There were nine days of mallet hitting wood before he found the courage to argue with his family, tie his bag, and leave. The hills were beckoning, he'd said. But as he walked up into the wilderness — his nostrils blocked, his feet raw, another mallet striking on his skull relentlessly — he could not find much evidence of god. The Galilee was full of god at that time of the year — new crops, flowers on the apricot, the lambs, the warmer nights . . . It was not hard to worship god in the Galilee. But here the spring had hardly made its mark. Jesus was an optimist. Look at the uncompleted land, he told himself, dry-tongued, enfeebled by the labours of the walk: the valleys waiting for their rivers, the browns and yellows waiting for their greens. Creation was unfinished here. This was where the world was not complete. What better place to find his god at work?

Unlike the four who had preceded him that afternoon and set up home amongst the poppies, Jesus did not follow any of the carvings in the rocks which indicated where hermits would easily find caves. He did not mean to leave his imprint softly in the clay. He was looking for much harder ground. He preferred the pious habitats of lunatics and bats where he could live for forty days, hanging by his toes if need be, and not have any excuse for shifting his eyes from heaven for an instant. He'd seen that there were caves set in the crumbling precipice which fell away abruptly below the camel trail, beyond the ambition even of goats. He'd choose one which was hard to reach and inhospitable, exposed to the sun and wind and cold. He set his sights on the remotest and the highest of the caves, a key-shaped hole. It had no more than a sloping rock as its yard, hardly bigger than a prayer-mat, the perfect perch for eagles. And for angels. But Jesus hesitated at the point where he should start to climb down. He surely had the right to drink before he embarked on his trials. It was not dusk. There was, as yet, no thin and bending moon to mark the onset of his fast. God would not come before day one. So he could drink. It was not a sin to drink. It would not be a sign of weakness, either, if he prepared for quarantine with, say, a simple meal, a wash, a rest.

He'd seen the batwing outline of Miri's goatskin tent, pitched on the flatland of the valley head. He walked towards it. There was no one to be seen in the open. But there were goats. If there were goats then there was water too. And milk and meat.

A tethered donkey announced his arrival while he was still fifty paces away. Jesus stood, as was the custom, a little distance from the open awning of the tent and waited for the greetings from within, and the invitation to come forward. He could not pay for food and drink. What little money that he had he'd left behind that morning in the keeping of the shepherd. But there are traditions, even in the wilderness. A traveller can wet his face and lips for free.

He coughed. He clapped his hands. He called out greetings of his own. But no one came. That was strange — the tent was unattended, and yet the awnings were still raised. Jesus took a step or two towards the tent, so that he could see inside more clearly. There were the usual signs of domesticity; the rugs and mats, the pots, some bread and dates discarded from a meal and being finished off by ants, the sacks of grain, the remnants of a fire, the skins of water hanging in the shade, the bundled blankets on a bed, the row of shoes. But no one there, as far as he could tell. Jesus looked around for signs of someone approaching, but there were none. He called again, without reply. His patience was not endless. He was keen, he told himself, to reach the cave before darkness and to begin his fast. He was afraid as well. Afraid that he might lose his nerve the moment that he reached the precipice, and go back home at once.

This was not theft. He took a few more steps towards the awning and lifted the nearest and the smallest of the water-skins off its wooden peg. He stooped and picked up the wasted heels of bread, the dates. He rubbed the ants off on his arm. Not killing them. Not trying to, at least. They dropped into the dust and went about their business, unperturbed. He picked some pieces of straw and the small stones from between his toes and off his heels. He squeezed out what thorns he could find. His feet were bruised and sore. His head had not improved. His body ached. Perhaps it would not matter if he went inside, out of the sun, if he sat cross-legged within the tent, those blankets as a seat, and took his final supper in some comfort. Again — with water, bread and dates held in his hands — he took some further steps. He left the sun. His eyes were baffled by the darkness. While he waited to become accustomed to the gloom he heard a whistling throat, as if the bunched-up blankets at his ankles were calling out for drink.

"Who's there?" he said.

Again a whistling throat.

"Who's sleeping there?"

Fevers will allow a period of short lucidity before their victims die. Musa became conscious for long enough to hear that one word *sleeping*, and then to register the pains throughout his body. His head was spongy like a mushroom. He could feel each vein and pipe, each gut and artery, each bone and nerve, highlighted by his agony. He was a parched and desert landscape, illuminated by lightning. And in that moment when he heard the word he saw the face as well. A Jewish face, young and long and womanly. A Galilean face. A peasant face. A robber's face, for sure, because the man had helped himself to water and was standing with their water-skin held in his hand. Musa would have struck the man if he'd been well enough. It would have been his duty to make it clear that theft, especially of water, deserved some bruises and a bloody nose. It would have been his pleasure, too. But he couldn't even clench his fist. He tried to call out Miri's name. He hadn't got the breath to make a sound.

"Allow me water, to soak these little crusts and wet my lips," the Galilean said in that compromise of tongues where Aramaic flirts with Greek. He sensed the silent answer he received was No. He knelt into the darkness of the tent, located Musa from the cursing sounds he made, and sat down at his side. "Do not deny me water, cousin," he said. "Let me take a mouth of it, and you'll then have forty days of peace from me. I promise it. The merest drop."

He put his fingertips on Musa's forehead. He stroked his eyelids with his thumb. "Are you unwell? I am not well myself." He laid his hand on Musa's chest and pressed so that the devil's air expressed itself and filled the tent with the odour of his fever and expelled the one word Musa had already formed, "Mi Ri." The cloth that

Miri had put across his mouth to keep the fever in almost lifted with the power of her name. His tongue was black. Again the Galilean put all his weight — which wasn't much — on Musa's chest and pressed. The sulphur of the hills. The embers of the chesty fire. Even Jesus could smell it. No further calls for Miri, though.

"A sip, a sip. And then I'm gone," Jesus said. "The merest drop." He poured a little water on his hands and smeared the dust of his journey across his face. He was immensely cold, but glad to have this respite from the sun. He wet his hair and massaged the water into his scalp so that his headache was somewhat dampened. He resurrected the softness in the bread and dates with water. He ate, hardly touching his lips with those long, craftsman's fingers. He drank some more. Then — an afterthought — he tipped a little water on Musa's cheeks and lips. He felt inspirited, newly released from pain, and powerful. He wet the cloth and put it back in place on Musa's mouth. He shook the water from his hands over Musa's face, a blessing. "So, here, be well again," he said, a common greeting for the sick.

What should he do? It didn't matter much. There were no witnesses or anyone to reckon with. There was as yet no thin and bending moon to mark the first night of his rendezvous with god. So he was unobserved. There is no choice, he told himself. He had to leave this sick man on his own to die. Otherwise he'd never reach the cave; he'd miss the start of quarantine.

He would have run away, except his feet would not allow him to. He hobbled out, an old young man, letting go the water-skin and pulling down the open awnings as he passed. He was embarrassed by his selfishness, perhaps? But Musa did not witness it. He did not witness anything. His eyes were closed. He was asleep at last, and dreaming plumply like a child.

CHAPTER
SEVEN

Musa woke again. The cloth, stiff and twisted like a loose root, was heavy on his mouth. He spat it off. He spread his arms to free himself of all the wrappings. He tried to sit up, never quick or easy for a man his size. First he'd have to turn his weight on to an elbow, push with the other hand, get on his knees . . . Camels were more gainly and less cumbersome. Musa did not like to be observed rising with so little grandeur from his bed, though normally Miri would be there to pull him by the wrists and elbows to his feet, to wipe him down, to hold his clothes. But now he could not even shift his weight. His head was loath to leave the tent mat. He couldn't quite remember where he was. Nor could he recognize the sickly smells of herbs, honey and incense. Embalming smells. He felt cold, no doubt of that. Baffled, too. Why was he bruised and powerless? Why was he still in blankets? Why was he feeling so melodic and so calm? More to the point — he tried to lift his head and look around — where was his wife? He clapped his hands. He wanted water straight away. "Miri. Miri." No reply. "Miri? Are you coming now?" The words were dry and splintery when normally his voice was reedy, adolescent almost. His saliva was caustic and his lips were cracked. His throat was wilderness.

He clapped his hands again and listened for some sign that she, or anybody else who had some water, was nearby. It didn't matter who, so long as it was free and fast. But there wasn't any sign. He should have heard the voices of his cousins and his uncles, and the blaring of the camels, the usual waking noises of the merchant camp. He could only hear goats, and the wheezings of the tent skins. Finally he found strength enough, though it was painful, to roll across the mat and peer out below the tent's heavy skirts. He recognized what he saw. Some of it, at least. This was the unembracing spot where, caught out by the dusk, they'd had to pitch their tents the night before. A scrubland in the wilderness too far from Jericho. There was the broken soil where Habak's tent had been. And Raham's tent. And Aliel's. Those fools. There was the blackened circle of their fire. The camel dung. The torn and broken bushes where the goats had fed.

There was — thank heavens — liquid within reach. Someone deserved a slap around the ears for carelessness. They'd dropped a water-bag by the awning of the tent. Musa dragged it across, pulled out the stopper, and wastefully — he hadn't got the strength to be more frugal — tipped water on his hair and down his face. Then he drank. He had to spit the water out at first. His mouth made it sour. But then the water went to work, reanimating him. He could almost trace the flow and billow of its irrigation; the freshet coursing through his mouth and throat into his stomach. At last the water percolated to his head. His breathing and his vision cleared. He was restored: a man of twenty-six or so, wedded to a life of bargaining, whose preferred self-image had him sitting neatly and cross-legged beside some market booth dispensing deals and judgements like a priest, implacably, too dignified to haggle with. It had him trading crackware lamps for damaskeen silver, figs for wine, wedding figurines for Roman cloth, papyrus for salt; there was no merchandise which could not be mated and transmuted in his hands. It had him envied and admired. And rich.

Indeed he was admired, but only in the market-place. He was a sorcerer with goods and prices there, the kingly middleman with his blued hair, his fringed and pampered cheeks, his crisp and spotless tunic, his swollen elegance, his cunning. But he was graceless in the daily commerce of the smile and hug. His embraces were the bruising sort. His punches and his kisses could not be told apart. It seemed that he both loved and loathed the trappings of his life; Miri his wife, the market-place, himself, his drink, the endless halt and harness of the caravan. He was their master and their slave at once. Two men in one; opposing twins, they'd said when he was a boy and couldn't reconcile his bossy tantrums with his bouts of weeping. No wonder he was large even as a child — two hearts, two stomachs, twice the bones, twin temperaments.

Now that Musa was a merchant and an adult, fearful of derision and defeat, he had learnt to suppress the lesser, tearful twin. Life was too hard and unforgiving for such a weakling. Anyone could drive that tender sibling to an easy bargain. Anyone could trespass in his tent. Anyone could make a fool of him. So Musa kept him hidden, a lost companion of his childhood, and showed the world his tougher self, the one which beat and bargained like no other, the trading potentate, the fist, the appetite. Why was this splendid fellow feared but not much liked by his cousins in the caravan? It baffled Musa, and it made him fierce. They are simply envious, he persuaded himself. But during those late and bitter drinking vigils outside his tent, his judgement was more fiery, and much simpler; They hate you, Musa. Hate them back!

For the moment, though, the lesser twin had been briefly resurrected by the water. Musa grovelled on his stomach like a temple slave, his hair and beard still wet and mossy, and thought of Miri and his uncles, the market cries, the camel snorts, with some degree of fondness. He was aware that he had almost lost them all, that he had nearly died, and that their loss would be insufferable. He peered out of the tent again, for signs of relatives and friends, a wisp of smoke, a shout. But there were none. Perhaps he had died after all, and this was hell.

What had occurred? Musa had to concentrate. A face was haunting him. A throbbing voice. He could not recognize it, though. He could remember his last journey, how the caravan had come out of the hills, delayed by badu herdsmen to the south, who'd wanted to trade yarn for copperware. He'd used his size and his impatience to force a bargain. He could shake profits out of sand, someone had said, and Musa had been proud to hear it. He could recall setting camp, and then the meal, the fires, the chill of night. He'd felt both hot and cold when he'd gone in to sleep the night before. Was it the night before? Or ten, or twenty nights? He'd told Miri to massage his shoulders. He'd sent her off for blankets. He'd almost vomited and had had to sleep on his back because his chest was sore and shivering. He'd had diarrhoea.

So that was it! He'd caught a fever, then. That much was obvious.

What was now becoming cruelly obvious as well — there was the evidence outside — was that he'd been abandoned by his comrades and his family to battle with the fever on his own. And that was pitiless. Left in the desert with . . . He counted what he saw. That useless donkey with the limp. And five, six goats. Camel dung. No bolts of cloth, none of the larger bulks of wool, no decorated copperware. No Miri, even. His feelings of melodic calm did not survive his growing dismay and anger. The lesser twin took flight.

The sun by now was fairly low in the sky, sinking and red-faced from its exertions like any other traveller who had passed a day in the desert. Musa knew it was late afternoon. The caravan would be too far away to chase. How could he chase it anyway? Ride the limping donkey? Ride a goat? He couldn't even lift his body off the ground. He lay — his shoulders in the tent, his head protruding out — and dreamed of chasing them on a relay of goats and catching them in some green valley to the north. He'd pull his merchandise from off the camels' backs, the copperware, the cloth, his wools.

(He loved the sensuality of wools, particularly the orange and the purple wools. They were the colours prostitutes would wear.) Those loving uncles and their sons would hide their faces with shame. Would he forgive them for abandoning him to snakes and leopards? Would he congratulate them on their thieving business skills? He'd sneeze at them. He'd drive them off with stones. He'd stand amongst them with a heavy stick and crack their heads. They'd know how dangerous he was. They'd seen him swing a stick before. Then he'd go to where the women were. He'd have a reason to attack his wife for once, and nobody would dare to lay a calming hand on his and say, "Be easy, Musa. Let her go." What could they say in her defence? He could disown her there and then. He had the right. Divorce her on the spot and turn her out. But he would take her to their tent instead, and everyone would hear her cries right through the night. The different cries which came when he was slapping her, the ones when he had pulled her tunic off and was laying leather straps across her back, and those when he had opened up her thighs and, with her hair held in his fists, was pushing into her until there was a trinity of pain and tears and fear. Kisses, punches? They were all the same to him. And then he would divorce her on the spot.

But Musa, if the truth was told, for all the bombast of his dreams, was feeling fearful and ill-used. He'd thrown water in his eyes, but there were tears as well. He was shivering, not only from the chill inside the tent. His prospects, frankly, were not promising. What kind of merchant was he now? A laughing-stock. An ass. A dupe. He'd been discarded like the casing of a nut. His mood was murderous, but there was no one there to murder, except himself.

His anger made him stronger, though. He tried again, turned on his side, brought up his knees, and found that he could stand, unsteadily. He shuffled round the inside of the tent as best he could, a cover on his shoulders, using the tent poles for support and taking stock of what they'd left behind. The goats, but not the best. His family goods. Rugs, bedding and utensils. Two woven sacks of grain. Salted meat. Dried fruit. Fig cakes. A flask of date spirit. A remnant hank of orange wool, some purple, his sample rod of coloured yarns, his clothes, his wife's, her loom. Some fragrant wormwood for the fire. He hurried to his saddle-pack, and was relieved to find his ornamented knife, the seven bottles of perfume that he'd traded earlier that year, and the little hoard of gold, coins and jewellery tied up in a twist of berber cloth. Abandoned, yes, but hardly destitute. He'd resurrect himself with trade.

He took the long wooden pestle with which Miri crushed their nuts and grain and, using it to help him walk, went outside past the tethered donkey into the fading light, with the water-bag hung round his shoulders. His knuckles whitened on the pestle with his weight. He turned in a full circle. Just in case. No sign of anyone who'd stayed behind. No sign of anyone to kiss and punch.

The donkey — an ageing jenny, older anyway than Musa — had been tethered by his wife. He recognized the kindness of Miri's knot. The creature had been lamed by her pannier harnesses which had rubbed to form a sore and then a boil at the top of her hind leg. The boil had hardened on the muscles so that the donkey limped, and was in pain. Her breath was bad. Her nostrils seemed inflamed, perhaps by the circulating poison of the boil. Musa leaned forward and looked more closely, not at the boil but at the donkey's nose, for signs of pus and infected membranes. Her top lip drew back like a baboon's and curled at the man's smell. She wanted him to keep away. He wanted to keep his distance, too. Ulcerated nostrils were a symptom of glanders. Glanders could be caught by men, and not only by jackassing the jenny as some people claimed. He was not sure if they were ulcers that he saw, or simply mucus. If they were ulcers the donkey would soon die. Then what use would she be, this legacy of his kind cousins and his uncles? He couldn't eat the meat; he couldn't even skin her for shagreen, unless he wanted to risk catching donkey fever himself.

That thought made Musa step away. Perhaps that was the illness that he'd caught already. Donkeys, it was known, were full of demons keen to set up home elsewhere. He lifted up his hand to check for the tell-tale swelling of the underjaw. But Musa's underjaw, beneath the beard, was loose and heavy anyway and it was difficult to tell if there was any swelling. He pushed his little finger into his nostrils. They were not clear, but then they were not painful either. Had he caught glanders then? Or had there been some other devil in his lungs? He was only sure of one thing, that both he and the donkey had been abandoned by his caravan companions with equal regard. They were considered worthless and infectious and as good as dead.

Musa loosened the donkey's knot and began to lead her away from the tent and the goats. Her illness angered him. It would be better if she died where her contagion was not dangerous. If he could make her move, that is. The animal was uninspired by Musa's prodding foot. She was reluctant to engage with him. She must have sensed his illness, too. He wasn't any stronger than she was herself. She knew that she could pull as hard as he could tug. Besides, a donkey is quite used to being hit. It is a condition of service almost, part of its contract of labour. A slap of the driver's switch on the donkey's cheek is rewarded with a shuffle forward and a bray. Beating donkeys is as innocent as beating mats. A hearty slap across its back brings out the dust. But this old jenny, for all the native half-smile on her lips, was made doubly obstinate by her ill-health. When Musa kicked her on the shanks, she did not move and bray. She'd seemed to buckle like a colt. She fell on her haunches, and dropped her head on to the ground, chin down.

There is something ill-conceived and comic about a standing donkey; the narrow hooves too dainty for the bony head, the long black dorsal cross that makes her coat appear as roughly stitched as patchwork, the fraying fly-swat tail, the pitcher ears. But lying down, her head between her forelegs like a dog, this donkey seemed neater and more dignified, and even with the pinkish overtones of her grey sides exaggerated by what was left of the sunlight — more beautiful.

40

Musa lifted up the pestle in both hands. It seemed as if his body was the only thing that moved in that shy universe of thorn and stone. It was too late and dusky for the high and beating flocks on their migrations. Yet he was not entirely without witnesses. Three hawks were arcing high above the scrub. Birds which could spot a vacillating beetle from such a distance could hardly miss a donkey sinking on to its chin, not in a landscape such as this where life was slow. There would be carrion, and there would be a fight. Three hawks to share two donkey eyes. They circled calmly, with rationed wing beats, above the narrow strip, then out over the tumbling precipice, across the side-lit hills, and never took their eyes off the scrub and its small drama — smaller and paler even than its shadows. Here — viewed from the dying thermals of the day — malice was at work, irresistible and rarefied: the man, a donkey, the two raised arms; the goats that couldn't give a damn; the stretched and brutal angles of the tent; and no one there to lay a hand on Musa's arm or press his chest so that the devil's air could be expressed before the pestle fell again.

Musa gave the donkey one more chance. "Get up," he said. The throat had cleared. His voice was reedy once again. He kicked her side. He jabbed his heel against her inflamed boil. No luck. He brought the pestle down on to her lower back, experimentally. "Get up," again. But here Musa had met his match. Her sickness was greater than his, and was defeating him. She could endure his bullying, but did not have the will or strength to stand.

She closed her eyes and even dropped her ears. Do what you will to me. You are invisible.

Musa could not stop himself, of course. A merchant always sees his business through. He had to bargain with the currency at hand. He knew that donkeys were like customers. They had long memories. Camels had none. A donkey that had got its own way once would expect it every time. It would resist the tether and the switch. It would shake its panniers off and bray for better food. He told himself he had no choice but to force the donkey to her feet, to make her move a safe distance away from the tent. For what purpose? Simply so that she could tumble on to her chin again and die where Musa had commanded. This, then, would be the final lesson of her life. There is a price to pay for disobedience, he thought. There is always a reckoning. He'd make her pay for his infection, too. For his abandonment.

Musa lifted up the pestle for a second time, but less experimentally. Now there were three good reasons why the donkey should be hit, and little to mitigate her punishment. He had to satisfy his anger. Anger was like phlegm and urine — best expressed at once. It was a shame there were no witnesses, he thought, warming to his task. He would have liked to have had an audience — Miri and his uncles. See what happens when Musa is upset, he'd say. Here's how to put a pestle to good use. He would divorce this donkey on the spot.

It was just as well there were no witnesses. When Musa swung the pestle he lost his footing. Its weight circled too widely behind his shoulder. His own weight was uncentred. He almost fell on to the donkey. His temper took a shaking, too. He had to start again, and use the pestle like an axe, chopping at the mortar of her head. Big men are often clumsy when they are violent. Their venom can seem comical and soft. They are too breathless and they have too many chins. Thin men, with bloodless lips and hollow waists, appear more dangerous. But Musa's frenzy was not comical. There was nothing jocular or soft about the way he used the pestle. Indeed, his clumsiness had made him angry with himself and that provided extra power. Killing did not bother him. It was natural. He'd slaughtered goats a dozen times. He'd wrung the necks of birds. He'd dealt with snakes. But this was more than slaughtering. This was a settling of scores.

It took two blows to put the donkey out. Her skull was thin, and she was old. She had sufficient spirit to bare her teeth at Musa's leg, but not enough to roll over on her side and kick at him. She only rolled when she was unconscious and had no choice. Musa did not stop when she was on her side. He wanted now to see some product for his efforts, some broken skin, some rips, some blood. He wanted to make the stubborn creature's head fall loose. It took him ten more blows to break the ridge of bones high on her neck, the vertebrae between her ears. They were protected by her short and springy mane. Musa had to twist the pestle as it fell so that he could strike the donkey on its uncushioned side, along the line of sinew between the cheekbone and the shoulder. Gradually her coat was rid of dust. The skin began to soften like so much grain had softened and split under the same pestle in Miri's hands. But the blood was slow to rise. When it did it surfaced on the donkey's skin like wine through bread, not running free but welling, blushing through the hair, thickening and darkening in curtains at her throat, as if the blood itself was so drained of energy it could not even fall.

Then Musa rested, watching while the blood-flow to the donkey's brain was blocked by the breakages and swellings. The nerves, first in her ears and throat, then in her flank, and finally in her damaged leg and at the end-tuft of her tail, shook and trembled as if the donkey felt nothing more than unexpected cold. Musa hit her once again. Her face was fruit. It bruised and split and wept. Her neck had broken at the shoulder-blade. Musa had succeeded in his task: at last the donkey's head was loose. He could not resist a final swing, although his shoulders ached and his heart was hammering. Was this exuberance or brutishness? He knocked her top front teeth into her mouth. They cracked out of her gums like stones from apricots.

Musa's exertions were exhausting for a man already weakened by the fever. He had to rest again. He put his hand on the donkey's rump, and lowered himself on to the earth. His hands and knees were splashed with blood, and they were shaking. He poured some water and washed himself. He knew he should take more care in case the blood was still contagious, but Musa held the simple view that the glanders would have died as well beneath the pestle blows, that death can vanquish all disease. Death can heal. He dried his hands in donkey hair and shook the water off on to the animal. He flicked the waste from his hands over the donkey's head, a blessing of a sort. Musa was feeling calmer, playful even, but he was never one for flippancy. So someone else was speaking through his lips. He was surprised to hear himself offer to the donkey the common greeting for the sick and dying. "So, here, be well again," he said. Fat chance of that!

"So, here, be well again"? The recurrence of that phrase made Musa shiver. There was a meaning to such repetitions. There always was. Everything that's stored will be restored, that is the chiming pattern of the world. Whose words were those, Be well again? Who haunted him? Whose throbbing voice was that? He concentrated hard. And, yes, there was a half-remembered figure now. A face within his fever. A peasant face. A robber's face. He could recall his eyelids being thumbed and stroked: "A sip, a sip. And then I'm gone." Not Miri's voice, but someone soft and male; his lesser twin but with an accent from the farming north. A Galilean voice, with open lazy vowels, and consonants which shot out like seeds from a drying pod, which shed their stones like apricots, which snapped out of the gums like donkey's teeth. "A sip, a sip, a sip." A healer's voice, belonging in the tent.

Musa looked into the tent. No unexpected shadows there. He searched for someone moving in the scrub. He hoped and feared to see the man again. He'd settle any debts. He'd pay the reckoning, if it was reasonable. Together they had travelled to the long black ridge and looked beyond into the ochre plains of death. Be well again. Be well.

* * *

So that's how Miri found him when she came. She had to stumble in the darkness for a lamp to see exactly what misfortunes had occurred. There was no body in the tent, and that was frightening. It didn't take her long to find the donkey and her husband. The corpse's smell was bad, and there were scrub dogs already gathered near the tent, hungry for the meat. Her husband's head was resting on the donkey's leg, and they were black with drying blood. At first she thought they both were dead. But no such luck. His chest was rising. He snored. His tongue was pink and healthy on his lips, not black from fever any more. It was a curse; it was a miracle. So much for death's discrimination. It had claimed the donkey, not the man.

Musa was woken by the lamplight. He wasn't feverish. He looked at Miri, her dirty hands, her bloody knees, her tearful eyes. "Hah, so you returned," he said. And just as well. He pointed at his bloody handiwork. But Musa's anger had been squandered on the donkey. He was relieved to see his wife. It showed. How could he manage on his own? It had been the oddest day, and he was tired. He did not know if he should celebrate or grieve. He pulled her fiercely by her arms, a tender, punishing embrace, and made her tell him everything that had happened, what his uncles had prescribed, what their plans for him had been.

"Where were you, then?" he asked finally. "Look at your hair."

What could she say? That she had run away from him? That she had dug his grave, and passed the afternoon quite comfortably inside? She couldn't speak. She was in shock, and trembling. Her liberation had been too short. At last she said, with what he might have taken to be tears of worry and concern, that she had thought that he was going to die.

"Well, you were wrong. A spirit came and brought me back. But not with any help from you," he said accusingly, though he released the hard grip on her arm and dropped his hand into her lap. "I saw his face."

"What face?"

"Somebody's face. The fever's face? I don't remember seeing yours."

"I couldn't lure the fever out," she said. "I sang for you. All night. It's true. I did . . ." Musa tilted his heavy chin at her, to let her know he hadn't heard her sing. ". . . I climbed the scarp to look for roots. To make a poultice. But . . ." (she opened up her hands to show her broken nails) ". . . I dug for nothing. The earth was hard. It's stones . . ."

She gabbled on, but did not listen to herself. God damn the spirit that has brought you back, she thought. Her wrist was still smarting from the fierceness of his grip. His hand was pressing into her and she was shrinking and retreating from his fingers. He was unsteady still. And ungainly as ever. He could not quite succeed — not yet, at least — in turning Miri on her back. But he was lucky with his lips, no longer dry and caustic. He pressed his kisses on her face. That was the trading profit of her day.

It had been an afternoon of hope, at least. She'd raised her hands into the unresisting air. The sky was soft for her. But now the sky became a hard and bruising dish again. Miri was reduced to one of scrubland's night-time residents, its seven people and its goats, its caves, its tent, its partial hospitality beneath the thinnest moon of spring. She was unwidowed and unfreed, the mistress of unwelcome lips, the keeper of a wasted grave.

CHAPTER
EIGHT

The four newcomers to the valley caves did not sleep well. They were bruised and battered. Their feet were sore. Their legs were stiff. They had been punished by the journey and should have dropped to sleep as readily as dogs. But the lodgings were too cold for sleep. Their scrubland host had celebrated the new moon and the onset of spring by calling up for them a wind which was old and wintry and mean. At first it was too quick and muscular to idle in the contours of the scarp or nose into the creases and the dens. It hurried past. But later in the night — just when they thought that they might sleep — the wind became invasive. A watery haze, distilled from the daytime's rising valley heat and turned gelid in the dark, had made the wind heavier and more sinuous. It came into the caves, shouldered out the skulking pockets of warm air, and put an end to everybody's sleep.

So there was at least a unity of damp and sleeplessness inside the caves, for these four travellers. What could they do, except slap out the cold? Or hug their knees? Or stamp their feet? Or blow into their hands, and wonder if they had the fortitude — or foolishness — to last for thirty-nine more nights like this? A fire would help, of course. But the old man's roots and branches had not caught alight. He'd evidently lost his adolescent luck with flint and kindling. His luck was creaky like his bones. So he and his unseen companions had to spend the night as cold and stiff and unignited as the fire.

They all knew darkness well enough. Who hasn't lain awake at night with nothing brighter than a cloud-hung star to add its feeble touch of light to looming shapes inside the room? Who hasn't cried out for a lamp? But this was darkness unrelieved — for starlight, no matter if it's moistened by the air, is never sinuous, unlike the wind. It will not curve and bend its way in to a cave. There was a blinding lack of light inside. They could not even see a hand held up before their faces. They could not see the demons and the serpents and the dancing bones. But they could hear them all too well. What better way to pass the time, and put the worry of the cold to one side, than by contemplating something worse than cold: sounds without shapes?

If someone coughed in their damp corner, then for the other three that was the certain presence of hyenas. If another — fearful of hyenas — whispered to himself for comfort, then his voice for all the rest became the soft conspiracy of thieves. A yawn became a stifled cry for help. A sneeze, the whooping of a ghost. The wind set bushes rattling: an owl browsed in the scrub: cave beetles, amplified by their raised wings, rehearsed their murders and their rapes.

The woman was not as sleepless as the other three, perhaps because she was protected from the wind by the few bushes outside the cave. Her name was Marta. She'd been married for nine years to Thaniel, the landowner of

Sawiya by Jerusalem. His second wife. She was — a phrase she'd heard too often in the song —

> The Mother of a threadbare womb,
> Her warp hung weftless on the loom.

Though she was over thirty years of age, she had no children yet, despite her husband's nightly efforts, and her experiments with all the recommended charms and herbs to aid fertility. She'd sacrificed a dozen pigeons with the local priest. She'd rubbed honey on a marrow, sent money to Jerusalem, worn copper body charms, endured — she could not see how this would help — her husband's semen in her mouth. She'd worn balsam leaves underneath her clothes for weeks on end until she rustled like parchment. She'd eaten only green fruit (and paid the price). She'd starved herself. She'd gorged. Now she was plump and getting plumper, not to satisfy her husband, but because a flat stomach was intolerable. A larger one and bigger breasts might bring good luck, she thought. Provide the dovecote, and the doves will come.

None of it had worked, of course. Her warp remained without its weft. A hundred times and more, she'd done her best to fend off with prayers and lies the monthly rebuff of her periods. Now she only had till harvest to conceive. Then, her husband said, he would divorce her. The law allowed him to. The law demanded that he should, in fact. After ten years of barrenness a man could take another wife. "You don't cast seed on sour land," he said. He had a right to heirs. It was a woman's religious duty to provide and bring up children. He'd had to divorce his first wife, because she'd failed to conceive. Marta had failed as well. So Thaniel would have to turn her out and look elsewhere. Of course it was regrettable and harsh, he said, but he could hardly blame himself. Not twice. He'd marry 'Lisha's daughter. She was young. Her father owned some land adjacent to his own. The prospect was a cheerful one. And sensible.

"I'll have a son within ten months," he told his wife. "And, Marta, wipe your face and show some dignity. What use are tears? You'd better pray for miracles . . . Come on. You will have had ten years to prove yourself, and that is fair . . ."

"I'll pray," she said.

"Pray all you want."

Marta took him at his word. She would do everything she could. So, despite the priest's objections that her plans were wilful and unbecoming, she had walked into the wilderness to fast by day and pray for miracles by night.

Now she was sitting upright inside the cave, her back pressed against the least damp wall, and watching the entrance for dawn's first smudge of grey. She was more tired than scared — and though she, like her neighbours, turned the clatter of each tumbling stone, displaced by nothing more ominous than dew, into a devil or a snake, she could not stop her chin from dropping on her chest from time to time. Her sleeping dreams were less alarming than her waking ones, and so it felt to her that she did not fall asleep but rather fell awake into the nightmare of the cave, alone. She woke inside a womb, a grave, a catacomb. But she was calm. These forty days could not be worse than the alternative — a life without a child, a husband or a home.

She despised the man, of course, and had taken hardly any pleasure in the marriage for at least eight of their nine or so years together. In that she was the same as many of the women in Sawiya. Marriage was a bumpy ride for them, though "Better ride than walk," they said, "even if the ride is on a donkey." Their husbands were an irritation, of course. But husbands were amusing, too. At least, they were amusing when they were out of sight. Their vanities and tempers could be joked about among women friends at the ovens or the well. Grumbling and laughing at their curdy husbands made the bread rise and the yoghurt set. But Marta could not find the comedy in Thaniel. He'd made her and his first wife barren, she was sure, with his dry heart and sparking tongue. They were like millstones without oil. But — Marta was an optimist — she still believed that everything would be a joy if she could have his child. She pressed her eyes shut with her forefinger and her thumb, her little finger resting on the corner of her lips, and she prayed that she could leave her infertility behind in this dark, barren place, where it belonged. She prayed for forty days and nights of ripening, that she'd be fruitful, that she'd multiply. Then she prayed that dawn would break the habits of eternity: Let it arrive early for once, and drive the night away.

Pray as she might, however, she could not entirely shut the noises out. She was certain when she stopped and listened hard that there was something, or someone, in the bushes just below her cave. She heard the small sounds that someone makes when he — of course, it had to be a he — is standing still and breathing through his nose. The snuffles, rustling of clothes, the lubrications of the tongue and mouth of someone waiting for her in the dark. One of her three new neighbours, perhaps? She had not thought of them as dangerous, though no man was trustworthy when a woman was alone, no matter who he was. She stopped her praying, and tried to breathe as gently as she could. There was more rustling, and then the someone seemed to shake a piece of cloth. It sounded like her husband flapping out the dust when he was taking off his clothes. The old man, then? The blond? The badu with the hennaed hair? Which one was naked at her cave?

Marta's measured breathing and her stillness made her drowsy. She tried to stay awake by concentrating on the sounds outside but, finally, she could not stop herself. Her chin went down on to her chest. She fell asleep.

Thank heavens for the charity of dreams. When Marta woke and heard again the scurrying below her cave, the naked man had been dismissed from her mind's eye. She listened to the noises more critically. They were too light and birdlike to be threatening. A man would make more weighty sounds. He wouldn't have the patience to stay so quiet and still. A woman then? A bird? Gazelles? The answer was obvious: it had to be the little straw-boned woman with the untied hair who'd evidently dug and taken up residence in a grave-like pit amongst the poppies; the peeping, rodent face, half-buried in the ground, and looking out across the scrub with moist and fearful eyes. Marta could have clapped her hands with pleasure and relief. She had forgotten that there was a fourth companion for the night. Might she still be hiding in her grave?

Now Marta had a reason to go outside. There was a friend at hand, a mad one possibly, but one that was too small to do her any harm. Women should seek each other out. She made her way towards the entrance, steadying herself with both hands against the cave wall, and stepped into the damp earth and the bushes at the foot of the cliff. She was surprised how sombre it was, and how blustery the wind had become. Surprised because she'd always thought that country skies at night would be much brighter than the smothered skies of villages. But the night was beautiful, nevertheless, more beautiful than any night that she had known at Sawiya, possibly because Sawiya was in the basement of the hills. This scrubland was the roof. From where she stood, the moon was level with her eyes. It was the thinnest melon slice, hardbacked, translucent, colourless. Its rind was resting on the black horizon, hardly bright enough to tinge the sky. But to her left, beyond the valley and its sea, the peaks and shoulders of Moab were boasting rosy epaulettes of light. The morning was approaching.

Marta walked towards the grave. She could hear the new friend scrabbling inside. There were flapping gasps of breath, like landed fish in nets.

"It's all right," she called, a reassurance for them both. "It's me. The woman yesterday."

But of course there was no other woman in the grave. There hadn't been since dusk. Miri was with Musa in their tent, and reunited by the blanket on their bed, her narrow, knuckled backbone pressed against his hip. Instead there was a shuffling and contented darkness in the hole. Here were the small, wet sounds that Marta had heard before. She couldn't place the sounds — they were too moist and feathery to be a woman, no matter how tiny.

She stepped too close. She knocked a loose stone in. That's all it took. There was a startled screech and then a gust of flapping, muscled wind as the pit made instant shapes from shadows and flung its contents in the air. It sounded like a hundred husbands shaking out their clothes. Damp bodies hurtled from the grave into the night, as headlong and as vengeful as demons hurled out of a nightmare and driven forwards by the seven winds of hell.

Marta screamed loudly enough for her new neighbours to hear, and to hear the echo, too. She dropped heavily on to her knees. Her face was wetly, firmly struck a dozen times. Her chest and shoulders took six or seven blows. She was assaulted by wings and beaks and smells. Then — almost before her scream had ended — they were gone, crying curses at her as they fled. She did not know what birds they were at first. She was too shaken. Her heart was beating faster than their wings. One of the birds had snagged its claws inside the loose weave of her cloak, and was hanging at her thigh, upside down, thrashing and spiralling. Marta, her panic equalling the bird's, beat at it but could not knock it away. Once she had caught her breath again and steadied herself, she held its wings and feet and pulled it free. Her hands were shaking. It was a heavy, barrel-breasted bird, with a mottled throat and muddy-coloured underwings. A scrub fowl of some kind. She knelt on the cold ground for a few moments, panting, warming her hands in the bird's breast feathers. She would not let it go. This was a gift. The evening meal, to mark the end of her first day of fasting. She held its feathers to her cheeks and lips for a few moments. It was softer than any cloth. But she understood this was no time or place for childishness. She broke its wings to stop it struggling. She ought, she knew, to slaughter it according to the rules by draining out the blood. But there wasn't any knife — or priest — to hand. Instead, she put her thumb against its neck and snapped its vertebrae.

There was a second unearned gift as well. Once the morning light had lifted high enough for her to see inside the grave, she found what the birds had gathered for. When Miri had dug the grave for Musa, she'd gone beyond the biscuit and the stones, and cut across the underground water-seep which drained what little moisture sank into the scarp. During the night, the grave had formed a perfect cistern; cool, straight-sided, and impossible for antelope or goats to raid and empty. The water was dark brown and little more than ankle-deep, but it made the forty days ahead seem almost comfortable.

Marta was not thirsty but she knew she ought to drink before the sun appeared and her quarantine began in earnest. She lay down on the ground, with her chin resting on the outer rim of the grave, and reached down to the water. Luckily, she was a tall woman and her arms were long enough to touch the bottom. At once a few black ticks alighted on her wrists. The water tasted rich and soupy, earth-warm, not appetizing but cruelly beneficial like herbal medicine. It tasted fertile. What would Thaniel think if he could see her spread out across earth, immodest as a girl?

She was not scooping water on her own for long. The blond, summoned by her involuntary scream and by the hubbub of the birds, was soon lying at her side, toasting his good luck and drinking palmfuls. The older Jew had trouble kneeling, let alone lying on his chest and reaching for the water. He held his side, and frowned with pain. Marta scooped water up for him, losing most of it between her fingers before she could get her cupped hands, still shaking from the fright she'd had, up to his mouth. He shook his head, apologized. It would not do to let his lips or tongue come into contact with her skin. He gave his felt skull-cap to her. It didn't hold much water but it absorbed enough for the old man to squeeze into his mouth. At first he tried to remove the scobs of earth from the felt before he drank, but he soon settled for the simple life by swallowing the water first and then picking the grit and sand off his lips and tongue. The badu was the last to come, evidently not alarmed by Marta's scream. He could not easily reach the water either with his hands. He jumped into the grave and got down on his knees to drink. He had the manners and the narrow backbone of a goat.

58

There's nothing like a desert water-hole for making good, brief neighbours out of animals that have nothing much in common other than a thirst. There is the story of the leopard and the deer, standing patiently in line while vipers drink. And the tradition amongst travellers that anyone who pushes at a well will die from drowning. Their bones will never dry. So these four strangers, gathered round the cistern, were more careful and polite than they might have been if they had met, say, at a crowded market stall, where the sharpest elbows and the shrillest voice would get the leanest meat. Even the badu, for all his childish, knee-deep impropriety, kept to his corner and was careful to avoid the other dipping hands. There was a good deal of nervous laughter, as well. They knew they were a comic sight — unwashed, unrested, far from home, and with the rankest water, hardly clean enough to irrigate a field, slipping through their fingers, down their chests and legs. So, once they'd filled themselves with water and were sitting on the rocks waiting for the sun to come and dry their clothes, they had no reason to behave as if they were entirely strangers. Like fellow travellers sharing tables at an inn, and knowing they would share the same uneasy stomachs in the night, they had to talk. They'd come into the hills for privacy, perhaps. But there were customs to observe. Customs of the water-hole. Customs of the road. And for the men, the awkward and restraining customs of language and demeanour forced on them by the presence of an unaccompanied woman. Who knows how these three might have spoken and behaved if Marta, handsome and imposing, her throat and arms and ankles close enough to study and to touch, hadn't been there? Who was the viper? Which the leopard and the deer?

Marta knew that she was disconcerting. Men stared at her, even in Sawiya where she was no longer any novelty, as if her presence made them uncomfortable. They stopped their work to watch her walking down the alleys towards the well. She could hang the sickle and stay the saw. The same men watched her coming back, balancing a filled pitcher of water on her shoulders. They hoped to see her arms lifted above her head. Her breasts would spread high and flat across her chest. Any man that watched would know that her stomach was still unburdened by a child, and — for reasons only understood by men and cockerels — that was arousing. But Marta misread their stares, and stared back at them, meeting eye for eye. Why should she feel ashamed? If they grinned or whispered amongst themselves, then she could guess exactly what they said and why they smiled. She was for them a fruitless tree. "Poor Thaniel," they must have said. "No sign of any crop this year. Two barren wives. Too much to bear."

Poor Marta, though. Despite her boldness in the alleyways, she was embarrassed by herself. Her sterility. Her size, which she considered to be too manly and ungainly. Her undernourished heart. Now she was embarrassed even more, in front of strangers. Her inadvertent scream had brought them running from their caves. It was as if she'd summoned them. Now she was exposed. Her hair, uncombed inside its scarf. Her wet and dusty clothes. The earth and water on her face and

60

chest. A married Jewish woman of her age was not accustomed to spending any time alone with men, apart from family or priests. Even Thaniel, her husband, did not spend much time with her on his own if he could help it. Thank god for that. So she was not comfortable to be displayed for strangers in this way. She tucked her feet out of sight, behind the hem of her tunic, wrapped her arms and shoulders as modestly as she could inside her cloak, hunched her shoulders like a raven so that her tunic hung straight down as a curtain and hid her body, and sat a little distance from the men. She put her hands on to the edges of her tunic and found the seeds that she had stitched inside the hem some years before, a good luck charm. There were ten seeds, each one an unborn child, each one hardened by the passing months. Five daughters and five sons, a balanced set of dowries if all of them survived. She ran them through her fingers like prayer-beads on a bracelet, counting them up to forty and then back to nought again. She counted secretly. She did not move her lips. She tried to turn herself to stone. She'd have to be discrete for forty days. She'd have to keep her distance from the men. The priest was right: it had been wilful, perilous and unbecoming to flee from home into the wilderness. No one had warned her, though, how fired and animated she would feel.

The old man did not worry her or even interest her, despite his frailty. He was a Jew. She'd met his type a hundred times before. Her uncles and her older neighbours were like him, meek and pompous all at once, slow to walk, quick to talk, and made babyish by any pain. This was her husband in old age. The blond

one, though, was odd and beautiful. A foreigner, she
thought. A disconcerting foreigner to dream about.
She'd seen that colour hair before, amongst the
legionnaires and sometimes on the merchants coming
from the north. A perfume-seller's hair. It was the colour
of honey. His neck and cheeks were as brown as
beeswax. She watched him from the corner of her eye,
not wanting to be seen, but not finding any reason to
look elsewhere. He sat cross-legged, self-consciously,
his legs entwined, almost in a braid. He had a staff, made
out of twisted wood, with perfect curls along its stem,
which he held across his lap. He ran his fingers round the
curls. He was a handsome man, she thought. More than
handsome. Statuesque. She wondered if his body hair
was blond . . .

Marta did not like the badu much. He'd jumped in the
cistern with no regard for anybody's cleanliness. She did
not trust the way he squatted on his heels, rocking like a
crib, twisting his hennaed hair between his fingers, and
ready to spring up. He was too small and catlike, with far
too many bracelets on his arm, she thought, to be much
of a threat to her. But there was something devilish and
immature about his face. If he had any body hair, it
would not match his hennaed head.

Marta had her numbers and her seeds for company.
She watched the men, and waited for the sun to warm
her up. The badu did not speak at all. He dropped
pebbles in his mouth. But the old man was glad to talk,
and the blond, though he hardly turned his head, seemed
resigned to listen. The old man did not whisper, but
spoke up loudly — in self-conscious Greek — so that

everyone could hear, perhaps. He gave his name, his place of birth, his trade. He was Aphas the mason, from Jerusalem. He reported on the complications of his journey to the caves, his attempts to light a fire, the discomforts of the night. All unimportant, unrevealing, reassuring facts. What other intimacies than these should be exchanged by strangers in the wilderness? Finally, when no one offered to reply, he turned towards the badu and asked for his name and his place of birth. But the badu only smiled — bad teeth, wet pebbles — and shook his head. He didn't want to give his family name, perhaps. He did not know his family name. What badu did? Or else he had no Greek. Aphas turned to Marta now and, with a chuckle at the badu's silence, tried to implicate her in his amusement. "Some chatterbox," he said. He almost asked her name, but then had second thoughts. Was it polite? One could not simply ask a woman's name, or say, "Who are your husband's family?" or "Why have you come here alone? What do you want?" Instead, he tapped the blond man on the knee — an old man can assume such intimacies — and said, "Yes, yes? Let's hear."

The honey-head, as Marta had thought, was from the north. He knew some Aramaic and some Greek, though many of the words he used were unfamiliar. Unlike the gabbling stonemason, he spoke as if he had eternity. She didn't recognize the name he gave for his home town, but she knew his own name well enough. It was Shim. An almost Jewish name. Though he was no Jew, he said. His grandfather had been a Jew, however, who'd left the valley of Jezreel in one of the dispersals, sixty years ago.

Now he'd come back to the land of his forebears, Shim said, to seek something that he could not name. "Perhaps there is no word for it. As yet."

"To meet with god," suggested Aphas, keen to show he was a man of culture.

"No, no, the word 'god' is hardly strong enough for what I seek." He would not look at the old man, but only concentrated on his staff and his own voice. "My god is not a holy king, an emperor in heaven. He's immanent in everything. In things like this . . ." he shook his staff, ". . . and in the human spirit. He will absorb us when we die. If we are ready. But first we have to find that something for which I have no word . . ."

"Enlightenment's a word . . ." ventured Aphas.

"Enlightenment comes to the ignorant. That is their candle in the dark and their salvation from the sensual impulses and appetites of public life. But for myself, I am looking more for . . . Tranquillity, perhaps. That's not so easy to acquire." He rubbed his fingers on his thumbs, as if his words were cloth. "I can encounter god at home. I can find enlightenment in tiny things. I do not have to leave the house. But here . . ." again he felt the cloth of words, "what better place to look beyond enlightenment and god for nameless things than here, in caves, far from the comforts and distractions of the world?" Aphas nodded all the while, though men like Shim — scholars, mystics, sages, ascetes, stoics, epicureans, that holy regiment — were a mystery to him. Why punish your body voluntarily when the world and god would punish it in their good time? It would not do to argue, though, with someone of Shim's undoubted

64

class and dignity. "I've understood," he said, although to Marta's eyes, he looked alarmed. "I know it, though there is no word for it . . ."

"As yet."

He had not turned his back on god, the emperor of heaven, Shim continued. Not on one god. Not on any of the gods. But he was Greek in his beliefs. He worshipped every living thing. "I worship this," he said, picking up a stone. "I worship those." He pointed at the birds. "I worship this." Again he turned the spirals of his staff.

"That's good. That's very Greek," said Aphas.

"I worship everybody here," Shim continued. His voice was slow, and hardly audible. "Excepting one of course." He lifted a hand from his staff and pointed at himself.

Aphas could not claim to have such selfless motives as Shim, he said. He could not claim to be so Greek. He'd come for quarantine because ("No need to wrap it up in complicated words") he was dying. These forty days were his last chance, his priest had said. He hoped to make his peace with god and with himself, of course. But most of all he hoped for miracles, that all the fasting and the prayers would make him well again. Tranquillity was easy to acquire, compared to that. He had a growth, he said. "A living thing, inside of me. No one could worship that. Bigger than my fist." He showed his fist, and pointed at his side. "You can feel how hard it is." He waited for a volunteer to press a finger into his side. Shim leaned forward on to his braided legs, put his finger on the growth, and nodded: "Like you say," he said.

"Come on." Aphas waved the badu over, and called to him in both Greek and Aramaic, and then translated it into finger-mime. "Feel this."

The badu sprang on to his feet and padded over as nimbly and as silently as a cat, grinning all the time. He lifted up the mason's shirt. Marta could see the stomach was distended. The skin was stretched. It looked as if the old man had an extra knee-cap placed between his thigh bone and his ribs. The badu spat out pebbles, laughed, and cupped the growth in the flat of his hand. He shook his head from side to side. He tapped the cancer with his fingertips and put his ear to Aphas's chest and grabbed hold of his hand. Nothing that he did made any sense. Aphas had to tug quite hard before the badu would let go. He wanted sympathy, or miracles, not this.

"He doesn't understand a word of it," Aphas said, retreating into chatter as he'd done for all his life. His nose was running and his eyes were wet. "Here, Master Shim, this fellow's yours. You love all living things, you said. Love him." He forced a laugh and wiped his eyes. He then repeated what he'd said, almost word for word . . . "Love him, I said." He turned to Marta, only looking for a nod or smile from her to rescue him from his embarrassment. She laughed for reasons of her own. Her three companions were absurd. Even the honey-head. Perhaps he was the maddest of them all.

They had hardly noticed that the sun was up and their forty days were underway. But soon — once Shim and Aphas had agreed that everyone would gather at dusk when they would light a communal fire and break their fast with Marta's scrub fowl and the free food of the wilderness if any could be caught or found — they fell silent, even Aphas. They concentrated on themselves. Finally, they sought the shade and privacy of their caves. The badu wandered along the scarp, crying out and kneeling down once in a while to pick up stones. Marta was relieved to stay alone, sitting in the sun, counting seeds. The birds that had been waiting in the thorns flocked back into the water, dipping beaks and wings. But very soon they were outnumbered. The water in the cistern smelled so mossy and the birds, excited by the unexpected boon of water, sang so unremittingly, that every living creature in the hills could smell and hear the summons to drink.

Swag flies, mud wasps and fleas blistered the surface of the water, dipping their bodies at both ends; one dip to drink and one to drop a line of eggs. Centipedes and millipedes, lonely lovers of the damp, gathered at the edges of the cistern in rare communion. Whip bugs and round worms celebrated in the mud. And slugs and snails, descending to the water and the bobbing body of a roach, signed the stones and rubble of the gravesides with their mucous threads. Star lizards blinked and turned their flattened heads in search of easy food. Overhead and in the thorns, more birds were gathering to breakfast on the throng.

Marta was still reluctant to go back to the cave. She hoped the little woman would return: "Hello, it's me. The woman yesterday." But all she saw were birds and insects, drawn to the water in the cistern. She was drawn as well. She went to watch them drinking and, perhaps, to catch a second bird. Her shadow fell across the grave. Again the birds shook out their wings and fled. She ducked and dodged. She did not scream. The lizards scuttled behind stones, and shut their eyes at her. The insects exercised their wings. Snails shrank into their shells, and mimed the secret life of stones. It seemed to Marta that she'd dipped her fingers into and drunk some holy essence. It was the fourth day of creation when god directed that the waters teem with countless living creatures and that the birds fly high above the earth, across the vault of heaven. She did not feel elated by god's work, but — like any other lukewarm Jew — she was repulsed. She'd have to overcome her fear of insects and suppress the edicts of Leviticus ("These creatures shall be vermin unto you, and you will make yourself unclean with them") before she'd find the heart to drink again.

CHAPTER
NINE

Musa was tired and disappointed. When Miri had told
him about the four cave-dwellers, he had presumed that
one of them would be the Galilean man. Why else would
he have followed Miri away from the comforts of the
tent to walk uphill into the heat and scrub? There were
better things to do. He could be resting, eating, taking
stock? He had the bruises of his fever to shake off. And
he had plans to make. How to turn his bad luck into
coins. How to catch up with the caravan with only one
pack-animal — and that one pregnant — to carry the tent
and all their possessions. How to get to Jericho where he
could buy a camel, trade some of his goods, and lay
claim once more to the title of merchant. But first there
was unfinished business with the water thief. He wanted
to see the man again. What for? He couldn't say. But, if
Miri's querulous reports could be trusted, the Galilean
had passed the night in caves. She'd pointed to the
coppery, pock-marked cliffs. "Not far," she'd said. Not
far, perhaps, for someone built like her. A chicken, all
skin and bone and beak. No meat on her, except for the
slight, high swelling of her stomach. But for Musa, this
outing was hard work. He was a duck to Miri's chicken,
flat-footed and ungainly. His thighs were so thick that

they required him to walk in opposing quarters: his right foot took him to Jerusalem, his left foot set off for Negev. He tacked his way across the scrub, with tiny steps.

At first Miri was required to walk behind with the water-bag and a mat, throwing her narrow shade across his back. Musa was not pleased with her. Everything had been her fault; the fever, his abandonment, his immobility, his loss of goods. He'd ordered her to pull the donkey carcass out of sight. It smelled. It bothered him. Even the vultures had only circled it, and gone away without tasting its disease. Something, though, less discriminating than a vulture had chewed its stomach out during the night. The scrub dogs, probably. Its eyes had gone. And there were flies. But Miri claimed the body was too heavy for her to move alone. She had refused to even try — and that was something she had never done before. For fear of a clout. What was happening to his wife? He'd caught her weeping in the night. Crying for the donkey? Surely not. Now she was sulking like a disappointed child, throwing things about the tent, making too much noise, complaining that her buttocks ached. Not that she had buttocks worthy of the name. Perhaps that was the price of pregnancy — disobedience, bad temper, aches. Did she expect that he would tolerate such disrespect for four more months?

"Keep out of sight," he'd said to her when they began their walk. But the ground was stony and uncomfortable. He did not see why he should suffer first, and so he sent his wife ahead to simplify a path for him. She had to clap

70

her hands to scare off any snakes. She had to kick away scrub balls and snap off any thorny branches in his way. She had to find the softest ground, and pull aside the loose rocks which might block his path. She hardly made a difference. It would have taken twenty men to clear a path. For Musa, though, his little chicken wife, clapping as she led the way for him, would have to do. He had his dreams. There would be twenty men at his command when he was rich. He'd be preceded everywhere he went by twenty men. They'd clear the path of stones. They'd throw down rushes. There'd be twenty girls as well — and none of them would look like chickens.

At last they reached the valley bed with its soft clay. Musa didn't have to stamp to make his mark. His feet sank in. His ankles twisted when he walked. He summoned his wife to his side, and leaned on her. His buttocks and calves were aching now. Compared to Miri's, his were buttocks ten times worthy of the name. So his pains were ten times worse than hers. His lungs were bursting. He wasn't built for hiking. He was built for litters, or for camels. Perhaps he had been hasty when he killed the donkey. He could, perhaps, have ridden on her back to meet the Galilean or got Miri to assemble a donkey cart. That would have been more dignified.

Except there was no Galilean there, as far as he could tell. When Miri had finally pushed him up the last few steps of the scarp, through the rash of poppies, to the shaded foot of the cliffs, and he had settled down with his exhaustion on the mat, there wasn't any sign of life at all, except the congregation of birds.

"Call out," he ordered Miri. "Unless, of course, a call's too heavy for you."

She obeyed, and called "Gather, gather!", her husband's market cry; and soon the quarantiners came down from their caves, one by one, and stood a little nervously in line in front of Musa while he looked each of them in the face as if they were for sale. He could tell at once what they were worth. Not much, the badu. Musa could trade two badus for one goat. Except this one had silver bracelets. The old Jew was an artisan and dying, by the looks of him. A man like him would be too proud to travel without money. The blond was carrying a walking staff, made out of spiralled tarbony. Quite valuable. Musa knew his type, a seasoned traveller and, probably, prepared for thieves. He'd have some hidden coins sewn in his cloak. The woman? Good clothes — a woven hair veil in fine material, a long sleeveless tunic, girdled twice as was the fashion, once beneath her bosom, once around her waist. Good cloth. Good skin. Good teeth. Good heavy purse, as well, he thought. And easy pickings.

The four cave-dwellers seemed to know they should not speak. The badu tugged and twisted his hair in high strands. The other three stood patiently, glad — so far, at least — of this diversion in their day. What was it about her husband, Miri wondered, that made strangers treat him regally, defer to him? His size? Were they afraid of size? Or was their meekness more deliberate, not signifying their respect for Musa, but a token of their own tranquillity?

"Just four of you," he said at last. The old one nodded in agreement. "And where's the other one?" The woman shook her head, and for an instant caught Miri's eye. Just half a smile. Miri had seen smiles like that before — from people who were surprised by Musa's adolescent, reedy voice.

The old Jew spoke for all of them. He thought, perhaps, there'd been a fifth when they were walking to the hills the day before. It might have been a boy, a woman or a man. He could not tell. His eyesight was not good. The figure was too far away. Quite tall. It might have been a shepherd even. But there were only four of them who'd come to carry out devotions in these caves. "My name is Aphas. From Jerusalem . . ." he began.

"And you?" Musa said, ignoring Aphas from Jerusalem. He pointed with his chin at Marta. "Why are you here?"

"To pray and fast. Like them," she said. "For quarantine . . ."

"Why fast? What will you gain from it?"

She shook her head. She didn't want to say. She smiled and shrugged and blushed. Musa watched her breasts and shoulders lift. She might be Miri's age, perhaps, but she was tall and generous, he thought. She was the kind of woman Musa would have twenty of when he was rich. She'd move a donkey without arguing. She wouldn't make a bother of her pregnancy. He wet his lips and smiled at her. "Where is the other one?" he asked. "The water thief?"

"Not us," the old man interrupted. "We have our own." He pointed to the pit in the ground behind his back.

"What's there?" asked Musa, indicating his own grave with, again, the slightest movement of his chin. Miri stepped back, out of Musa's sight. She put her hand up to her mouth. Would anybody say, "That's where your wife spent yesterday. She dug that grave for you"? Miri pinched her lips between her fingers.

"Our water cistern," Aphas said. "It was already here . . . For god provides."

Already there? Musa was inspired. His mind was as quick and direct as his body was clumsy. He could see a trading opportunity at once, and a fast solution to the problems of his unsought delay in the wilderness. Here was an opening for him. God provides, indeed. He looked from face to face to satisfy himself that none of them could be the Galilean and that none of them were worldly or local enough to spot his lie. And then: "It's there because I put it there," he said. "My land. My water." He pointed to the rows of caves up in the cliff. "My caves."

Miri took her hand away from her mouth. She had to smile. Her husband was the demon of the mat. She listened with her mouth open while he recounted how he had dug that hole himself, with some help from his wife. He turned his head as best he could and closed an eye at her. She should keep quiet.

It was hard work, he said. The ground was full of stones: "My wife is pregnant. Look at her. She's not as young as me. She isn't fit to dig a hole in mud let alone in stones. She isn't big enough to even lift a stone. She broke her fingernails. Show them your hands." Miri did as she was told. "Hard work," he said again. He wasn't at this point quite sure why he and Miri had dug the hole. He needed time to think, and this he gained by making

74

Miri show her damaged fingernails to each of them. By the time she'd come back to his shoulder he had found the next verse to his song. "My little donkey died," he said. She was diseased. It was a cruel kindness to end her misery. She was an animal he'd owned since he was a boy. She was his sister. "That pit . . ." (the slightest movement of the chin again) ". . . was to be her grave." He couldn't let a donkey rot, out in the open, not a donkey so much loved, he said. She would attract wolves, or leopards. He didn't have to tell them how dangerous that was. For everyone. What, then, should he do now? Put the donkey in the grave and bury her under stones, as he had planned? Or let his hard work come to nothing for the sake of a drop of water, and some strangers? He closed his eyes and hummed to himself as if even Solomon would be taxed by such a choice. Here was a further opportunity to think of ways of turning these four into profit.

"And then, of course, there is the other matter, too," he said at last. The matter of the caves. Accommodation is not free, he explained. They wouldn't call in at an inn and expect to eat and sleep for nothing. That was not dignified or rational. This was not common land, and travellers would have to pay a tribute of some kind. A token tribute. Nothing large. A gesture only. "A sip, a sip, the merest sip," he said, and liked the sound of it. They did not have to pay, of course. They could choose to move elsewhere. And that was free. They might imagine they could stay and not pay rent. "You can imagine, too, how sad I'd be if you decided that," he said. "And how my hundred burly cousins in these hills might feel justified to come with sticks and turn you out. I only have to belch round here for there to be a storm. Your choice." He'd give them till midday to make up their minds.

While the badu concentrated on his hair, the other two men debated what they could do about the water and the caves and Musa's uncouth cousins. It looked as if their quarantine was doomed. Musa entwined his fingers in his lap and closed his eyes. He made himself too large and placid to defy. His world was such a shapely place. He had the sweetest, simplest plan. He'd stick around until he'd shaken all their pockets out. It wouldn't take him forty days. He'd have his fingers on the spiralled staff, the silver bracelets, the old man's purse, the hidden coins in the cloak, in less than ten. He'd have his fingers on the woman's breasts, as well, if only he could bide his time. She was worth the forty days, and more. He liked her fabrics and her cloths. Her textiles made his penis twitch. His eyes were not entirely shut. He looked at Marta through his lashes. He liked the way she lifted up her tunic hem, and ran the fabric through her fingers like a set of beads.

Marta knew that Musa was watching her. He was as subtle as a hungry dog. Her husband, Thaniel, was a jewel compared to him. She would not want to be married to a man like that; his little wife was hardly better than a slave. But Marta was jealous of Miri, nevertheless. The woman was enslaved perhaps, but sinewy and spirited . . . and pregnant. Here was the person that Marta would like to be herself, the one that took her place in dreams, whose warp hung heavy on the

76

weft. Marta had held Miri briefly by the hand when she had come to show her broken fingernails. Their touching skins could not have been more different, the one as full and oily as an olive, the other parchmenty. Marta longed to put her hand on Miri's stomach and feel the wing-beats of her child. Would that be parchmenty as well? If only babies were contagious, like a fever . . . If only she could pass her hands through flesh and cup the child inside her palms . . . If only Miri would agree to sell . . .

Marta pulled up the little bag tied into the material of her tunic top, and felt its weight of coins. She could pay. She could pay for Miri's baby, if only four months could be compressed into the forty days and there was a child for sale. She was prepared to pay for water and for rent, as well, so long as Miri was around. In fact, it was a comfort in some ways to pay, because it guaranteed she would not starve or freeze to death, and it would buy her access to Musa's little slave. She let the bag drop down again on its drawstring, into the warmth and darkness of her clothes. It made the slightest bulge, and made her blush, because she knew that Musa watched the dropping bag and that his eyes had travelled with it underneath the folds of cloth. She pulled her hair veil down across her face and waited for the old man and Shim, the honey-top, to finish their negotiations and make their bid to Musa.

Musa often claimed that seeing inside the heads of his adversaries was, for him, as easy as judging melons by their skins. He knew when they were sweet and ripe. He knew if they held any juice, and where and when to squeeze. He knew when they were cavernous and dry. It was an easy game to play. He was the champion. He judged and squeezed his clients in the marketplace, and knew, before they even knew themselves, how much they'd offer as their initial bid as well as what they'd end up paying as the final price. They nearly always gave the game away. Their fingers moved, and spelled out twos and threes and fours. They smiled too much or met his eyes too levelly if they were cheating him. Their breathing changed if they were feeling pressurized. There was a whole vocabulary of casual coughs, finger-tapping, tongues on teeth, false frowns, which told the emperor of trade if his suppliers or his buyers were underbidding, backing off, or ready for the deal.

So Shim and Aphas were no contest for a man like Musa. He watched their conversation from his mat — the old man urgent, pressured, volatile; the blond one shamming his indifference to money, numbers, water, rent. If they had any sense, Musa thought, they'd recognize their trading weaknesses and not attempt to better him. How could they better him? They were townspeople, by the looks of it, and far from home. They wouldn't know the customs of the scrub. Their reasoning would be that every stretch of land inside a town was owned by someone. All land was good for goats or corn or rent. Why not the country too? Why not the wilderness? And so they'd end up paying for the water and the caves. They'd not make any fuss, or ask for any proof, not with a hundred cousins in the hills. They might plead poverty at first, and ask that Musa earn a place in their devotions by showing them some charity.

But he'd refuse. Charity and loans were the commerce of a fool. No, no, they'd either have to pay, or start their quarantine again, elsewhere, he'd say. No other choice. Perhaps they'd like to gather up their things and go? He'd tell Miri to prepare the donkey for burial in their water cistern. That's when they'd start to empty out their purses like prodigals and wedding guests.

Musa put his fingers in his lap and tried to calculate what his profit on the day might be. What was the going rate for muddy water and for caves? What could he charge? As much as he could get. The badu with the hennaed hair could hardly contribute, of course. He couldn't pay in cash. That much was obvious. He couldn't even talk. "He doesn't have a tongue," the sickly Jew had said. But what about the sickly Jew himself? A purse-proud little working man, too dignified to beg for anything, too dull to ever shirk a debt. Such a man would never travel far from home without some silver pieces for the journey. He'd have a money-belt beneath his cloak like every artisan, containing coins and, perhaps, some salt crystals for good luck, plus a twist of sweet resin to catch his fleas. Musa even smiled to himself, though Musa's smile was thinner than his lips. No fleas on me, he thought. They can't afford the rent.

This Aphas, though, according to Musa's reasoning, would do his best to pay the rent. He looked exhausted by the journey, and withered by his sickness, too. He wouldn't want to move elsewhere. He couldn't move elsewhere. For this — the water and the cave, the right to rest and stay, the licence to breathe desert air — he'd pay out eight pieces, Musa judged. He'd pay out ten, if pressed. But not, perhaps, a coin more. The blond one would pay eight as well. He'd say it made no difference to him whether he was rich or poor. He would not wish to argue over rent. He'd claim he didn't need the shelter or the water, that he would settle for the stars and dew, that a thousand cousins did not bother him. And then he'd get his money out and pay.

The woman? Musa peered at her again, and ran his tongue along his teeth. She could afford as much, or more, as the two men. Look at her clothes. Look at her unmarked hands. But let her pay the eight as well. Musa looked up from his calculations. Three eights were twenty-four. That was enough. He'd drop to twenty if he must. He coughed, and motioned to the two men with his chins. "Yes, yes," he said. He didn't have all day.

He let them have their say. They were intemperate. They offered twenty-five between the four of them, fifteen at once and ten in forty days. Musa was more easily persuaded by their case than they had expected. Twenty-five was not enough, he said. He was insulted by their twenty-five. But it was wrong, perhaps, to deny them water for the sake of principle. That much he would concede. There are traditions even in the wilderness. A traveller can wet his lips and face for free. So, yes, he would accept just the twenty-five pieces of silver, but they would have to pay it all at once. He could not have them in his debt. And he accepted, too, their inconvenient request to leave the donkey's grave unfilled. And in return for his forbearance? The three men could come down to his tent and help to drag the donkey to the precipice.

"Be friends with me," he said. "Stay here for forty days. Drink all the water that you want. Pray till you have a camel's knees." He would be neighbourly and could supply them with their daily needs. He had some dates and olives he could sell. Fig cakes. Dried fruit. Goat's milk. Goat's meat, if they could match his price. And there was grain which she — his chin was lifted at his wife — will grind and bake for bread. There were rugs and rush bed-mats which they could hire. Lamps, with oil. Camel dung, for fuel. Everything to make their stay more comfortable. Best of all, they could be sure that they were well protected. With Musa as their landlord, no one would dare to come and trouble them, or take advantage of their devotions. His name was known and respected by everybody in the hills and far beyond. Everybody was his cousin, even the scorpions.

Musa spat on to his hand and called the three male quarantiners forward to close their deal. "Just one more thing," he said, "and then it's done": when the forty days were up, then they could show their thanks by helping him to carry his possessions and the tent down to the track which led to Jericho. They could be his donkeys for a day. In return, he wouldn't make them pay him any passage tax for travelling through his territory. That much was free.

"What do you say? Is this not better than you hoped?"

Musa felt — as ever — pleased to be himself. He had found the morning unexpectedly amusing, and satisfying, too, despite the absence of the Galilean man. Already his retinue and his clientele had grown. His wealth increased. His dreams came true. The caravan and his deceitful uncles could be buried beneath the pleasures of the day. Everyone he met, it seemed, except the badu (and he would have to pay some other price) was opening a purse and inviting him to put his fingers in. And why? To pay for earth and air and water that was the property of god. If every market-place was full of fools like these three fools, he'd only have to dig a pit and watch while people threw their money in. All this — and all within a day of riding fever to the open gates of death. He was invincible.

He made Shim lend him his staff for the walk back to the tent. It was downhill but hardly easier than coming up. His feet, unseen beyond his waist, descended into empty space. Musa had to place the staff ahead of him, feel for solid ground, and send his weight along its spiralled length, before he dared to shuffle forward. His fever had weakened him. He was immensely slow. But languor was the right of merchant kings when they were weighed down with the prizes of the market-place.

Luckily, his five companions were in no hurry for themselves. They had forty days to fill. This interlude with Musa was, at least, less wearying than unbroken prayer. Aphas, anyway, was glad to be as slow as Musa, but his steps were weightless. He did his best to listen to Shim's teachings and expostulations, to nod with recognition at the places that he named, but he could only concentrate on his increasing pain. His ankles felt as fragile as an unfired pot. His cankered liver nagged and lobbied without cease. The heat was punishing. He'd been a stonemason all his working life, perhaps, but none of these stones in his path offered any solace.

They were only nuisances. A little distance to the side, and behind the men, Marta walked with Miri, their bodies brushing, their hems in unison. The badu ran ahead and cleared the path. He was a volunteer. He seemed to find the rocks and stones amusing, laughing at them as he turned them on their sides. The badu's cries were strange — unformed and blustering. A vulture looking down on them and smelling death and fat and pregnancy, as they left their thousand footprints in the clay and emerged from the little valley on to the plateau of the tent, would be hard pressed to guess which one would be its carrion.

Musa was exhausted when he reached the tent. He went inside for rest, and for some private moments with his flask of date spirit. He felt the fabrics of the bed. He ran his fingers through his wools, and thought of Marta, naked, waiting to be draped in narrow lengths of cloth. The women sat cross-legged in shade, outside. They were whispering, but Musa didn't care what women had to say. He lay back on his cushions, looked out through the open awning and watched the three men circling the donkey's carcass, holding their noses, shaking their heads like undertakers. Aphas shook his head because he did not want to help with burial. He was too old and tired and ill. A Jew that touched a donkey corpse would be unclean until the night, and then would have to purify himself in water that should, at least, be cleaner than the water in the cistern.

The other two shook their heads because they'd never seen an animal so bludgeoned. Musa smiled. So now they'd understand what kind of man he was, what sort of landlord he could be. He watched the badu and the blond man stoop to test the donkey's weight. Miri had been right. The carcass was too heavy for a woman to move on her own, despite the loss of blood and eyes and entrails. But these two men were strong and evidently not concerned about the weight or smell. The blond one, Musa noticed, was more powerful than he appeared to be at first. The badu was not powerful at all, but sinewy. They disposed of Musa's jenny with speed and energy. He watched them drag the donkey by her legs, leaving a trail of blood and flies across the scrub to the smooth and stoneless slope which led to the rim of the precipice. He could not see the donkey now, just the shrinking heads and shoulders of the two men.

Musa — already resurrected by his drink — half expected that a fifth figure, the water thief, would appear out of the wilderness to lend a hand. The air was heavy with the presence of the man. Would he shake water on the donkey's face, caress her eyelids with his thumb, and bid the donkey to "Be well again"? Or would he join the hennaed hair and the blond as they pulled up the back legs of the animal and tipped her body off the precipice to float for half a moment in mid-air and then to drop into the grieving shadows of the cliff? Shim shouted with excitement on the steep decline, "Let fly, let fly", as if the donkey were a dove.

CHAPTER
TEN

A lesser person, Jesus thought as he departed from the dying body in the tent on that first afternoon, would lose his nerve and head back for the way-marked caves, up in the hills. That was the easy path. He had seen the footprints of the little group of travellers who had preceded him, deviating from the camel trail. He could have followed them and passed his quarantine in company, tucked into the folds of clay, amongst the poppies, and exposed to nothing worse than forty days of boredom and discomfort. But Jesus had a harsher challenge for himself. Quite what it was he didn't know. He only understood that he should choose a way that was more punishing. The worse it was, the better it would be. That, surely, was the purpose of the wilderness: He knew the scriptures and the stories of the prophets. Triumph over hardship was their proof of holiness.

He had decided to climb down to the key-hole cave that he had spotted earlier that morning, when his mood was still reckless and ambitious. He was elated by the distance he had put between himself and his parents. Anything seemed possible. He had not yet begun the hard, dispiriting ascent up the landfall into the hills.

Perhaps if he had been more tired when he had seen the hanging cave he would have set his heart on somewhere more attainable. But, invigorated by a shepherd's breakfast — goat's cheese and bread — and a good night's sleep in sweet straw, it was not difficult for Jesus to believe that god had drawn his eyes to that cave in the precipice, and for a purpose. God was testing him. God was waiting for him at the cave. If only he could face the climb down — and Jesus, even as a boy, had never cared for clambering on cliffs, or trees, or rooftops — he could spend his quarantine with god for company. He could tuck himself into the folds of god.

Here was a man who'd been a simple-hearted child, much loved and loving, nervous and obedient; quick to listen, happy to believe whatever he was told; observant in his prayers and rituals. Unremarkable, in fact. Except in this: by the time he was thirteen or so, he was the only one among his friends who behaved as if the customs and routines of their religion were anything more than tiresome duties. He was the only adolescent in the neighbourhood who demanded more from god than festivals and regimens and rules. He loved his prayers, like a child. They were a comfort to him. More comforting than food or sleep, it seemed. And just as well, because he didn't sleep enough for someone of his age, his mother thought. He didn't eat enough. He dozed and grazed on his devotions, like a priest. Except, unlike most priests, his devotions did not make him mild and fat. He was as skittish, pale and narrow-shouldered as a goose. The neighbours called him Gally, a common nickname for a Galilean boy whose accent was strong, but ideal for Jesus. He was like a gally fly. He could not rest.

In his mid-teens, Jesus grew much taller suddenly; long and timid and even more preoccupied with prayers. "His head's in heaven, with the angels and the doves," was the local joke. "Any day now, and his feet'll leave the ground." It was a judgement that satisfied Jesus. He was indeed in heaven, for he had discovered ways of praying that were more than simply comforting. They were chaotic and exalting. When Jesus prayed, there came a point where the words were speaking him; and he became their object, not their source. Sometimes these prayers spoke him in Greek or Aramaic. He would listen to himself and try to memorize the wisdoms that he heard. Was this how Moses kept in touch with god? But there were occasions, more mystifying, feverish, and blissful, when the language was unknown, a tripping, spittle-basted tongue, plosive and percussive and high-pitched. Then, if he was left undisturbed for long enough with these wild rhapsodies, he might feel his spirit soften and solidify at once. He was an egg immersed in boiling water, a fusing and dividing trinity of yolk and white and shell. In that respect, he was transformed by god like other boys his age were changed by girls.

His mother and his father would not leave him undisturbed for long enough to be transformed as often as he liked. They shook him by the shoulders when they found him sodden with his prayers, or sent one of his brothers to distract him. Devotion, yes; by all means let him be a righteous Jew, they said. They would encourage it. But unremitting piety like his was suitable for old men, not for boys. Why was he not more like their other sons, dragged unwillingly from their cots each morning by their exasperated parents? Jesus was unnatural; an adolescent dragged unwillingly from prayer. His mother feared she'd never find a wife for him, he'd never put on any flesh, not while he prayed so often and with such riotous solemnity.

Finally, his father took advice from the priest, a subtle and subversive man, who understood the fervours and elations of the young and liked to keep the company of less pious adolescents than Jesus. He took the mumbled prayers to be, like sniggering and whistling, an irritating habit for a boy. He recommended that Jesus's devotions should be more actively discouraged. "He has to learn that there are important duties other than prayer," he said. "Give him more things to do about the house. Get him to help you with the carpentry. Make him so tired he only wants to sleep. Throw water on him if he starts to pray in gibberish. Don't be ashamed to use a stick. He'll grow out of this the moment that he starts a beard. It's just his age."

The priest was right. By the time Jesus's chin and upper lip were wispy with hair, the prayers seemed to have abandoned him. His private languages disappeared, like adolescent boils. He resembled the neighbours' sons at last, except he was more nervous and more serious, a touch bereft perhaps. At least he wasn't rising off the ground and nudging angels with his head. He even ate and slept.

88

Yet, despite appearances, Jesus had not lost any of his passion for god. He did not need to move his lips to pray. He'd reached the stage where every breath was prayer, where all the steps and sounds he made were verses for god, where everything was touched with holiness: a heel of bread, the soundless corners of the house when he woke up, the cobwebbed shadows on the clay-white walls, the motes of sawdust hanging in the window light, the patterns on his fingertips. God in everything and everything in god. Even with his father in the workshop, cutting wood and making frames, he found there was a rhythm to the bow-drill and the draw-knife and the plane which took the place of prayer. Every movement was a repetition; every repetition was a word. The timber and the tools took on new meanings. The knots in wood were sins. Twisted wood was devil's work and should be thrown out or burned.

Once or twice, immersed in reveries of light and work and wood, he had neared and glimpsed the large and inexplicable itself. To be alive amongst the sawdust and the stars was beyond understanding; to be this person, in this place, and now. Even to contemplate that puzzle was to stray too far from safer paths, to sweat and shiver in that hollow room which has no doors or walls, where Never End and Never Start hold their invisible debate. There'd be no echo there to comfort him, or anyone. No dark or light. Not even any time. And only god — if only god would show himself — to make much sense of it. Faith or dismay, that was the choice. Choose Never End or Never Start. Choose god or pandemonium. When Jesus chose and put his faith in god, he blinked away the hollow room. He brought the wood, the tools, the workshop into focus once more. His spirit softened and solidified again, as it had done when he was in his teens, except more bleakly. It formed a question to be put to god. A question taken from the hollow room. A question that a child would ask. This was his question for the wilderness. The question of a simple-hearted, fragile man — guileless in his love of god, spontaneous and vulnerable in his beliefs. You see these motes, this dust, this bread, these soundless corners hung with webs, these fingertips, engraved with tiny lines? What for, and why?

No wonder Jesus was a clumsy carpenter. He would have built a leaking ark. He concentrated on the large and inexplicable, and neglected what was on his bench. He cut or hit his fingers far too many times. God's patterns on his fingertips were scarred. But he was happy to have wounds. The wounds were prayers, and answers to his prayers. His prayers drew blood.

The wilderness was large and inexplicable as well. Only an innocent would try to tackle it with nothing on his feet, and leave his water-skin and overcloak behind. But Jesus had to put his trust in god's provision for the forty days, and could hardly pack a bag with clothes and food as a reserve against shortfalls. He did his best to persuade himself that god was at his shoulder at that very moment, supplying all the courage that it took to get up from the woven comforts of the dying merchant's tent and set off in the falling light towards the cliff-top. But he had found it difficult to pray, away from home. It was hard to concentrate on god when his feet were so sore. He found it easier to summon up his parents and his brothers, and his Galilean neighbours, and their priest. They were transported to the scrub to witness him. At first, they would be laughing at his foolishness. Their god-struck, visionary boy, too shy to look them in the eye, who'd hid himself in gabbling scriptures, had gone off in a temper to the hills. Their Gally was absurd. Look at his bleeding feet. Look at his flaking lips. Observe that holy, love-lorn look across his face. See how he hardly manages that little climb up to the ridge. They would expect him to be weak, to turn back at the challenge of the landfall, to take the easy path up to the poppy caves, to fall asleep inside the merchant's tent. But when they saw him persevere they would wonder at his fortitude and say, "We never knew him after all." He could not quite admit it to himself but Jesus took more courage from the thought of surprising his parents than he took from satisfying god.

But, in these final moments of his journey, between the tent and cave, Jesus was a tired and disappointed man. He did not feel much welcomed by the scrub. Its textures were harsh and colourless. Its skies were far too large and low. He'd been naive. He'd hoped for greater hospitality, that the path would rid itself of stones and sweep away its thorns for him. God's unfinished landscape would provide a way, he thought. The scrubland would recognize his simple dress, his solemn purposes, his modesty. Its hills would flatten. Its rocks would soften. It would protect his naked feet. This, after all, was the path that led to god, still at work on his creation. So the path should become more heavenly, more freshly formed, safer at every step. It should become an infant Galilee. The winds should be more musical. The light should shiver and the air should smell of offerings. But god had left the thorns and stones in place across the scrub.

At last, in the approaches to the cliff-top where Jesus had to find the way down to his lodgings for the night, the scrub began to slope, eroded by flash floods and centuries of wind. There were no plants. Here, the soil was smooth and crumbling and dangerous. All the loosened stones of any size had rolled away and fallen to the scree pans on the valley floor. Somewhere along the precipice, the latest rock fell free. It made its noisy, tumbling farewell to the slope, and bounced into the weightless silence of its fall. Any nervous man like Jesus, only used to Galilean heights and daunted by the receding ground, would feel afraid of being like that stone. He should not, therefore, have felt ashamed of getting down on his hands and knees and edging forwards on all-fours, like a sheep, towards the fragile brink of the cliff. But Jesus was ashamed, and frightened, too. Frightened that he would end up amongst the scree. Frightened of the night ahead. Frightened of his quarantine.

This was the final opportunity for Jesus to turn around and go back to the tent. It would not be hard to justify such a short retreat — his religious duty was to help a dying man. Perhaps he ought to settle for the easy caves up in the hills. That might have been god's intention all along. But Jesus was too nervous to stand up and flee.

He felt like Yehoch, perching on the temple roof, calling out for angels and for ropes, because he could not tell if he should put his trust in god or men. The optimist and innocent who had set off that morning from the shepherd's hut had now become a pessimist. Jesus had persuaded himself earlier that day that creation was continuing in these hills. Look at the lack of trees, he'd told himself, the thinness of plants and grasses. God would be at work still. This was the edge of god's unfinished universe. But what on earth could god complete on this despairing precipice? Where were his fingerprints? What work was there to do? Every Galilean knew that vegetation was the fruit of god's union with the earth. There was no vegetation on these slopes. Perhaps there was no god either. Perhaps this was the devil's realm. The stones were sinners. And the scree was hell.

Jesus hung on with his naked hands and feet. He was ashamed. His neighbours and his family were watching him. They were his witnesses. "Ah, yes," they'd say. "He's fallen now, down on his knees. Look at him crawl."

He had no choice. He hung his head over the precipice, and looked from left to right, for a descending path, and any evidence of caves. The light was poor, but he was lucky. He could not see his cave, or any cave, but he could see a sloping rock similar to the one which formed the front deck to his chosen sanctuary. The perfect perch for eagles, and for angels, he had said. Except there were no eagles nor any angels, just ravens and the falling debris of the cliff.

One of the ravens landed close to Jesus, turned its head a dozen times, inspecting him for food, and then flew off, calling out its disappointment — tok-tok, tok-tok, tok-tok. Its voice was unmistakable, more like a carpenter's than a bird's. He'd made the noise himself a thousand times — the impact of a tool on wood. But, although he tried his best, Jesus could not take it as a sign that god was calling him. He had expected signs all day, it's true. Some shaft of sunshine, picking out a rock. Some burning bush. A distant voice, perhaps, to tell him how he ought to reach his cave. A white dove, yes; or the elated song of a warbler might carry messages from god. But tok-tok-tok? God would be more eloquent than that. Jesus had to wait for quite a while, clinging like an insect to his slope, before a better sign was offered him. A steady flight of storks, coming up from Egypt to the north — the Sea of Galilee, perhaps — were passing overhead. A sign of spring. One dropped below its companions and flew along the massive, sheer cliffs of the valley. Its white shoulders and body were briefly highlighted by the sun against the greys and browns. Then it shrank away so far that it became a duck, a dove, a fading speck of white, a mote of sawdust in the window light. The moment that it disappeared, Jesus told himself, would be the moment that he moved.

So Jesus took his courage from the stork to edge along the cliff on hands and knees, looking for a way down to his cave. It was not difficult. It was not long before the ground grew rougher underfoot and underhand. There was a rockfall, where the land had split and slipped, like a broken crust of bread. Jesus started to climb down. The marl was soft enough to crumble between his fingers. There were struggling signs of god's creation, at last. A few opportunist plants — morning star, hyssop, saltwood — had taken root in the crevices and on the leeward side of rocks. They lent their odour to the climb and left their muffled blessings on his palms whenever he took hold of them. Hyssop was familiar, a herb for eggs and fish, but now it was the smell of vertigo and fear. When the rockfall steepened, Jesus descended on his thighs, facing outwards. The ground was loose but firm enough to take his weight. He did not trust his feet. They were already torn and bleeding from the walk and now were further scratched and battered by the earth. He tried to put as much weight as he could on to his hands and thighs as he went down below the level of the slope on to the precipice. He had to hurry. It was almost dusk. The cliffs were facing east. The sunlight ended sharply. He was climbing on the dark side of the world, his back pressed hard against the earth.

He reached his lodgings for the night more easily than he had expected. The route was steep but well provided with handholds and platforms for his feet. His fear of heights and falling rocks made him quick and nimble for a change. He was propelled. He almost found the climbing pleasurable. He was the boy he'd never been.

The entrance was much larger than he'd thought. The cave was deep. There was no sign of life, not even any bird lime on the rocks, or sand-fish burrows. No screaming bats. No perching angels. He called out from the rocky platform at the cave's mouth. The echo of his nervous greeting came back twice. "Is anybody there ody there ody there?" He wept, of course. What young man, alone in such a wilderness, wouldn't weep to hear his own voice mocking him and reassuring him? No echo would be worse. He couldn't light a fire or lamp. There wasn't any food or drink to comfort him, but he had eaten anyway, in the merchant's tent and in the shepherd's hut. Two meals that day. He couldn't think what he should do. Give thanks? Protect the entrance of the cave with stones? It was too cold to sit outside and watch the stars come out. He hadn't brought a cloak to wrap around himself. So he found a pocket of warm air, out of the draughts, and curled up on the dry clay in the cave, in his thin clothes. He made a pillow of his open palm, still smelling of the hyssop, and protected his body with his elbows and his knees as if he thought he might be kicked by demons. Would there be scorpions or snakes? Would there be nightmares? He closed his eyes. He brought his lids down on his fear. He put his trust in god; an optimist again. He could rest. He could rely on god's provision, yes. The travelling was over. He fell asleep, almost at once.

Sleep is a medicine. When he woke up on his first day of quarantine, his spirit was repaired, as was his confidence. There was no walking to be done that day. He did not have to climb. He only had to shake the stiffness from his limbs and go outside to meet the day. The rosy epaulettes of light on the peaks of Moab which Marta was admiring at that same moment from her own cave entrance, seemed heavenly to Jesus. He sat cross-legged on his angel perch. He could hear the bluster of a wind, blowing on the cliff-tops and the hills, but not descending to his cave. God was taking care of him. Jesus would explore the cave when it was fully light outside, but for the moment he simply waited for the epaulettes to spread into a cloak, and for the cloak to throw its warmth across his shoulders. Time was slow, of course. He filled it with prayer, and thinking of his parents watching him pray. They couldn't come and shake him now.

There was nothing else for Jesus to do, except to simplify his life. Repentance, meditation, prayer. Those were the joys of solitude. They had sustained the prophets for a thousand years. And they would be his daily companions. He started rocking with each word of prayer, putting all his body into it, speaking it out loud, concentrating on the sound, so that no part of him could be concerned with lesser matters or be reminded of the fear, the hunger and the chill. He seemed to find his adolescent rhapsodies. The prayers were in command of him. He shouted out across the valley, happy with the noise he made. The common words lost hold of sound. The consonants collapsed. He called on god to join him in the cave with all the noises that his lips could make. He called with all the voices in his throat. He clacked his tongue against his mouth, Tok-tok tok-tok tok-tok.

He must have recited a hundred prayers that morning, before the sun obliged and warmed him through. His prayers brought up the sun. His prayers suppressed his appetite. His prayers picked out the sunlight on the dead and silver sea and hardened it. It turned it into jewellery. The water was as solid as a silver plate. It rose from the distant valley into the mid-air haze. Jesus had to look at it through half-closed eyes, it was so bright. The more he looked, the more transformed he felt. He could have taken this to be the natural way of water and light. But Jesus had not come this far to witness only godless routines of the sun and sky and sea. He had to take each shift of light, each colouring, each shadow of a bird to be the evidence of god. He had to persuade himself, before the forty days were up, that he'd been awarded a brief view of god's kingdom. Let the silver plate be paradise. Let god be calling out to give to him his new commandments, as he had given all his laws to Jews in this same wilderness. What would his parents and his neighbours say when he went back to preach the word of god? They would not shake his shoulders, send his brothers to distract him, use the stick. They would rejoice in him. He could congratulate himself, and did. He was shoeless, homeless, without food. He'd slept on naked ground. But he was at last without fear or sorrow. "Am I not free?" he asked himself. "Am I not blessed?"

Finally it was too warm to sit out in the sun, and he was thirsty. He put a pebble in his mouth. He went back to the cave and slept again, just inside the entrance. He dreamed he was a common fly and climbing down a crust of bread. It broke away. He fell with crumbs of bread between his legs. His wings weren't any use. He fell awake. Flies on his face were feeding on the mucus of his nose and eyes and lips. There was indeed a noise of falling without wings. A few stones dropped outside his cave. A little further along the cliff a new landslip was underway. God's footfall made its mark on earth.

The earth had quietened by the time that Jesus went outside. There was nothing on the precipice to see, but there were voices and movements on the rim above. He turned his back to Moab and looked towards the summit of the cliffs. Dust fell on his face and hair. A pebble hit his shoulder. His company had come at last; his guide, his god, his friend. He would not pass his quarantine alone. He waited for a face to show itself. Perhaps there was a face already; he was not sure. He thought he saw the blond hair of an angel and a face the colour of a honeycomb. He thought he heard a joyful voice call out, in a mocking echo of his dream, "Fly, fly . . ." Were they the words? There was a further fall of earth and then there was a vision that he could not understand. Its meaning was obscure and dark and troubling. A donkey seemed to come out of mid-air, falling through the sky at him. It dropped down the precipice to the right of his cave. It turned. It hit the rocks and bounced once more, high above the valley. Then it fell towards the silver plate. A sacrifice towards the silver plate. Its legs were wings. It seemed to have no weight, no eyes. Its head was loose like cloth, as if the bones along its neck were less substantial than the air.

CHAPTER
ELEVEN

As soon as Shim and the badu had begun to drag away the donkey's carcass, the women — separated from the two remaining men by the customary seven steps — set to work themselves. They searched the camel panniers inside the tent for the rods and beams to assemble Miri's loom. They laid the pieces out in order of size — the largest breast beams and shed sticks at the back, then the warp and heddle rods, and then, closest to hand, the beating hook, the stick spools, the leashes and the pegs.

Miri was glad to be distracted by something other than Musa's piping voice. Her husband was sitting in his blanketed emporium, a pyramid within a tent, his flask of date spirit half consumed, his goods displayed on the mat in front of him, his stomach folding on his thighs like dough expanding into dough. He was biding his time. He knew his tenants would be tempted by the prospect — once their daytime fast had ended — of some of Miri's fig cakes or dried fruit, some salted meat, some herby cheese. Fasting's hungry work. He judged the old man, Aphas, would be the first to be enticed. Old men near death have no one to indulge, except themselves. Then, where Aphas had succumbed, the other three — perhaps the missing fifth as well — would follow. They'd have to understand they could not simply plunder the free food of the scrub. This was his land, he would remind them. The birds and roots were his. They had to buy their food from him or go without until their forty days were up. They had to pay his price. He owned the water and he owned the sky. A sip, a sip, the merest sip, could not be had for nothing. He chuckled at his own audacity.

This was Musa's quarantine. He would not fast or pray. He'd rest. His wife would milk and bake and cook; he would display the goods; his tenants would walk down from their caves each day for their supplies; and he would drink his spirits and his wine and dream of future caravans. So this detainment in the hills was working out unexpectedly well, he thought. Bad luck had almost turned to good. He had his health. He had some rent. He had some modest trade. He had some porters for the journey down to Jericho. He'd have the woman, Marta, to enjoy, if he was patient. In the meantime there was a skinny second-best at hand who would require no patience. He'd take hold of Miri's wrists that night and press her bony little thighs into his lap. He'd close his eyes and rub the fabric of her clothes against himself and call her Marta underneath his breath.

Miri was as nervous as a doe. She did her best to be invisible. She could see and smell that Musa was in a skittish mood. Date spirit had revived him. His veins were full of blood and drink and mischief. He was playful and expansive for the moment, but that could change. So far the spirit had only reached his heart and mouth but it would travel to his cock and fists, and then there would be danger. She would have to keep out of his reach once the donkey had been disposed of and these four visitors had gone back to their caves, unless she wanted to be pummelled by his hands and mouth or forced to masturbate him with a ball of wool or made to kneel.

Miri hid behind the woman Marta from Sawiya, and concentrated on the loom. She kept her face as blank and still as clay. But Marta was as open-faced and undefended as a young girl. She did not seem afraid of Musa's eye. She touched Miri's arm and hand and back; she was a sister for the day. She smiled to herself — and once she even laughed out loud — at the datey monologue that Musa was imposing on Aphas. The old man would have dearly loved to sleep, she saw. Instead, he had to listen to their landlord's endless, hypnotizing tales of profits, bargains, deals, the buy-move-sell of merchant life, the mysteries of trade. Here was a man who knew the wider world, the land behind the middleman where everything was cheap, the hill behind the hills, the village that you reached when all the villages had ended, the sky beyond the skies where blue was silver and the air was heavier than smoke. That was where (according to Musa's narratives that day) he'd seen deserts which made this scrub seem like paradise, where he'd survived on nothing else but camel leathers for his meat, the mist of mirages for drink, and promises for merchandise.

"Nothing you have seen compares to what I've seen," he said to Aphas. But he was watching Marta while he spoke. He did not want to miss her bending over with the pieces of the loom. How would the fabric of her clothes spread on her back and thighs? How would her buttocks spread?

If only Musa had been talk and nothing else, Miri thought, then he might have been mistaken for a tolerable man — for there was something admirable about him, on first encounter. Everybody was agreed. When he was fuelled by drink, still good-humoured and telling stories about the market-places of the world, the gourds and henna, ivory and olive oil, the grain and chalcedony he'd bought and sold; the carbuncles he'd traded for ambergris, the gold for slaves, the aggry beads for ostrich feathers; how he'd turned honey into salt and salt into silver, then, yes, he was captivating. "Like a snake," in Miri's view.

She'd been captivated once herself. A short and bitter memory. She'd first encountered Musa in her father's camp less than a year previously. He'd made her laugh. The way he looked. The words he used. The stories that he told. His self-esteem. He'd promised her that she would marry him and travel to the hems and pockets of the world. He'd show her valleys with so many flies that all the cattle had two tails. He'd take her to a land where all the chiefs had jewels so large that visitors could tether horses to them. He'd find her villages where women gathered gold by dipping pitch-smeared feathers in their lake. They spread the gold like honey on their bread.

How gold and sweet his voice had been that night.

Now his voice was pitch for her. She'd never seen the jewels, the lakes of gold, the cattle with two tails. She'd seen the flies. She'd seen the wind-whipped camel

103

tracks, the dusty camps, the stultifying market towns. She'd felt her husband's fingers and his fists. What was there captivating in the life she led with him, other than his talk? How simple it would be, she thought, to earn some instant silence and some widowhood with a single blow from a loom rod. Musa's head was round and red and tufted like a pomegranate. And it would split as easily. The man was full of pips and piss. She and Marta could drag the body to the precipice and push it off to join the little jenny on the valley floor. Two donkeys, yes. Both lame. Both dead.

Thank heavens that there was the loom to think about instead. Miri was the sort of woman who could be stoical only if her hands were busy. Then she could endure the heat, her aching thighs, the aimless gossip of the goats, her husband even. She couldn't simply be inert like Musa, her fingers twined across her lap, talking, drinking, dreaming wealth and luxury and lies. If there was nothing else to do, she'd rather scratch herself or pick her broken nails than keep her fingers still. Why should she dwell on the misfortunes of a marriage in which even fever could not intercede?

But, for Miri, there was never nothing else to do. Her life was knuckles marching, fingers-on-the-move: making bread, sieving cheese, seeing to the needs of goats and men, a thousand tasks and still a thousand more to do . . . She had to find the time as well to carve the wooden talismans which Musa sold for prices beyond sense as the propitious work of holy men. Now she would take the opportunity, while her husband was sweet-tempered and loquacious with his drink, while there was a break from caravans and market-places, to work for once on something for herself which even Musa would not dare to sell. She'd peg the loom in some cool spot. She'd beg some yarn from Musa's store of wools. She'd weave and embroider a birth-mat for her confinement. She'd have the best part of forty days to weave a birth-mat fit for queens.

Marta, her daytime sister, could not help to build the loom. She'd hardly ever touched a loom before. In Sawiya the looms were fixed, in workshops, and there were families of weavers to provide everything from birth-mats to shrouds. But she was glad to do what Miri asked, carrying the wood and putting down the pieces. It was neighbourly to help a pregnant friend. She'd known of women who had miscarried because they had bad neighbours who hadn't helped with heavy loads. Yet though Marta was no good with looms she could choose wools. She had an idle eye for colour. A birth-mat should be white, of course. But white wools do not travel very well. They pick up flies and dirt, as Musa had discovered to his cost on one occasion. He'd bought a length of fine-weave cotton cloth which he meant to sell for shrouds ("Moon white," he said. "Spun in the sky at night") and carried it for too long in the camel bags on a journey to the Sea-meets-sea for the spring markets. He'd rolled the cloth out for a Greek who was preparing for the burial of his son. The moon was yellow streaked with fungal green. The urine in the bleaching lye had activated on the camel's back. "First came the stench, and then the cloud of thread-flies," Musa said. "Then fled the Greek." So from then on Musa only bought and sold the darker-coloured wools with well-fixed dyes, and cloths which could stand a little dust and were not bleached.

Musa was indulging his two women. He let them pull out his stock of wools from the dark recesses of the tent and smiled as sweetly as he could while they sorted through the yarns. This was a combination that Musa enjoyed — the fabrics and the flesh. He liked his wife to lift her clothes and straddle him, sometimes facing his huge chest, sometimes looking at his toes. He liked her clothes to fall on to his naked thighs and chest. Fabrics were more sensual than skin, he thought. He was a merchant, after all.

Marta shook her head and pushed aside all the rusts and browns, the wools which Miri seemed to prefer. A birth-mat which could not be white should try at least to be distinctive. She took Musa's sample rod and let the coloured yarns drop loose. She showed them to the sun, but they were not transformed by light. These were the colours of a Roman's robe. There was nothing worthy of a birth.

"Take these," said Musa who, now that Aphas was asleep, had been commenting, with unusual animation for a man, on every sample that the women fingered and rejected. But he did not want them wasting decent wools on Miri's mat. He reached across and pulled two half-hidden, remnant hanks of wool on to his knees — the vibrant, eggy orange, and the purple that he'd considered prostitutes might wear. He freed the yarns a little and spread the strands across his hands, so that the women could inspect them. They were his customers.

"Good wools," he said. "The brightest in the market-place. Find a brighter wool. Or one more flattering." He could imagine Marta, reclining like an empress on a purple-orange mat, and he the emperor. Too late he saw the wool was badly spun. He tried to hide the broken strands, but too many pieces fell loose, like unpinned hair. "Good wool," he said again. "Some threads have snapped. You see? But you can knot the ends and weave them in. It's free. No need to haggle for a sweeter price. Be quick." He flicked the purple wool at Aphas's sleeping head. "This fellow here might want to show his purse and take a bargain home."

The women laughed at first. Musa had surprised them. Was he teasing? They recognized poor wool. Besides, his colours were comically ill-judged. The orange and the purple were bickering on sight, a florid uncle and his gaudy niece. The women frowned and rubbed their chins, and tried to visualize the finished mat. This wouldn't do. They shook their heads.

"What do you want for nothing then? Gold thread?" asked Musa, raising his voice and narrowing his eyes at Miri. "Don't shake your head again. A wife should never shake her head." He shook the wools. "It's these or nothing. Go without a mat." He closed his eyes, and wiped his face dry with the wools. His wife had slighted him. In front of Marta. There was a price to pay. The wine was draining from his heart. He'd beat his wife for this.

"Give birth on straw," he said. He half-opened one eye, like a lizard, to see what effect his firmness had. His wife, of course, had no expression on her face. But

Marta seemed embarrassed. Perhaps, for Marta's sake, it would be wise to seem more generous. "Miri does not want to bear her child on straw," he said to Marta. "Speak to her. She's stubborn when she wants." He held the remnants up, the merchant and the liar once again. He'd have their custom yet.

"Take, take," Musa said, feigning impatience. He threw the wools down at Marta's feet, so that she had to bend to pick them up. At last, the lizard opened up its second eye. He ran his tongue across his lips. If Miri was a skinny goat, he thought, then Marta was a horse. "Those colours bring good luck," he said, back in the market-place. "You'll have a boy. You'll have two boys, Miri. As strong as bulls. Two little gods. An orange god, a purple god."

A good luck mat that promised sons? Marta pushed the wools together. She bunched the yarns. Perhaps the orange and the purple were not incompatible, after all. These were the fertile colours of the darkness and the day, the harvest sky at night, the ready, outer leaves of maize. She smiled at Miri. Helping Miri with the weaving might bring good luck to both of them. Miri shrugged and took the wools. Her husband had decided on the purple and the orange. That was that, and not another word to say. There wasn't any point in bargaining for better wool, or any of the yarns in the earthy colours that she preferred. She'd have to bear her child on the sort of mat that a perfume-seller would use to lay out his wares.

"The orange one. You see? Your choice is good," Musa said, congratulating the women and himself on their good taste. "This is the very best. It's from the swamps. Beyond the swamps. A hundred days by camels, then a hundred days by boat. And then you have to walk, up to your knees in weed. They take the colour from the plants. Everything is orange there. The sky. The leaves. The people's eyes . . . They all wear cloaks of orange wool and disappear against the land. They are invisible. The purple one? It's Tyrean. The weavers there take dyes from fish. It's fish or snails. They never say."

He told them how each year he went to Tyre to buy and sell. "They only have the purple wools," he said. "The women can't stand the constant smell of fish or snails. But when they see my orange wools, and put them to their noses, they run to fetch their husbands or their fathers. It doesn't matter, Miri, that the yarns are thin. Who cares about a broken thread when the colour is so strong and sweet?" The women didn't disappear when they wore orange cloaks in Tyre, Musa explained. They were as madly visible as butterflies. As were the women in the south when, on his return from Tyre, they bought his stock of purple wools and could be seen at last against the orange leaves and sky.

"Sometimes it seems to me that I am trading only in colours, not in wools," he said, keen to end the transaction on a magic and unworldly note. "I am like someone who sells sounds instead of drums and pipes. I deal in smells instead of food. Old man, wake up. Here's something wonderful." He tossed his empty flask into Aphas's lap. "Imagine it, old man. A caravan of colours, music, smells. So light a cargo. Watch how the camels run. A man could make a fortune out of that. Ask her. She'll see." He pointed at Miri. What did he mean, "She'll see"? Would Miri see her husband make a fortune? Or would she travel to the south with him, a hundred days, a hundred days, and then a walk, her baby strapped across her chest, his camel panniers leaking sounds and colours on the path, shedding smells into the knee-deep waters of the swamp?

CHAPTER
TWELVE

"That's it. The donkey's gone," Shim said, when he and the badu came back to the tent and joined the others amongst the wools in the shade of its awnings. Then, "There's someone there. A boy, I think." He wiped the perspiration from his forehead. He ran his tongue around his lips. He puffed his cheeks and blew out air. He wanted everyone to see how tired and thirsty he'd become. When Musa offered him the water-bag, as hospitality dictated that he should, he could firmly shake his head, the handsome man of principle and fortitude. He'd hold his hands up, palms out, as if the very sight of water in a bag offended him. He'd spit, to show he would not even swallow phlegm to ease his thirst. Here was an opportunity to gain respect and admiration — some recompense for the rent and water tax which the landowner had exacted from him. He was beyond temptation, they would see. He would not break his fast until the sun was down. He would not cheat, as evidently they had done. He saw the range of food and drink at Musa's feet, the empty flask in Aphas's lap, and held his fellow cavers in contempt.

Shim did not have the chance to spit. Musa snapped his fingers for the women to be quiet. He waved the

111

blond forward impatiently. He wanted to hear exactly what he had to report — not because he cared that Shim was tired and dry and beyond temptation, or that the donkey was gone, or that the badu, swaying like a hermit in a trance, had twisted his hanks of hair so tightly that there was blood — and flies — on his scalp.

"What boy? What sort of boy?" he said. "What do you mean, There's someone there? Say where."

"Below the top," said Shim. He vaguely gestured at his toes. "A good climb down . . ."

"What did he say? Was he the fifth that you saw walking? Was he a Jew? The one I saw was just a villager. Is that the one? He had an accent from the Galilee," said Musa.

Shim shrugged. What did it matter who it was? "Such heavy work," he said. "Animals weigh twice as much when they're dead. I'm parched . . ." He remembered the badu. "Him too."

"A skinny man. Was he a skinny man?"

Another shrug from Shim. "Not. . ." He paused. He didn't like to say "Not fat" to Musa. "Not fat like you." "Not strong," he said instead. "We didn't speak to him. We only dropped the donkey off. That's what we promised you. It fell . . ." Again, a gesture with his hand. "It missed him by a whisper. But it was thirsty work."

"Describe him, then. What kind of person, do you think?"

Shim spread his hands and laughed. How should he know? His landlord was a tiresome man, obviously obsessed with taking rents and picking profits off every creature on his land. He'd not co-operate with such a

112

cormorant. "Someone who hasn't any wealth, I'd say. Don't waste your time on him . . ." He held his hands up, palms out. He shook his head. "You'll not get rich." At least Musa was silent for the moment. His mouth had fallen open and his eyes were wide. Here was Shim's opportunity to have his say. He stepped three paces further into the tent and stood where he could speak softly and with dignity, and still be heard by everyone. "And do not think to offer me your waterbag," he said. "The spirit of my quarantine is that I must refuse all food and drink while there is any light. Others might be less exacting with themselves. An older man, perhaps, might be forgiven for his lapses. And women by nature cannot be as spiritual as men. They are false treasures, as the scriptures say. And who can blame them for their modesty? But for me denial and enlightenment are twins. We only meet the god within our true selves through suffering. We seek the wilderness because in this solitude we can hear ourselves more clearly . . ."

Perhaps this was the moment he should spit, and then deliver them a homily on the higher disciplines of fasting. He rolled the phlegm inside his mouth, looking for an uncovered patch of ground, but once again he did not have the chance to spit. Musa, with surprising speed, had fallen forward and was holding the handsome man of principle and fortitude by the ankle, pressing with his nails into the hollows of the heel. "How does that hurt? Is god here yet?" With his other hand, he pulled the little toe out of Shim's sandal, bent it back from the other four, and tugged, like someone snapping the bone out of a piece of roasted chicken.

"Don't speak," he said, though Shim hadn't got the breath to do anything but whine. "Be quiet. Do what I say. Go back and bring him here, the fifth."

"He . . . might not . . ."

"Go back and bring him here." He gave the little toe a final, warning tug and let go of Shim's foot. "Did that feel good? Is that the suffering you're looking for?"

Shim stepped back out of reach. The pain persisted. His toe was red and oddly angled.

"Hurry," Musa said.

Shim's ankle would not take his weight. He made the most of standing on one leg. "He will have gone by now," he said at last. He did not recognize the tremor in his voice. "It was a shepherd. Just collecting eggs. Or looking for a stray."

"Go back and see."

Shim could have said, Go back yourself and see. But he didn't want to risk more pain, another dislocated toe. He must stay calm and dignified. "Pain and enlightenment are twins," he said instead. And then, "Send her, your wife. Send him." The badu was still squatting outside the tent. "Send someone who can walk." He turned his back on his landlord. He was a holy man. He'd return to his own cave at once — if he could bear the pressure on his ankle and his toes — to continue with the solemn business of his quarantine.

Musa wished he had the pestle close at hand. He'd show what damage he could do to this man's hands and knees. He'd never pray again. Musa did not like to be defied. Men were just like donkeys, and their memories were long. If he allowed this Shim to succeed in challenging him just once, then he would challenge Musa at every turn. If the caravan had not gone off, and there were cousins close by, then it would be a simple matter. Musa would only have to clap his hands and there would be five men to teach the blond the rules of tenancy. But there weren't cousins. His only ally was his wife, and she could hardly break the blond man's fingers with a rock, as he deserved. Revenge would have to wait. Musa would pretend to compromise. He'd seem to be a diplomat — if that was what it took to see the Galilean once again.

He waved his hands at Miri. "Up, up," he said. She held him by his wrists and pulled. The dates were heavy on his breath. His breath was heavy on her face.

When he was sitting down or standing up, Musa was an imposing man — but anything in between and, like a camel, he was vulnerable and comic. Miri had only got him halfway to his feet; his legs were doubled up, his knees were spread, his buttocks were just clear of his bed-mat. She'd had to hold him like that many times before, when he was drunk or, merely lazy, he demanded help with defecating beyond the tent. If she let go on those occasions, her husband would collapse on to his own waste. A mesmerizing thought. She always wanted to let go. She never did. She didn't now, though it was tempting. She had so many grudges to express. She held him steady while he threw his head and shoulders forward so that his weight shifted from his buttocks to his knees, and then she pulled again. Musa was standing on his feet at last, and he was slow and dangerous.

Shim was by now a hundred paces from the tent, and hurrying — only limping when he remembered to. His toe and ankle had survived. He had alarmed himself, and yet he was elated too. So this was why he'd travelled all these days into these numb and listless hills, he thought. Musa was sent to test his fortitude. Musa would be his quarantine. He'd kept his dignity so far, he thought, and he'd been admired for it, by the old man and the Jewish woman at least. But he would need to be alert and cautious from now on. Musa would be an unremitting enemy. He was the sort who'd come up to the caves at night and smoke his tenants out, or take away their water rights, or worse. There would be no escaping him. So when he heard the fat man's oily voice calling to him across the scrub, he stopped and turned. He felt a little nauseous, to tell the truth, when he saw Musa standing up so solidly, with one arm hidden behind his back and all his pleats and folds of flesh made smooth and monumental by the falling, heavy cloth of his tunic. What magic was afoot? He'd not be the least surprised to see the fat man running in the scrub towards him, leaping boulders like a little deer, or somersaulting at him, as fast and weightless as a tumble bush. He'd grasp his ankles once again and pull his toes off, one by one.

Shim's hands were shaking. So were his toes. He could not move. He stood amongst the goats and cupped his ears to hear what Musa was saying.

"What have you forgotten now?" the big man called. There was, at least, no anger in his voice.

Shim had no idea what best to say. Had he forgotten to ask permission to depart? He'd not apologize. Had he neglected some propriety? The question puzzled him. He could not speak. He was a fish caught on a line. He took a step or two back towards the tent. Then ten, then twenty more. He was prepared to talk at least.

"You have left this," Musa said, when Shim was half-way back. "Look here. Come on." He showed his hidden hand. It held Shim's spiralled walking stick, his talisman, his peace of mind, his one companion on the road. It was his sign of holiness. He had forgotten it.

Shim would not be safe or comfortable without his staff. It was not Greek or logical, but he loved the twisting wood, each curl a cycle of his life. It was as much a part of him as curls cut from his hair. It could be used, like stolen hair or fingernails, to torment him with pains and nightmares if it fell — as now — into ill-meaning hands. He had to get it back. Should he retrace his steps more slowly, to show his unconcern? Or should he hurry with a careless stride to demonstrate his fearlessness? He hurried, almost ran back to the tent. He saw that Musa held his walking stick in his two fists, ready to hand it over or to strike. An image of the donkey came to mind. He understood her bruises now, the blood, the broken bones. The donkey was his little toe.

"Go back and get the little Gally. For me," Musa said, as soon as Shim had returned and stood inside the tent, just out of reach. Musa's tone was meek and pacifying. He was the merchant forced to drop his price. "Or at least let me keep this walking stick for just a while and lead me to the place where you could see him . . . You are not frightened of the precipice? You are not frightened of a fall, I hope." Musa reached forward and softly, oddly, touched the end of the staff on Shim's leg. Shim neither shook his head nor spoke.

"Miri," continued Musa, "bring honey water for my cousin. And some dates. Put cushions down." Miri frowned and shook her head at Shim. He'd be a fool if he came close. She could not tell if Musa meant to murder him or simply make him look a fool.

"It is my quarantine," said Shim, staying put. Miri nodded at him, smiled. "I will not eat while there is light. I will not drink. I do not allow myself to recline on cushions. There is no compromise, no matter that the task of seeing to your donkey was exhausting." Here was his opportunity. He spat into the sand at last. "I cannot even swallow phlegm for fear that it might slake my thirst."

"Are you allowed to swallow words?" asked Musa. "Then, perhaps, it would be well if you consume what you have said today, and start afresh. Begin again. Do what I ask. Accompany me. Show where he is. If it's the man I think, then he's as close as you will ever get to angels. You're wrong, you see. He wasn't only someone looking for his sheep or hunting eggs. Some nobody. He is a healer and his flock are men. His eggs are . . ." No, he couldn't think of anything for eggs. "There's holiness in him. If it's the man. He is the one who saved my life."

Musa liked that final touch, ". . . who saved my life." A useful lure, which he had used before. "This gemstone is blemished. That is true," he'd told a customer earlier that spring, and made the sale. "But it has healing properties as well. This is the stone that saved my life."

118

Musa didn't need to talk to Shim now, or even look at him. He could forget him. This was another market trick. Address your comments to the crowd. Ignore the buyer. Let him battle with himself. And there was a small crowd of eager listeners. His wife, of course, whose listening was dutiful; the woman Marta; the old man. Everybody lived in fear of death, and everybody was beset by age or sickness. So everybody liked to hear of healers. The badu — though he did not stop his rocking or let go of his tortured hair — turned his attentions towards Musa. Even if he didn't understand a single word, he recognized the storyteller's tone.

Musa sat on his rugs again, with Miri's help. He pulled his hands across his face, and let them drop into his lap. Where should he start? This one was hard. He only had to tell the truth. Just tell the truth and see the man again. He was hungry for the chance to see the man again. He'd even pay to see the man again. Musa did not recognize himself. Was he in love with that frail voice, those hands? Had he gone mad? Or had he simply drunk more than he'd realized?

"Two days ago," he said, "I had the fever. I was as good as dead. Hot, cold and wet. My tongue was black. Ask her. She sang for me all night. Her voice is like a goat's. A voice like hers could drive the devil off, and clear the sky of birds. But even so she couldn't lure the fever out. Miri, tell them it's true." He waited while his wife obliged with a nod. "What could she do? Except pray? Already she was grieving for her husband. There wouldn't be a man to take good care of her. I was a piece

119

of meat, and soon to be as numb and silent as a stone. I don't remember anything, except death's door."

Where there were market-places, there were preachers. So Musa knew the words and mannerisms he should use to lend a touch of holiness to what he said: "She went to look for herbs to make a poultice for my head. And when she went a stranger came into my tent. He was my light and my salvation. He came from nowhere. And he was here, right by my bed, then not quite here, then gone, then come again. The air was flesh. But still I saw his face. I heard his voice. From the Galilee. He said his name. I can't remember it. He put his holy water on my head. He pressed his holy fingers on my face. He held a conversation with the fever in my chest. He said, This man is loved by god. This man is loved by everybody's god. This man is merchandise that can't be touched. I will not let you take this man from us. He put his fingers on my chest. The hot and cold went out of me. He plucked the devil out as easily as you or I might take the stone out of an olive. He pinched death between his fingertips. He flicked it on to the ground, like that . . . as if it were an olive stone . . ."

Musa coughed to gain a little time. He could not think how olive stones and death were quite the same. He tried again, ". . . I knew that I would live to be white-haired because . . . You must not take my word for this. Ask her. Come back in twenty years. This very place. And you will see me with white hairs. So now you understand?" He looked at Shim finally. "That man you saw, that boy, he made me live again . . . The little Gally drove death away." Again he pointed at his wife. "Ask her. She left a dying man and then she came back to a miracle . . . You see?" He slapped his chest. He pulled the flesh out on his cheek to show how soft and large he was. "I am restored."

It was exactly as Musa wished. He had his way; he had his company; he had the blond man's staff.

"Let's see this holy man of yours," Shim said, glad for once that he was no longer the centre of attention. "Come, come." He called his fellow quarantiners to his side. The more they were, the safer he would be. They did not need persuading. Marta could not miss the possibility of further miracles. Aphas found the energy to stand and join the pilgrim group. A healer was his only hope. The badu followed them like a dog, always glad of expeditions. Would someone draw the demons out of him? They set off for the precipice in the middle of the day, when only mad men left their tents, to find the Galilean man, if it was him. He was the purpose of their quarantine, perhaps. He was the answer to their prayers. Like Musa, they would be restored.

Miri and the goats were left behind. They had no need for miracles. Miri was unwidowed by a miracle already. She had no wish to meet the healer face to face. She'd want to slap his cheek. She'd want, at least, to have the devil's eggy breath returned to her husband's mouth. She'd want to have the days rolled back like parchment on a scroll to times when Musa lay across his bed with a blackened tongue, blurting fanfares of distress. But Miri did not believe in Musa's healer, anyway. He was as real to her as cattle with two tails.

She watched the five pilgrims disappear towards the crumbling decline of the scrub, their pace set by her husband's flat, unsteady step. She could have wept. She could have taken Musa's knife and scarred herself, as widows do. Instead she turned again towards the warring hanks of wool and the small world of her loom.

CHAPTER
THIRTEEN

Miri normally preferred to weave in daylight outside the tent. The masters working in the towns would say that weavers who set their looms in open ground have first to find the landscape's warp and weft, the shadow lines, the tracks, the spirit paths. The weaving and the landscape should concur or else the cloth would lose its shape. The wind, the water and the threads, the lines of scree, the strata of rock, the patterned strips of wool should run in unison and then the fabric would be true. The weaver and the ploughman should align. It's not enough to know your yarn. You have to know the land as well, they'd say.

But Miri simply liked the light of open ground. She liked the privacy. Most of all, she liked the moment, early in the morning with the sky still pale and unprepared, and no one else awake, when a piece of cloth was underway and she could step out, bare-footed, to inspect the new weave on the loom, its warp threads tightened by the cold and damp. She'd pick off any tiny snails that had climbed to feed on lardings in the wool. She'd twang the freshly wefted cloth to shed the dust or dew. If the weave was square and true and tense, the loom became a harp. The cloth would hum a single note to her. She could not wait to see what note the birth-mat would provide. First she had to find a place to peg the loom.

Miri would have liked somewhere a little distance from the tent where she would be left in peace, out of Musa's reach, and out of hearing. She'd already seen a flat place without too many rocks, on the leeward side of the tent. It would be safe and comfortable, once she had kicked away the stones and cleared the scrub weed. She would not bother with the landscape's warp and weft. She'd travelled enough to know she'd find no patterned unison in this tumultuous scrub. No weave could match such stringy wind or cluttered light or rock, and only someone from a town would think it could. She would concern herself with duller matters and set the loom where the soil was firm enough to hold the pegs, and where the sunlight came in from the left, so that her working arm did not cast shadows on the cloth. The yarn, for her, was more important than the land. Yet, yes, she would allow the masters this — a weaving done in open air, informed by sunlight and then allowed to stretch and dampen overnight beneath the stars, was best. It would outlast a workshop weave which had not been toughened by the sun or tested by the wind and dew. A workshop weave was like a coddled child, pent up indoors all day. As soon as it encountered rain or heat or cold, it sagged and frayed.

As Miri walked towards her chosen patch of ground, carrying the base beams of the loom, she realized she could not peg them out away from the tent as she had wished. The site she'd chosen was the perfect place, except in one respect. There were six goats. The five females were untethered. There was no goatherd to prevent them wandering. There were no dogs. Or other wives. Miri could not leave her birth-mat unattended. In the night the nannies would join the snails in feeding on the weave. Goats thrive on cloth. They love the taste of it, the colours too. They love to dine on cloaks and blankets. They'd strip a sleeping goatherd naked if they could. They'd eat the devil's hat.

At first she thought she'd try to stake the female goats alongside the billy. But she was pregnant. It was hot. The goats were spread out widely over the scrub, foraging for food. Chasing goats was work for boys. Besides, goats staked in dusty scrubland such as this would not feed well, and hungry goats did not produce good milk. She had no choice. She'd have to peg out her loom inside the tent and suffer Musa's company.

She was not used to constructing her loom inside. She did not know the rituals or the rules. A loom, assembled in a tent, should always face the entrance squarely, she'd heard it said; the awnings should never be allowed to fall closed while the weavers were at work. You might as well throw out the cloth, half done, if the awnings were closed by mistake. There were prayers to recite before the loom was warped, and other prayers for when the finished cloth was cut. Unfortunately Musa's bed already faced the entrance to the tent. She would not want to weave within his reach.

So Miri loosened the pinning on the side wall of the tent between the hand pole and the leg pole. She rolled the goatweave back on to the roof and fastened it with leather ties and stones. She'd opened up a gap three paces wide which she could close against the wind and goats at night quite easily. It gave her access to the dark part of the tent, beyond the woven curtain which she'd made herself some months before. This was where she slept when Musa did not want her, and where the stores were kept. It smelt of mildew, from the flour and the skins. She cleared a space, two paces wide, four paces long. A large birth-mat. She fetched the pieces of the loom which she and Marta had already stacked — too hopefully — at the entrance to the tent.

Miri had her mother's loom. She'd set it up so many times before, outside, and made so many lengths of cloth and in so many different camps — tent panels from goats' hair, shrouds and cloaks, hair cloths and veils, mats and carpets, woollen camel bands, dividing curtains, travel bags — that weaving was her kith and kin. There, in the tent, was the little rug she'd made in grey and red, in carefree days before her mother died and she'd become her father's burden. There were the goat-hair panniers, the cotton flour bags she'd made in undyed yarns. There was the blue-green curtain, in twined weft weave, that she had started when they'd camped in hills above the sea and her father had sent out word that she would go to any man that asked. Musa's caravan had stopped and she'd been bartered for a decorated sword and a fleece-lined winter coat. "And you can take the loom," her father said. There was the black cotton dress she'd woven for the wedding day, with its cross-stitch embroidery in red and blue and its plaited woollen girdle and its cowrie shells. She'd spun

126

the cotton and the wool herself. All her history was made of cloth. Now there would be a birthing-mat in purple and orange.

She set to work. She tied the broken orange threads of wool into one long piece and wound and stretched it round the two warping rods. She lashed the rods, pregnant with their orange thread, to the breast and warp beams. She pegged one beam into the ground, using a stone as a hammer. She pulled the other beam as far away as it would go, so that the tension on the wool was uniform, and pegged it to the ground. She carried stones into the tent and packed them round the pegs to stop them slipping. She put the leashes, the heddle rod and shed stick in place, opened up the warp threads, and checked the tightness of the wool. She tugged each thread, looking for the loosest ones which would meander through the weave if not fully stretched before the weft was started. The orange wool, unbunched, looked less garish than it had in sunlight. Perhaps her husband had been right to choose such cheerful wools.

The gap she'd opened up in the side wall of the tent gave open views across the falling scrub, towards the precipice and the distant purple hills, a lesser purple than the wool. Somewhere below and out of sight, Musa and his tenants were hunting for their miracles. What kind of self-deception were they guilty of? Would the Galilean man or boy, this godly creature who'd crept so memorably into their tent, expel the old man's cancer, fertilize the woman's crabby womb, make Shim's heart as handsome as his face, expel whatever madcap spirits had taken residence inside the badu's head, bring god

127

down to the precipice to transform Musa, shrink him to a proper size?

Miri cupped her stomach in her hands. She knew that life did not improve through prayer or miracles. The opposite, in fact. So let them go and waste their time. She didn't care. She only hoped their quest would take them far away and leave her there in peace all day, all year, to lose herself in woollen threads. She sat cross-legged before the loom. She rubbed the beams with her fingertips, exactly as her mother had, exactly as her daughter would. She plucked the warp. She played it like a harp. There were no orange notes as yet. It was too soon for her new mat to sing.

CHAPTER
FOURTEEN

Jesus had not expected anyone to come. There would be god at hand, of course. Invisible, unprovable, perhaps, and shy to intervene. But ready to provide. If needs be, god would show Jesus how to turn the stones to bread and take his water from the clouds. All things are possible to him that believes. And at the end of quarantine he'd give him faith enough, if he so chose, to jump off the precipice instead of climbing to the top. He'd have no fear of death. The angels there would fly out of their eyries in the sky and take him by the arms back home to the Galilee. In their good care he'd not so much as strike his foot against a stone.

Jesus knew exactly what he believed where angels were concerned. He put his faith in them. They were as real to him as birds. He was no rigid sadducee. But he was not so clear on any of the other, weightier and wingless issues of the day. He'd sat cross-legged and done his best to follow the arguments held in the temple court by older men, but he could find no pleasure in debate. It was too easy to agree with every idea put to him with any feeling.

Of course a Jew should take the laws of Moses literally. He saw the sense in that. He nodded, rapped his knuckles on the ground, a young man wise beyond his years. But should a righteous Jew reject everything not found within his laws — the immortality of souls, for instance, or the cheering prospect of messiahs — for fear of being reckoned false and being cast aside by god? He could not nod or rap at that with much sincerity because, like every fresh-faced follower of god, he harboured hopes of immortality himself, and prayed to see messiahs too. He prayed they'd come to earth to make god tangible, to mediate for god in all the conflicts of the world. But would messiahs drive the Romans out or let them stay, unharmed? Again, Jesus would not claim to have a single view. He did not like the taxes, tithes and tributes that the Romans levied in the Galilee to pay for their great marble works, their aqueducts and unremitting roads, but still he could not bring himself to hate the frightened, pink-skinned boys from far away who were the local legionnaires. He pitied them. They were not circumcized. They were not Jews. They had no covenant with god. They had no place in paradise.

Jesus had a simple view, a village view of god, that was not scholarly. He believed he was the nephew of his god, a god who many years before had chosen from all of the families of the world the family of Jews — not Romans, note — to be his kin. He'd rescued them from captivity and led them to a promised land, the Galilee. If god required the Romans to depart and retreat with their taxes down their roads back to the city of their birth, then he would do it all himself. He had the strength, for he was hard and muscular. His nature was not womanly. An engineer like god who kept the great machine of stars and planets voyaging through air could have no trouble with the Romans if he chose to drive them out. The fact he did not choose to drive them out was evidence that god was not concerned with matters of the body. His empire was the mind and soul, the spirit not the flesh, the age to come and not the world of days. There'd be a battle, then, bitter and divine, not with the Romans but against the legions of evil. All the demons would be killed and every sin defeated. Then God would call his family to his clearing in the fields. God would separate them, one from another, as a shepherd divides his sheep from the goats. Then waters would break forth in the wilderness and streams in the desert; the burning sand would become a pool and the thirsty grounds a spring of water; the haunts of jackal would become a swamp and the scrub would flourish with its reeds and rushes. That's what the scriptures promised.

Jesus had sat inside his cave and looked out on to the poisonous mists rising from the sea and expected to witness in his loneliness a vision of god's mossy paradise. He'd not expected to be disturbed by visitors. But first — with hardly one day of his quarantine endured — there'd been the tumbling donkey, then the faces on the ridge, and now this gathering of five. He sat entirely still, too scared to hide himself in prayers, and watched the timid delegation taking risks to reach a crumbling promontory a little way along the precipice. He watched the blond man — not an angel now — pointing out to his four strange companions the stony perch and the entrance to his cave. He sank back further into the darkness and looked out like a cat. They must have seen a shadow move or heard the rattle of a displaced stone, because they stayed, standing or sitting on the sloping earth and looking across at the key-shaped darkness where he hid as if they had no business in the world except to wait for him. He could not hear the words, but he could hear their voices. They were thin and querulous, like lambs. That was a slightly cheering thought. He was a cat. And they were lambs.

If they had been five shepherd boys, five camel drivers, five legionnaires, five matching anything, he might not have found their presence quite so sinister — but these five were like animals in Noah's ark, unlikely and disturbing friends.

There was a second face already briefly familiar to Jesus from the falling of the donkey, an impish, restless figure, as brown-skinned as a honeycomb, with red-black hair. There was an old man, bent and hesitant, his legs like twigs. And a woman, sitting at a distance from the men.

There was another man he recognized as well. The large man from the tent, the one whose dates and water he had taken, the almost dead man he'd abandoned only yesterday. He'd offered no more care and charity than to rub a little, borrowed water on his lips. The merest drop. He'd left the man to die without companions. But Jesus was not troubled by any guilt. He was afraid. He could remember the man's blackened tongue, and the heat of fever. And he could still recall the eggy odours of the devil on his breath. Yet here he was, recovered, big, beyond the grave, against all probabilities. He was holding a stick or walking staff in one hand, and that — to a timid man like Jesus, lonely, inexperienced, far from home — seemed ominous. It was the twisted wood that should be thrown out or burned. It was so fractured by the distance and the heat that it seemed to curve in spirals like the demon's baton he'd heard about from stories older than the scriptures. The sort of stick that could strike flames into a bush, split rocks, become a snake, turn wine to water with a single touch, turn holy bread back into stone again, make brothers fight and mothers chase their sons from home. It could fly through the air into a cave and beat its cowering occupant. It was the sort of playful stick the devil used to drive good Jews away from god.

The man put down his curling stick and cupped his hands around his mouth. "Come out. And talk to us," he called in breathless bursts. His voice was like the echo of a voice, an almost-dead man's voice, reduced and watery and pale. "Come out, Gally. Let's see. Your face." Gally? The big man knew him, knew the nickname that his Galilean neighbours used. He knew where he was from. "Gally. Gally. I'm the one. From yesterday." A chilling phrase. "You drove the fever out. A miracle. Come out and. Show yourself. . ."

Jesus knew that angels and devils could not be told apart just by their looks. Handsome was not virtuous. It was not sinful to be fat. But he could tell the difference. Angels left you calm of spirit when they stepped into your life. Devils left you troubled. Here was a devil then,

133

sent to the wilderness, with death and fever as his friends, attended by four mad, unbelonging souls, to be adversaries to god. Jesus would not come out of the cave, no matter what they offered him. They'd come to tempt him from the precipice with their thin cries.

CHAPTER
FIFTEEN

Slugs came in the night and marked their silver maps on Marta's legs; and when she woke she had to shake the cave lice out of her clothes. She felt as if a kittle bug had crawled across her face while she was sleeping and laid its gritty eggs along her eyelashes. Her head was full of flies. It seemed she'd swallowed something in her sleep. It left its scales and bitter mucus on her lips. It bruised her throat. It wrapped itself inside her abdomen and jabbed her stomach every time she moved. A sand-fish or a heavy snake, perhaps? The galling spirit of the scrub fowl whose vertebrae she'd snapped? The cave had made her grubby, panicky and ill.

She had to walk off several times a day, and in the night, to the plug of boulders where the valley ended, to retch and defecate. There wasn't any privacy amongst the rocks. She always had an audience of lizards, birds and flies, and there were snakes and leopards observing her in her mind's eye. Her husband, Thaniel, and all the elders of Sawiya gathered round, disguised as shadows. "She's giving birth to dung," he said. "That's the best she can do." Once, beyond midnight, her clothes bunched up around her waist, her bowels hot and mutinous, she'd been discovered by the badu. He'd leapt between two boulders, above her crouching body. His naked foot had almost struck her head, and both of them had cried out their alarm in unison. This was only the second time she'd screamed in almost ten years, since her marriage night with Thaniel, in fact. The first time had been a day or two before when she'd been struck in the face and chest by the birds hurtling from the grave. If anybody in Sawiya had cried out so loudly there'd be a crowd before the echo died. But this was scrubland, out of hearing of the caves. No one came.

At first she feared that she'd caught Musa's fever or that something venomous had bitten her. Anything was possible, in that haggard and incautious land. That's why she'd persevere with her quarantine, despite her sickness, and the filth. She would not flee back to Sawiya as her good sense and her stomach told her to. If anything could happen, then it would. The good, not just the bad. She was a practised optimist, and her optimism was enhanced by fasting. The desert mystics that she'd heard about from scriptures, prepared a path for god by emptying their stomachs and their heads until they went into a trance. Moses too. So if she felt giddy-headed all the time, a touch delirious, in a raptured panic, then that was good. Even ill-health could be taken as a portent of her improving fortune. Ill-health had brought the Galilean man to Musa's bedside, after all. Might ill-health bring him to her cave as well? Would he kneel by her side as Musa had described, and place his hand above her womb and say, "Be whole again"? Might he declare her pregnant, by some miracle?

She'd heard of women — unmarried, some of them, or widows and grandmothers, or wives whose husbands were away — who had conceived a baby without the maculate involvement of a man. Angel children, they were called. A thin and comic telling of the truth, she thought. But it was comforting to imagine that, in stories anyway, a woman might conceive without enduring a husband between her knees, that life could be created chastely.

With the Galilean healer so close, it all seemed possible. The almost-sight of him, the shy and nearly-shadow on the precipice, had made her pregnant with hope at least. When Musa had stopped calling out — "Come on, Gally. Show yourself" — the templed silence of the afternoon had seemed trapped and amplified by the valley's vaulted walls. She'd listened to the conversation of the gnats, the dry remarks of crumbling soil. It had seemed that she could hear the living rocks around the healer's cave, breathing, humming to themselves, praying even. She'd stared so long into the bashful blackness of the key-hole cave that amongst the visions she had seen were spectres of herself with angel babies at her breast and on her knee. All girls. No heirs for Thaniel, and no divorce! She'd been like the seed pod of a scatter bush. A little sun or wind or time and she would burst.

So Marta let herself enjoy the fantasy of being sick with child. Her symptoms were the same: stomach cramps, diarrhoea and nausea. Her head was steam. Her back and thighs were bruised. Her face was flushed. She even fancied that her nipples hurt, that they had broadened and were darker. Even if not pregnant by some miracle — or if not pregnant *yet* — then, perhaps, these pains were smaller miracles and brought about by those changes in her womb which she had come into the hills to pray and fast for. Perhaps her stomach was disturbed by all the sterile acids being driven out by juices of fertility. The diarrhoea and the vomiting would empty her of all the poisons of her past. The bad luck in her life was passing out of her like brackish water leaking thickly from a bag. She'd be sweetened and renewed. If anything could happen, then it would.

Of course, there was a nagging part of her which recognized and feared that other godless, uninspiring possibility, the dismal scripture that everybody said was kept sealed in cupboard vaults by priests who'd stolen it from devils. There'd be no answers to her prayers, not in forty days, not in forty years. There were no miracles, nor angel children, nor even any rewards for a blameless life. There was only time and talk and making do, and then the rough-weave shrouding of the everlasting earth. Her face was flushed because she had been touched not by the floating hand of some glimpsed healer but by the scrubland's harsh and unforgiving wind. The hurting back was due to sleeping on the ground in damp and draughts. The water from the cistern was to blame for her bad stomach. Or, perhaps, the culprit was nothing more angelic than the scrub fowl that she'd caught and eaten, barely cooked, at their first meal together.

But Marta was in no mood to think of life as godless and intractable. That cupboard vault would stay sealed, for forty days at least. She was not calm, sedated by prayers, the fasting and her loneliness as she had expected. Instead, her mood was turbulent. One moment, a fear of animals and darkness. The next, a tumbling faith in god. Dismay at being ill, unclean and living in a cave, then sudden rapture at the prospects of her life transformed. She'd lost control of her stomach, heart and brain, perhaps. She trembled and she wept, she laughed out loud, she mumbled to herself, she hardly slept, but she was possessed by hope, as madly and absurdly, as sweetly and as helplessly, as a melon taken over as a nest by bees. You'll be alone, she had been warned by her sister and the neighbours' wives, who feared for her safety and her sanity as she set off from Sawiya. You'll live on rain and leaves, if there are leaves. You'll lose yourself up there. You'll fry. But no one had foretold how she would find a godly pattern to her journey to the hills. No one had mentioned wayside marks carved into rock which would lead her and the men so safely and so simply to the caves. No one had promised there would be a water cistern, ready dug. Or that an evening meal would flap into her hands. Or that the landlord, Musa, despite his charges and his rents, would be heaven-sent to provide some decent food for her, and keep her safe from thieves and wolves. No one had prophesied, You'll make a friend, the pregnant woman with her loom, whose hand she'd held, whose stomach she had touched, whose child she could imagine as her own.

There was one prophecy, of course, which Marta had heard at least twice a day in Sawiya, whenever she'd recited the introit to prayers. She'd always spoken it as if the words referred to worlds ten thousand days away. But here, so close to heaven in the hills, so close to no-such-thing, the more she ran the verses through her mind, the more it seemed the prophecy was meant for her alone. Its garments fitted her. Those were her tears described, her barrenness, her quarantine, her desert places. The scrubby hills beyond Jerusalem, the scriptures said, would send down to the world through David's seed a holy king. He'd heal the sick. He'd bring comfort to the broken-hearted. He'd build up the empty spaces. He'd spread fertility on earth.

Once Marta had decided that there was a holy pattern to her quarantine, she was softened to the possibility that what was prophesied through god's own word would come true. If anything could happen, then it would. That was her latest article of faith. What was destined for ten thousand days would come about at once. So she had listened to Musa's tale — how he was healed by the man that he called Gally — and she had recognized immediately what it must mean. That fifth figure, dogging them from Jericho, that shadow on the precipice, that man who, if Musa spoke a quarter of the truth, could drive out fevers, devils, death, was sent by god to put the world to rights. He would not have travelled to the scrub and clambered to his cave only to minister to rocks and ants. He would have come, her daydream promised, to minister to her. Their meeting was ordained. There'd come a time, during the forty days, when he would swell into the holy king. He'd reach out from his cave into hers and hold her, cupped inside his giant palm: "Be well . . ." He would build his kingdom in her empty spaces.

These were her waking dreams. But there were others, more troubling, in which less godly prophecies came true. Her neighbours worried her. Not just the leaping badu or the dying Aphas. They were beyond her help and understanding. She was glad of that. But Shim too. She dreamed about him almost every night, perhaps because she was uncomfortable and cold, and hardly ever slept deeply. Sometimes she dreamed he was amongst the men who watched her in Sawiya when she went down to the well, the only handsome one. Sometimes he was confused with Musa and the Galilean man; the tent was caves, the fat was thin, their quarantine became a feast of uncooked meats, and all three men leaped over her while she was squatting in the rocks. They were a trinity as silent and as elegant as deer.

But on the second night of their quarantine, after they'd gone down to meet the healer and then had come back to their perching valley in the dark to break and celebrate their fast on Marta's strangled fowl, she'd had a dream of Shim that would not fade when she woke up. He came into her cave on draughts of air. His body was as hard as wood. His arms were snakes. It was he who swelled and cupped her in his palms and said, Be well. His seeds were insects running up her leg. Even in her sleep she knew they were as mad a match as the orange and the purple wools on Miri's mat. But Marta did not shake herself awake or let him go. She let her hair and his, the black and blond, entwine and spin a yarn across the cave's damp floor — one-ply, two-ply, a braid, a knot that no one could undo or cut. She'd have to go back to Sawiya with Shim tied into her hair as evidence of what she'd dreamed.

Marta knew that dreams like this were little more than moths. They flew by night. They showed their colours in the dark, and then, once there was any light, they shut their wings and disappeared. But she was waiting to be blessed by god and fearful that her sins would show. She wondered if such shaming dreams as hers might still be visible by day. See how she walks, see how her face is flushed, see how her nipples have grown broad, they'd say. Was there a blond hair clinging to her clothes? Could anybody tell by looking in her eyes that she had spent her dreams with Shim; how silent and how beautiful he'd been for her, how fertile she had been for him? On other nights she dreamed that Gally came to work his miracle, but he found Shim inside her cave and went away.

So it was hard for Marta to face the men. She knew it would be wise and less embarrassing to spend her days at rest inside the cave, protected from the sun and wind and from the piercing judgement of her neighbours. A woman should be out of hearing, out of sight, when she was sick and volatile. But Marta was too restless to sit still, and too excited by the sober freedoms of the scrub to stay in darkness. Besides, there was no way of avoiding her neighbours entirely. They all woke up before break of light to meet at the water cistern, and to pray — although, of course, a woman could not stand amongst the men in prayers, even if she were not sick

142

and volatile, or tainted by her dreams. Marta had to stand a little distance off, behind their backs, and she was content to do so. If she did not arrive in time for their dawn hosannas in praise of the water and the light, Shim or Aphas shouted her name or let the badu throw stones at the bushes by her cave. They were being neighbourly. "Come out and drink," they said. "It's almost dawn." So she would tie her hair veil tightly round her head to make herself invisible and join them at the grave. Even when Aphas begged her to reach down into the water to fill his cap, she did not speak to him beyond the common courtesies, or show her face. She did her best to close her wings against them all, to hide away the mothy colours of the night, to keep her ardours to herself.

No one there gave Marta much thought, to tell the truth. The men thought only of themselves. The badu grinned at her with an expression which seemed both childish and lascivious — but then he grinned at rocks as well, and rocks could have no reason to be nervous of a grin. The old man wheezed and limped as if his illness was only real if acted out. And Shim had greater matters on his mind than floating into Marta's cave by night on draughts of air. It was his habit, as soon as there was any light, to impose himself upon the largest rock on the sloping ground below the caves and meditate, his chin too high, his back too straight, his eyes and tongue just visible. He would not speak if spoken to. He let the flies stay on his eyes and lips. He let the lizards run across his hand. He set himself the task of staying still. Marta hardly recognized the man by day. The light was cruel to him. How unexciting he'd become. She would not want his hair in hers. He was a better man in dreams.

She understood, of course, that Shim had reasons to be proud and petulant. Their landlord had humiliated him on that first day. Shim had nearly had his little toe pulled off. She'd seen him shaking with defeat as he hobbled back towards the tent. Musa had the curling staff behind his back. It looked as if he meant to strike Shim down, and when he did not strike him down but chose instead to win with words, then Shim's abasement seemed complete. Even anger had looked comical and weak on him.

Shim should despise their landlord, then. That made sense. What Marta did not understand, and what neither she nor Aphas could bear to listen to, was Shim's dismissal of the healer. He hadn't even spoken to the man, the boy, as far as she could tell. He'd only seen him for a moment, from the brink of the precipice. Yet Shim took every opportunity to ridicule Gally (that had become the name that everybody used) and anyone who took his side.

"What saintly person would squander a miracle on such a man as Musa?" he asked Aphas one morning at the cistern when the old man had called a verse for Gally in his prayers. Aphas merely shook his head and shrugged. It was too early in the day and he ached too much from sleep to grapple with the wisdom of the Greeks. Even shrugging made him wince; the pain ran up his veins like fire up oil-soaked thread.

"Come, come," persisted Shim. "Won't you agree with me?" Their landlord's story of his rescue from the

144

fever was not believable, he insisted. Musa was a man who would not tell the truth unless there was a price on it. The donkey they had dragged away and dropped was more honest than Musa, and more saintly than Gally. Perhaps it was the donkey, according to Shim's mischief-making, that had come to Musa in his tent and passed some of its holy water on his head, and pressed its holy hooves on to his face, and plucked the devil out between its teeth. "What can you say to that?"

Another shrug from Aphas. And then, "There is, at least, a mystery . . ."

"Where is the mystery?" asked Shim, unused to any judgement but his own. "It was an animal, perhaps. Or one of our landlord's cousins put in the cave to make fools of you all."

No, Aphas would not be shaken from his latest faith. He was sure he'd seen a shape, quite tall, and hardly making any sound as if it floated on the ground. It must have floated down the precipice to reach the cave because, so far as he could see, the entry was beyond the reach of normal men. It was beyond the reach of goats.

"I felt . . ." he said, but did not finish. He dared not use the word enlightenment again. He'd used it once before, only to hear it mocked by Shim: Enlightenment comes to the ignorant. "I felt uncertain . . ."

"You felt uncertain if you saw a man at all," said Shim, beginning to enjoy himself. Aphas was not a scholar and the only other audience was a blushing woman and the madcap badu, who betrayed no sign of listening, but at least here was an opportunity for greater wisdom to prevail: "A floating shape is not a man. If it were, then — look around — this little valley would seem as populated as a market-place. It's only the sun and wind that make the rocks and bushes seem to float and tremble. No mystery."

"She saw it, too," protested Aphas.

"Our neighbour, yes. The nearly-shadows and the humming rocks that she claims as her experience are not evidence of anything beyond the natural." He didn't point at Marta or even say her name. "Who else then? Our fine landlord? You cannot cite his narrative, even if he really thinks he tells the truth. At best, his were the visions of a fever. Hot dreams and make-believe. Who hasn't had a fever, and then seen shapes? But why blame fever when he's so obviously a drunk? So what is left? The badu's word? We'll take his word for it." Shim laughed. The badu couldn't speak a single word. "Whose testimony should we trust that there is anybody there at all?"

"Your own testimony," Aphas almost shouted. Had Shim forgotten what he'd said to Musa? "You saw him from the top. There's someone there, you said. You almost dropped the donkey . . . didn't . . . ?"

"It was the truth. The donkey hardly missed his head," said Shim. "He looked at me. I looked at him. You see, I have the final word. My logic has you trapped. I'm the only one whose testimony is more substantial than a shape or a shadow or a dream. And this is strange. What should one make of this? Those three of you who did not see him *quite*, convince yourselves that he's a healer and a holy man. While I, who stared him in the face, who can describe his nose and chin and ears, can

146

tell you he is not. It seems I have to persevere with what I said. The man's a boy, at best, collecting eggs or chasing sheep . . . What's holy there? And where's the mystery?"

"No normal boy could climb down a cliff like that. It's dangerous. It's almost sheer," insisted Aphas, defeated by Shim's reasoning but irritated too, and close to tears. At home, he had three sons of Shim's age, and older. They had been taught to listen to their elders, and to be respectful of every priest and holy man. Certainly they knew it was not right to argue with a dying man, a man in pain. He turned his head away from Shim. He did not want to hear another word. He'd dreamed, like Marta, that the healer's hand had come into his cave. What else would save his life? He spread his fingers on his side, despairing at the unforgiving ache. He should have put his fingers in his ears.

"A normal boy will take a chance to snatch some eggs," said Shim. "All normal boys can climb. The stupid ones take bigger risks. We're talking of a very stupid boy."

Marta coughed. She sniffed. She made impatient movements with her legs. The bees inside her melon head rose up in fury. She was surprised that Shim could strike such a cruel note, as if it mattered to him that she — and evidently Aphas, too — needed to believe in healers and in miracles. What otherwise was the point of prayer and fasting, far from home, unless the grating noises of the world could be turned tuneful by the charms and cantrips of some holy conjuror? Shim's god might be a god whose greatest trick was curdling milk or taking mould to bread. But Aphas and Marta's was a god who parted seas to take his people out of slavery, who punished wickedness with floods, who summoned water out of rocks, who only had to whistle for the towers and the bastions to fall. Theirs was a god who showed his hand through miracles.

She'd like to do what the widows of the slaughtered men in Maccabee had done to their false prophets and stuff Shim's mouth with clay. He'd have to listen then. For once she could be angry in ways which were not approved, a woman shouting at a man. She would be happy for the chance to scream again. This was the scrub. No one would come to help. She'd tell him that she knew his mind. He was clear water. She could see the bottom of his pot. His scoffing at Gally was nothing more than his cowardly revenge on Musa. But Marta was not fooled, she'd say. She had not travelled much, she could not read, but Marta was not mystified by him. She even saw what hid beneath the bottom of his pot. She saw the deeper level to his mockery, and she understood that Shim was simply jealous of the Galilean man.

Shim was a practised traveller to holy places, as he'd told them many times. He boasted that he could read Greek letters, converse in Aramaic, Siddilic and Latin, tell fortunes, compose and sing his own prayers in a voice of mesmerizing evenness, and sit as sinless and as motionless as a pyramid, possessed by half-a-dozen gods, competing with the rocks for soberness. He said that he was used to deference, that he was used to supplicants seeking his advice and wisdom. At religious gatherings throughout the provinces more simple pilgrims than himself — and that included the likes of Marta, Musa and Aphas — would treat him as the pious and the holy one. They'd seek him out. They'd kneel to touch his gown. They'd give him alms and shelter for the night. Why should he not expect the same to happen in the scrub? His landlord and the quarantiners ought to come and stand a little distance from *his* cave. They ought to pray for him to drive their spirits and their fevers out. They ought to sit in hopes each day that his portentous shadow would fall on theirs. Instead, he was ignored at best, or made to look a fool, or argued with by one — Aphas — whose character was not enhanced by travel, or another — Musa — whose mind was not refined by study. Instead of deference and alms, he had a dislocated toe. And all these simple pilgrims in the scrub were seeking help and wisdom from some meekling youth whose only credo seemed to be that it was wise to turn his cheek against the light and cower in his cave.

"Or else we frightened him," he said, to end his conversation with Aphas. "That is the measure of his holiness. He scrambled down. He hid inside the cave and now he's stuck. He can't climb up. He's too ashamed to show his face. He's sucking wild birds' eggs for food, and praying for rain. Perhaps we ought to go with rope and rescue him." With that, he shut his eyes and settled down to meditate, his fingers spread out on the rock, with just an eyelid flickering to show he was alive, like a lizard boasting in the sun.

CHAPTER
SIXTEEN

God had not provided a ready-dug cistern for his Galilean son to take his water from. There were no rock pans by the cave for the dew to gather. Or any salt shrubs within reach, so that Jesus could tear his nails off digging for their liquid roots. There were no barrel bushes with their wax skins, or tamarisks with hollow, swampy trunks. If there had been any spring plants, vain enough to defy the precipice's nude and excavated rocks, then they had already flowered, seeded and retreated underground into their bulbs. Jesus searched inside his darkened cell but he could not find any sopbugs, their knapsacks full of pap, which could provide some short-lived moisture for his tongue with their sweet explosions. There were no nesting birds, or bats, or even any ants to eat, so far as he could tell. There was no rain. He thanked the lord. He'd found a place opposed to sin and nourishment, and he could starve himself of both without distraction. God in his generosity had removed all earthly sustenance and cleaned the cave of all temptations. Jesus only had to conquer his tormentors on the promontory — and time, of course.

A single silver bush was growing in a seam of marl above the cave, scarcely showing leaves. It spread its skeleton across a rock as if it meant to suck the quartz from it. It drank its colour from the stone. Jesus jumped to snatch the lowest leaf, an oddly adolescent act, but men are boys when they are bored. He was surprised and gladdened by the effort that his jumping took, how tired and jarred he felt. It meant he was already weakened by his fast and that much closer to god, therefore. He hardly touched the leaf, but it snapped its stem and fell into his hair as dryly and as heavily as furnace scale. He would not put it in his mouth. He would put nothing in his mouth for all the quarantine. He would not even break his fast at night, unless it was with help provided by his god, a meal placed at his head by angels while he slept (as god had provided a cake baked on hot stones and a pitcher of water for Elijah's forty days of fasting). But even though he would not place the leaf on his tongue he was still curious to see what sustenance the precipice might give to him. The moist leaves of a pair bush, common in the scrubland by the tent, could be rubbed on to the lips or sucked for sweetness. A sprig of morning star, tucked between the teeth and lower lips, would taste of peaches for a day. But this was only canker thorn. He snapped the silver leaf. It fell apart like ash. No sap.

By now he had no sap himself. He'd urinated two or three times on that first evening when he'd climbed down the precipice and taken up his residence, and that was normal. He'd always had a nervous bladder, forever wanting to pass water in the middle of the night or as soon as the priest began his readings from the written laws and no one could leave the temple without offence. He'd learnt to put his discomfort to good use: his bladder was a messenger from god, a sign of his unrighteousness. It was said by some of the older family that possession by spirits or by unclean thoughts was marked by such an excess of fluids. Sneezing, vomiting, a salivating mouth, diarrhoea, passing too much water — these were all signs that evil was in residence. It should be first resisted, then forced out. His bladder woke him in the night with a purpose, he told himself — it was an opportunity to say more private prayers, to practise tongues, to quietly endure the ache, the guilt, until dawn for fear of waking up his parents or setting off the hens if he went outside to urinate. Likewise, his bladder plagued him in the temple when he sat cross-legged before the speaking scroll so that he had the opportunity, not given to the other worshippers, to battle with his imperfect body for the glory of his god.

It was in part a pleasure, then, and in part a self-indulgence devoid of any glory, to be able to empty his bladder as he pleased. Once he'd settled on the precipice, he could obey his impulses at once, and edge along the cliff-face as far as was safe, to pass his water where it would not contaminate his cave but without regard to parents, temples, hens. Such open privacy had not been possible in the Galilee.

Here was a man who was in the mood to divine grand meanings in the simplest acts. There'd be no god without such men, prepared to make the little cause responsible for large effects, quick to find the lesson in the most everyday events. So it did not go unnoticed that his first day's urine was produced by drink stolen from the merchant's water-skin which he had lifted from the awning of the tent. It had only been a sip, the merest sip, and Jesus had drunk nothing since. But if there had been any sin or lack of charity on his part, then it would show its stains. There would be murkiness. These early waters had been copious, though, and odourless, and clear, and free of guilt. But by the end of the second day of fasting his urine was already dark brown, like pitch water. It sank into the ground too thickly and with cloudy bubbles. Even Jesus, whose sense of smell had not recovered from the journey, could recognize the eggy fragrance of sulphur. This was the devil's urine and Jesus's bladder had become a battle-ground. The patch of watered dust dried within a few moments. He scuffed it with his heels. He was contaminated by himself but he could not expect a ritual bath for weeks.

On the third day of his quarantine, he had to go along the cliff a dozen times. He stood and waited with his back turned to the sun to no avail, and then he tried again, facing outwards towards the sea, but he was completely drained already. He strained himself until it burned and stung. He pressed his bladder with his fingertips. The impulse to pass water did not go away, but he showed nothing for his efforts, except, again, the thinnest trace of sulphur in the air. He could not wet the soil. His body was an empty bag.

This was a lesson he would not forget: water is more valuable than gold. He hunted for the well-shaped proverb. That was the line that he could preach when he got back to the Galilee. He briefly saw himself outside the temple gates on market day, raised on a cart, with sermons for the multitude. An empty purse is better than an empty pot, he'd say, and his neighbours in the audience would put their hands across their mouths and whisper, It's Gally, see. Listen to him now. We never knew him after all. But for the moment he was more concerned with his own empty pot. Perhaps he had been arrogant and profligate. He almost wished he'd saved the urine that he'd passed so easily on the first day. To break his thirst, if he grew desperate. Let god forbid that he was ever as desperate as that. He'd heard tales of badu who in a drought would drink their own waters and the acrid waters of their camels and think nothing of it, but badu lived close to the earth, like animals themselves. The water that they nominally drank from wells was bladdery, and shared with all the desert creatures anyway. The badu had no god to satisfy, or rituals to obey. They did not have to wash their taints away. Jews, though, were a people governed by the laws brought down by Moses from the mountain, and cleanliness of body and of spirit were the paving stones to god. Those that forsook the laws, Isaiah said, would be consumed.

Jesus was determined that he would not be consumed so easily. He shook his head and stamped his feet and beat his shoulders with his fists until all thoughts of water went away. He would not let his hunger and his thirst lay traps for him. The spirit had to beat the flesh. I am not hungry, he told himself. This is not thirst. The dryness and the stomach pains are false. I do not want to eat. It is the nourishment of home I miss, not bread and water. It is the nourishment of god I seek, not wine or meat.

154

That's what he told himself, but in his heart and in the middle of the night he was less certain. He was plagued by thoughts of rolling back the days, back to the shepherd's where he'd left his overcloak, back to his father's carpentry, a chisel in his hand, back to the times when he was small and unremarkable and prayers had been more comforting than food or sleep. Here, in the scrub, his prayers were fickle; sometimes a single verse would strengthen him, but more and more he found no courage in his prayers. The cave had swallowed them. The precipice diminished them. The darkness muttered to itself without pause but was not listening to him. At those times, he turned away from prayers and concentrated more on finding some reclusive strategy by which he could survive his quarantine.

First of all, he set himself what Achim the psalmist called "the Task of Not", the discipline of wanting nothing from the world. Seek wakefulness instead of sleep, the psalmist said, and pain instead of comfort. If you are offered apricots or galls, then put your fingers in the bitter dish. And look only for the peace that's found in wretchedness and not the peace that's found in love. There were hermits even in the Galilee that lived to Achim's recipe: they put ashes in their mouths; they would not let themselves sit down, even at night; they broke their finger-bones with rocks; they stripped themselves of clothes and walked about like animals. Jesus had seen such men himself. He'd watched them hardly flinch when they were stoned by villagers.

Jesus, then, would be an achimite. He had to look for peace in wretchedness. He took a young man's pleasure

155

in the prospects of his suffering. There was no other choice but to embrace discomfort as a friend. The scrub had offered him few hospitalities, little sleep, no love, but it could readily provide all the suffering that he might seek along its paths, and show him torments in a thousand shapes. He could not bring himself to smash his hands, not yet. He would not break his fast, even with dust or ashes. But he could at least be naked like an animal. Angels go naked, he reminded himself. He hardly wore any clothes, and only those for modesty, but he removed the few that he had — a tunic, and a cloth, the prescribed undergarment of the Jews — and took them to his rocky perch and set them free like doves, the poor man's sacrifice, to wing their way down to the valley floor where Musa's donkey lay without a shroud. The words of Achim called to him again: Come for me now, come for me in a thousand days, for I am naked, I am yours, and all I had is thrown to the wind.

Jesus — naked on the precipice, his garments irretrievable — felt both foolish and triumphant all at once, and even briefly aroused by his own nakedness. What would his parents say? What would his neighbours make of him? Look at their Gally now. He had reduced himself to flesh, when he had expected and boasted that the fast would subjugate his flesh and cause his spirit to be clothed in gold. But Jesus really felt no shame. There were no witnesses. The air and sun were satisfying on his skin. He was a child again, and he had entered into Eden.

It was not long before his body grew too hot to stay for long in Eden, and the first of many headaches started. He withdrew into the cave where the borrowed light and temperatures were more forgiving, at least by day. He leaned against the inside wall, the perfect achimite, until his arm went numb, and then he squatted on his heels. Not sitting, quite. It was a compromise. He muttered resolutions to himself, rocking with each word, although his feet were cut and painful. He bore the cramp and deadness in his legs as if they were a blessing. But he gave up on Achim within a day, although — too late — his clothes were gone for good. The darkness undermined his appetite for wretchedness, and he had reached the point in his fast when he was vulnerable.

Now he made himself more comfortable, and did his best to drive all thoughts of Achim from his mind, although the psalmist's songs were thumpingly insistent. He devised a second strategy for himself, to deal with quarantine, to conquer thirst. It was more kindly and more homely than the Task of Not. He would not embrace discomfort, after all. That was a vanity. Instead he'd be a resting camel, aimless and unthinking, and with no memory or hope to complicate his life. Every boy in the Galilee who'd ever run out of his yard at dusk to watch the caravans arrive knew that a camel could travel with its panniers full without water for ten or twelve days before its hump began to hang. A resting camel with no pack to carry could stay for twenty days at camp with nothing in its mouth but teeth and tongue and still be fit enough to canter with the herd. A fatted camel, if it kept out of the sun and stayed down on its haunches, could survive a quarantine without water. It would, like Moses, have just enough strength to carry a stone tablet from the mountain-top to the water-hole, where it could be refreshed. Was not a man a finer and a stronger creature than a camel? Could a man not go as far and further without water and last the forty days, unthinkingly, like a beast? Jesus nodded to himself. He'd be a resting camel, yes, and not go anywhere. He'd stay down on his haunches. He'd not expose himself to heat or sun. He'd not explore the precipice or even sit out on the rock to feast on Moab and the sea. He'd stay inside the shaded halo of the cave by day, seeking out the coolest air and asking nothing of the thriving sunlit, moonlit world beyond, except that it should rescue him from memory and hope.

That did not last. Jesus had another strategy. I'm like the canker thorn, he told himself at other times. I have no need of sap. I'll spread my skeleton across the rock and root myself into this marl. Sometimes he was a camel and a thorn at once.

Again, particularly at night when he was cold and desperate for voices, Jesus turned back to his prayers. Old friends. He'd force himself to be more disciplined with them. No matter that his friends were fickle. He was not fickle, nor was god. He prayed out loud without fear of offending any of his family with his fervour. If he could not excel at prayers, then no one could. But no one — not a priest, a saint, a prophet from the hills — could pass the countless moments of the day engaged by prayer alone. There always came a time when the repetitions made his chin drop on his chest, so that he woke with a falling shudder after just a moment's sleep. At other times he simply could not concentrate. His worshipping became more conscientious than spontaneous. The prayers lost weight, like ashes in a fire, and floated off. Sometimes he stopped the verses halfway through and caught himself paying more attention to the dirt beneath his nails or an old woodworking scar across his hand than to the holy words. Sometimes a prayer became a conversation that he half recalled. He called on god to answer him, but all the voices that he heard were from the Galilee, a cousin's voice, a neighbour talking harshly to his wife, a peddler calling out his wares.

Most of all Jesus was disrupted by the silence of the cave, the depth of night beyond the entry, the scrub's indifference. Perhaps this silence was another test, he thought. Like hunger was a test. And boredom, too, and fear. Instead of prayers, he tried to concentrate on god in other ways, by listing all the prophets that he knew, the holy books, the laws. He repeated all the alliterating finger songs he'd learnt when he was small, each joint an attribute of god, the wise, the merciful, the generous, the enemy of sin . . . He took to marking patterns and holy signs on rocks and on the ground and touring them each day to run his fingers round their shapes, so that these dusty journeys of the fingertips became his wordless prayers. And that was comforting. He took it on himself to pass the time by marking rocks with all the words he knew.

He had taught himself at home to recognize a few words in written Greek script, more words than anyone else in his family. He could read and write his own name, and the name of god. He could roughly translate the inscription on the local temple stone which promised death to gentiles if they strayed into the inner court. He knew the meaning of TI.CAES.DIVI, the truncated Latin on the tribute coins. It designated Tiberius to be an Emperor and God. A blasphemy, the priest had said. The priest had little sympathy for Rome, although when it came to collecting tithes he much preferred their silver blasphemies to the copper ones.

Jesus also knew the scripts for a dozen or so words in Aramaic. He liked their timber squareness. They were shorter and less angled than the Greek or Latin; no vowels. The marks were simpler and more cheerful, doing all they could to bend in natural shapes. They'd been designed by holy carpenters, not masons. Their corners had a little curve to them, the work of planes.

After his boyhood years of study at the temple school, steadying the scrolls and holding down the parchments beneath the pointing finger of the priest, Jesus had learnt to match some of these Aramaic shapes to sounds — the little candelabra of the letter *sha*, the lightning strike of *enn*, the falling plough sign of the *kaoh*. He liked the places on these parchments where scribes were changed. The one who'd stitched his way across the page with wary, threadlike marks passed on his verses to the playful and untidy one who let his muddy sparrows leave their tracks in undulating lines. Then came the scribe whose writing always toppled backwards, as if the meanings of the words were riding faster than the shapes which soon would fall on to their spines.

This was a happy ignorance for Jesus, only knowing a dozen words amongst so many thousands. He would not

160

want to read as easily as scholars, he told himself, for that would only help to split the meaning from the sound, to divorce the music from the shape. If he could read like his priest could, by simply dragging his forefinger underneath the script and speaking every word he touched as if these were not verses but an endless rote of errands to be run, then the scriptures might become little more than strings of tiny tasks, a list. There'd be no mystery. But in his ignorance, he could both listen to the words of the reader and marvel, too, at the unspoken narrative of shapes, or concentrate not only on the script but also on the spaces in between. God was in the spaces, he was sure. God went to the very edges of the page.

Now, at the entrance of his cave with all the light of day removed, only the voice of the priest was missing. There was still a scroll for him to sit beneath. Jesus could look into the stars and see such spaces and such shapes as he had followed in the temple, spread out across the boundless parchment of the night in silver verses; again, the little candelabra, the lightning strike, the falling plough, the wary, undulating, toppling constellations which were the work of just one scribe. The sky was like the scriptures, written down in Aramaic too.

So Jesus took great care in marking down his list of words. It was a sacred act, and one which brought the vastness of the scriptures and the sky into his cave. He cut the three square Aramaic letters which signified the name of god in the soft clay walls and scratched them on the harder entrance stone. He made a temple of his cave. He consecrated all the surfaces. He marked his own name, too, but lower in the clay and smaller than the name of god. He'd not scratch in the truncated titles of the caesar — TI. CAES. DIVI — but he attempted to reproduce the Greek warning to all gentiles that they risked their lives by coming too close. He wrote it where it would be seen if anyone came too close, in the weathered earth at the entrance to the cave. He hoped that *anyone* could read. He faltered after seven of the twenty words. The shapes were blurred. He used to know them all by rote, but now his memory was failing him, like his bladder. It was an empty bag. He finished off his warning to the gentiles with the Aramaic *enn* and *sha* and *kaoh*. A word that made no sense, but Jesus found the letters comforting. The lightning lit the candles, struck the plough.

When he had finished writing out the word for god, laying claim to every stone and any flat face of clay which had room enough for lettering, he chose something simpler to occupy his mind. He took up his pointed writing rock and scratched a basket of three circles in the sun-dried floor, just inside his cave, and cut the circles into quarters with a cross. It was a rough grid on which to play the mill-game. This was how bad boys avoided temple lessons, hiding in the medlar trees, and playing on the mill-board for prizes of dried grapes, with sacrilegious forfeits for the ones that lost: put grass snakes in the priest's side room; steal walnuts from the temple tree; rap on his door and run . . . And this was how old men killed time until the time killed them, sitting with their backs arched in the shade, above a mill-game board, waiting for their girls to serve a meal

162

or for the moon to send them home. Jesus searched for tiny stones to act as counters — six blackish-brown, six white or grey — and spent the day as best he could in opposition to himself, testing all the blocked and ambushed routes around the grid. He'd never been much good at the mill-game when he was young. He had not practised. He'd prayed instead. He could not see the point of games.

Now he had all the practice that he wanted. He could enjoy the dodging conflict of the little stones, the way they tussled for the cross-roads of the board, and did their best to flee the outer ring and hold the centre ground. There was another sermon there, he thought. Outside the temple gates on market day, raised on a cart. The mill-game as a symbol of the world, with god its inner circle and the stones as pilgrims hunting for the centre of the cross. It was a holy game.

He could, therefore, persuade himself not to mind the guilty times when he abandoned prayers, when he lost heart in the repetition of the scriptures. Instead, he contested with himself in the mill-game and played both parts, the winner and the loser. Indeed, it seemed the game itself was a sort of prayer, with just one supplicant and no one to respond except himself. The mill-game worshipper, alone in quarantine, could not presume the company of god. Nor could the man at prayer. Both of them had to play both roles, and be in opposition to themselves and make all moves, and lose and win in equal part. God would not show himself. He would not sit cross-legged on the far side of the board, replying to each move of Jesus's with his own stratagems, drawing

163

in his breath when he seemed bettered, crying out when he had Jesus trapped, dispensing charity and hope and forfeits when he had placed the final stone inside the cross. He would not simply run up like a dog wherever Jesus prayed.

It was no comfort, knowing that the winner was the loser too. Jesus could not sleep, even though he had relented in his disciplines and allowed himself to lie naked and depleted on the ground, out of the draught, his shoulder as a pillow. His skin became as cold as clay. Where were the camel and the thorn? He rolled into a ball, his knees pulled up towards his chin, his thin arms clasped around his shins, his backbone bumpy like a rabbit's gut. It was the fourth night of his quarantine, and he was weak.

CHAPTER
SEVENTEEN

Marta wanted female company. Aphas and Shim could
look for wood and maintain the fire at night. The badu
could make traps for birds — his only skill, it seemed.
But there were female tasks they would not do. They did
not think it was their place to fetch their food from
Musa, or cook it, for example. Marta could do that. Once
her stomach had begun to settle, she was glad to
have their errands as an excuse to flee the caves. Of
course she had to pray, but her devotions did not take up
much time. She was an indecisive worshipper of god.
Her liturgies were brief and shy. Once she felt safe and
strong enough to leave the perching valley of the caves,
she took to hurrying each morning down the valley to
the tent, where she could bargain with Musa for some
bread or dates or curd. She hired a reed bed-mat from
him, which she could soften with a cushion of sand.
She'd get half her money back if she returned the mat at
the end of quarantine unmarked, he said. Sometimes she
bought a little stiffened goat's milk in a pouch, as well,
and some of Miri's sweet cake. To eat in secret after
dusk, not to share.

"I feel responsible for you," Musa said, when she
stood at his bed end one morning to offer her respects

and money. "A landlord and his tenants are like cousins. Brothers, sisters, even. And now you worry me. Look at yourself. You're losing weight," he said. "And that won't do. We have to keep you plump and strong. Don't be like her. My wife's a stick." He turned his head towards the curtain and the rattle of the loom, and called out to his wife, "Feed her, Miri. She is my guest. She is my sister for today."

"I mustn't eat," Marta said. "Not now."

"Who'll know?" he asked. He wasn't pleased. He wished that he could pull her to the ground and make her eat. He'd stuff her mouth with bread, not clay, and pick the crumbs off with his tongue. He turned away from her, and fell back on his cushions. An insult to a visitor. "You do not have to be our sister for the day if you don't want. The choice is yours. Be thin."

The thought of Marta — thin or plump — made his mouth go dry. The fleshy twist of leavened dough, tucked in his lap, began to uncurl, bake and form a crust. Patience, patience — she'd be his within the forty days. She was alone. Who, or what, could stop him going to her cave one night? His plans for Marta kept him busy for a while. But otherwise, he only thought of being in the market-place, the centre of the crowds again. He wished that he could simply clap his hands and be elsewhere. He'd leave tomorrow if it were possible, except he could not make his escape out of the scrub until those three fools at the caves would put his bags and tent on to their backs and take him to the river valley. He was the warder of other people's quarantines. He was the prisoner, as well.

He entertained himself with thoughts of leaving Miri behind in Jericho or, better still, exchanging her for Marta. What would he do when he got north, apart from looking for his uncles and his cousins? He'd have no trouble getting restitution for the merchandise they'd taken — they'd think he was a ghost — although it might be many seasons before he traced his old companions. How would he live, what would he buy and sell until that day? He asked the question to himself a thousand times, and every time, it seemed the Gally's face imposed itself on Musa's mind. "Be well," he'd said, and driven out the fever.

Yes, patience was the watchword now. Everything would turn out well if Musa could only wait until he found the healer for a second time, and enticed him to his tent again. In his dreams and in his drink, he'd lured the Galilean from his cave and asked, in lieu of rent, to be taught the trick of healing. He learned to fill his saddle-bags with prayers and spells, to dig up roots, pick leaves. Then he travelled to the pleats and pockets of the world and sold long life, and health. He was mistaken for a holy man, and people emptied out their purses in his lap. He drove out fevers for a price, turned water into wine. He made barren women pregnant with his Galilean tricks, and caused the lame to dance for him. At last he was respected for himself.

He could not stop himself inventing new, unholy miracles. He knew — let's say — the art of seeing through the women's clothes, so he could watch them naked as they lined up at his stall. He practised this new skill on Marta. He'd find some task for her close to his bed, so that he might see her bend or lift her arms and watch her fabrics shift across her skin, so that he might enjoy the smell of her. He made her wait at his bed's end, while he made plans.

But for the most part of the day, Marta and Miri had their privacy in the screened end of the tent and with the goats. They hardly spoke at first. What should they say? You only had to read the parchment of their skins to know these women had little in common apart from their age, perhaps. Marta's face was hardly marked, except for a few lines around the mouth, and two almond-shaped wedding scars on her cheeks. But Miri's face was an empty water-bag — squint lines round the eyes from travelling too long and often in the sun; dry skin across the forehead and the nose; chewed lips; and battle scars.

On the first occasion that Marta had gone beyond the curtain, Miri's face was bruised. Her smile was puckered by the swelling at her mouth; one eyebrow was bluey-grey and swollen. Hers was a beggarwoman's face. The elders of Sawiya would drive her sort out of town, with Thaniel leading them. There was, nevertheless, something jaunty and unquenchable about the little woman that Marta found irresistible. She had to reach across and touch the bruise, a healing gesture of her own. The two embraced, and held each other's hands like sisters. It did not matter that they did not talk at first, for women always find some soundless intimacy with which to occupy themselves.

Marta simply followed Miri. Sat when she sat. Watched when any work was done. Smiled when stared at. Passed the hanks of wool. She held the nannies by their ear tufts during milking. She helped to shake and separate the curds. She took her turn with blowing into the goatskin from time to time to clarify the yoghurt into butter, and collected herbs from the scrub. She reamed to slap the unleavened dough against hot fire-stones to make platter bread, cooked in moments. She reamed to check and block the pegs on Miri's loom, and to tie the smallest knots in the broken yarn. She was like a child in some aunt's yard, clumsy, willing, slow, engrossed, her tongue between her teeth, eager to be praised, and quite content to be ignored. But soon the intimacy of weaving, of sitting side by side on the woven fabric as the mat progressed and lengthened, to help maintain the loom in tension, turned the women into twins. A muttered conversation started. Their shoulders and their fingers touched. Their knees collided on the wool. They talked about their lives, about their marriages, and Marta wept — sad for herself and sad for Miri — on the day that Miri asked how many children she had got at home. Not one.

They shared a bowl of water when they washed. Behind the curtain, Marta let all her clothes drop to her waist and took her underliner off, while Miri brought a dampened cloth for her to wipe herself, and a head of lavender to make the water sweet. Then Miri matched her nakedness, though less majestically, and washed. She let Marta put her fingers on her stomach and feel for heels and heartbeats. Once they heard the curtain drop. It was still swaying when they'd pulled their clothes back

169

on. They knew that Musa had been watching them. But still they laughed. These were the fullest forty days they'd ever lived.

Late in the afternoon, the men arrived and readied Musa for his daily walk. They left Miri preparing bread behind the tent, and went off through the falling scrub to look for signs of Gally. A path was worn where there had never been a path, between the caves, the tent, the precipice. Musa with the curling staff. Aphas with a bending stick he'd made from sapbush. Shim, safely at a distance, lost — or hiding — in his meditations. The badu, following and leading, low-shouldered, like a herding dog. And Marta last.

Again there was no sign of anyone in the cave. No healer waved at them. No Galilean shouted out for food. There were just shades and shapes. The rocks were shivering.

Aphas could hardly breathe, he was so disappointed. His lungs felt squeezed. "I'm not a very devout man," he said, when it was almost time to leave. "If I'd prayed more, and bathed and followed rules, observed the sabbath better, I might've not got ill. Who knows? I might've not got this." He touched his bulging liver, and gasped several times. The constant pain was wearying. It took him to the edge of tears. "But this is what I feel when I am here. This air is . . . sweet . . . There is someone."

Aphas could not stop himself from weeping now. His illness and his imagined eloquence were more than he could bear. His voice was smothered by his sobbing. He was recalling Musa's words, how Shim's very stupid boy had pressed his holy fingers on Musa's face, and said, I will not let you take this man from us. How he had plucked the fever out; how he might pluck the cancer out of Aphas as easily as he could pluck the stone out of an olive and toss it to the ground. Those were the very words, more powerful than scripture. "I did see someone move," he said at last. "Forgive my tears."

"Someone, perhaps. A shepherd . . ." said Shim.

"Why not a holy man?"

Shim would not allow that possibility. He spoke from personal experience. He'd seen holy monks several times before, he explained. He'd sat with them, in temples to the north, in Greece, in other caves. He'd seen a prophet once. He'd been with men who knew their scriptures off by heart, and others who could discern the future of the world from studying the stars. All of them looked wise and old, as dry and silvery as weathered timber. Enlightenment took time. Their beards were long and grey; their skins were lined like parchment scrolls. There was a light around them, not like light from a fire, but cold and pious, coming off their skin like phosphorescence on a fish. Such a light was the mark of holiness and such a light, people said, could heal. It was a light he hoped to earn himself. It wasn't easy to acquire without long years of seeking it, far from the comforts and distractions of the world. It wasn't given after forty days. It wasn't squandered (on the likes of Musa). It wasn't found in shepherd boys. "It does not climb down cliffs to hunt for eggs," he said. "You mentioned shapes and shadows when you saw something in that cave, but

171

you did not notice any light, I think." He closed his eyes. He concentrated on the light to come. "Don't give up hope." He meant that Aphas ought to hope that Shim would soon begin to glow.

"I do hope," Aphas said. "What else is there for me but hope, and prayer? We ought to pray. As loudly as we can. Then he'll come. He'll come to join the prayers, if he's a holy man."

It was not easy to kneel in prayer on that rough, sloping ground. Marta felt she ought to help the old man, but once she had, Musa demanded help as well. She had to hold him by his wrists, and take his weight while he sat down, and then she had to pull him forwards on his knees. He held on to her hands too long. His nostrils flared when she got close to him, as if she were a meal. They rocked in prayer until there was hardly any light remaining in the sky. They asked for cures, fortunes, changes in their lives. But still there was no sign of Gally.

"He's gone for good," said Shim. "I told you so." But Musa, Marta and Aphas would not hear of it. Musa pushed his borrowed staff into Shim's back. A warning to stay quiet. It left a puckered indent in his clothes. They watched for tremors in the darkness of the cave. They heard odd sounds, thin evidence of hope. It seemed, as well, that there were marks of movement that looked like lettering on the sloping rock in front of the key-hole entrance. Some stones had been displaced since their last visit. Perhaps by birds. Perhaps by someone sitting on the rock.

172

"He's there," said Musa, almost the first words that he'd spoken since they'd left the tent. "I'm sure of it. And we must tempt him out. A hundred prayers won't do the job. He isn't short of prayers. He has his own supply. But he needs food and drink or else he'll die." The next time that they came, he said, they'd bring some dates and bread, and water in a bag. "We can tie them to some yarn and lower them on to the rock. He'll show his face for that. If he's a man."

The pilgrims pulled each other to their feet and stood on the promontory for one last view of the cave, like mourners, their shadows dropping out of sight. No movement on the precipice. There was no one to look at but themselves. Then not even themselves, because the light betrayed them. They had to scramble back to safer ground up slopes which had no shape or colour, through scrub which still was waiting for its moon. Meanwhile, elsewhere, in candlelight, the purple and the orange wools embraced.

CHAPTER
EIGHTEEN

Jesus wanted to believe that a flapping pigeon had landed in the canker thorn above his cave. Some proper company at last, out of the ark. Grey feathers and red earth, black wood. He was familiar with pigeons. They roosted underneath the beams of his father's workshop, and lived off garden scraps and chicken feed. He knew their sounds, especially the alarm of their wings if they got trapped by cats or caught in the twig nets put down to protect the beans and peppers in the family patch. Then he'd be the first to run outside and set them free. God's work.

From the noises that he heard, he judged his visitor to be a single bird, caged by the thorn. He recognized the sharp and frightened chirps it made, the heedless way it shook and banged its wings. Come down, he whispered to himself. He hardly had the voice or faith to call out loud. He longed to press its feathers to his face. That's what the fast had done to him. He no longer prayed for god to come. He'd settle for the bird.

His pigeon dislodged a cloud of dry marl, which floated at the cave entrance, making speckled columns of the sloping sunlight, making temples of the air. His pigeon knocked off some of the thorn's few silver

174

leaves. The tree was shedding sins at Jesus's feet. He could have put his arms out into the sun and caught a leaf if he'd had the strength and could have stopped the trembling in his hands. As it was, he did not move at all. He let the leaves make their pattern on the ground, uninterrupted. He only watched and counted them, telling fortunes from the way they fell. It would be bad luck if any leaf was touched or covered by another. And then — when bad luck was heaped up on the ground — he would outlive the fast, escape the scrub, only if the falling leaves exceeded forty. Or, every leaf was one more year of life. In that hard light, with his poor eyes, the piles of leaves looked like a hoard of silver jewellery.

Soon there were leaves enough for Jesus to escape the scrub and live another sixty years. All he wanted now was for the pigeon to come. It was bound to be a bird from home, he told himself, a grateful pigeon sent from the Galilee to be his witness. He sat in darkness, his ankles crossed, just his toes amputated by the hard edge of the sun, and listened to the frantic beating of its wings. He waited for the pigeon to liberate itself, and fly down with its narcotic *ookuroos* to hunt for chaff at his feet. There was no chaff.

Jesus rubbed his knuckles in his eyes, he pinched the bridge of his nose, hoping to clear his sight. The entrance to the cave appeared hard and sharp, a jagged pyramid of light, but anything beyond was out of focus. His eyes had weakened in the gloom, and one was watery and blurred from an infection. The tears drained from his sinuses into his throat; that was the moisture he had drunk for thirteen days. His tongue was dry and stiff and silvery, a thorn leaf in his mouth, a mouth stuffed full of sin. The only sounds that he could make himself were little more than *ookuroos*. He and his pigeon were cousins, then, tongue-tied, inconsequential in the scrub, and insubstantial to themselves. They were soft creatures, naked, dislocated and afraid, and tired beyond the boundaries of sleep.

Jesus did sleep, though, or fainted. When he woke, the pigeon had grown larger and more threatening. There were no chirps or beating wings. What he'd mistaken as a bird now struggled with the thorn too heavily to be so small and feathery. It tugged and tore too madly at the branches. The sheer cliff-face above his head, where surely nothing larger than a single bird or bush could find any purchase, seemed to be making noises fit for a rock cat or a wolf. Bigger pieces of the marl began to fall, and cover the jewellery. The leaves seemed curses now. Sixty years in hell.

Jesus was not too tired or ill-nourished to be afraid. He closed his eyes, squeezed the bridge of his nose again, and concentrated. His hearing was still as sharp as reeds. He heard the bush grieving for its last few leaves, the crumbling marl, the tetchy bluster of the valley wind, his own uncushioned heart-beats. At last and in the distance, high and thin, coming from the naked air above the precipice, there was the turbulence of agitated men. Another flying donkey then?

A branch snapped loose and fell on to the sloping rock in front of the cave. Then a small leather bag, much reddened by the marl and snagged by the canker thorn in which it had become entangled, dropped into view. It hung on a plaited wool rope in front of the key-hole opening at knee-height from the ground, and swung from side to side, its weathered leather chirping sharply — a cowering pigeon, indeed — until it lost momentum and only swayed when it was tugged from above.

Jesus did not even sway. He put a finger in each ear and pressed his palms into his eyes. He would be deaf and blind. But he could not shut out the world for long. He had no doubt what sound would be the next, a voice too high and reedy to be a normal man's. No soothing *ookuroos*. He'd heard and feared that voice a dozen times before, because each evening of the fast the fever-giant he'd left for dead in his black tent with its bat wings had come on to the rocky promontory a little to his right to tempt him from his quarantine. He shouted out his messages in short and breathless bursts, like some trinket salesman, as if long phrases would not have the wings to fly between the promontory and Jesus's cave. "Come out, Gally. Let's see your face . . . My name is Musa. I'm your cousin. And your friend." No answer? Then, "I'll make you rich . . ." At other times, "At least put up. Your hands. To pray for us. You can't refuse. This woman's barren, see? This uncle's dying. From a canker. A canker in his ribs. These other two. Have been possessed. The one. Won't speak. The other one. Can't shut up. Come. Up to the tent. You are. You are the healer. Come up. And heal."

Jesus concentrated on the leather bag, and waited for the voice to start again. He could imagine Musa and his retinue — the blond, the tall woman and the limping man, the cat-like madcap with the hennaed hair — now inventing their beguilements in the company of serpents and hyenas on the summit of the precipice. He could imagine them with wings like vultures, and with yellow eyes. When they had lured him into their tent, amongst the fingered cushions and the seeing lamps, they'd rub their sins against him, flesh on flesh, and defile him with their food — their mildew and their carrion, their sabbath fish, their cups of blood, their geckos and their pigs.

It might have been wise, if Jesus wanted any peace of mind, to impose upon himself the cheerful, undemanding view of radicals and city Greeks, that the devil was simply an excuse; someone to justify a person's own shortcomings, someone to take the blame. It was their creed that devils had no place on earth, that evil was not a living creature in the world. There was no one to blame other than oneself. There was just good luck and bad, god's rules observed and broken, the clumsy juggling of happiness and guilt. And death of course, but death without a reckoning, and death without eternity. If Jesus could persuade himself of that, then how much more comfortable his quarantine would be. The leather bag would be nothing more than an irritation, and the big man on the precipice would be no angel out of hell. His shouted words would only be another earthly test of Jesus's patience, simple to combat, safe to ignore.

Jesus, though, was young and inexperienced. His life so far had been unGreek. It was cheerless and demanding. Death was still far enough away — and too improbable — for him to want to believe that there might be no reckoning. He was, besides, a villager, too direct and untutored to take much comfort from abstract notions that life was finite or that the devil was not flesh and blood. For him — although he could not put the words to it — the living devil was just as real as god. Indeed, the devil was the living proof of god, for everything that god had made was weak and blemished and imperfect by design. God's pot had cracked inside the kiln, so that his sons and daughters could by their labours and their prayers restore perfection to the pot. The devil occupied the crack, and lay in wait like a thief. God put him there. To deny the presence of the devil was to turn against the perfect blemishes of god.

So Jesus was in little doubt that, should the devil choose, he could easily appear as Musa on the precipice. He could produce a thousand leather bags. He could invade his soul and jostle for a perch inside his heart as truly and as tangibly as a raiding jackdaw could invade an open nest and jostle out its chirping innocents with its black wings. That was the drama and the cruel romance of Jesus's theology. That's why he clung so greedily to god. This was not the Galilee, with its flax fields and walnut groves and rain, its cousins and its fig-shaded yards. He only had to stare out of his cave to know for sure. The evidence was large. This was the devil's kingdom. Hot winds. Hard rocks. Dry leaves. A barren universe, and death disguised.

Jesus, then, could not be calmly Greek and radical in this demonic scrub. How could he be when the devil called him from the precipice, when the jackdaw's matted wing was hard against his face? He was alone, exposed, a chirping innocent. And yet he felt triumphant

179

too. Thank heavens for the devil, even, for the devil was the herald of god. "The devil and the bee obstruct the way to heaven and to honey. The path to sweetness is a stinging one," according to the country psalm. As he grew closer to his god, the devil's fat hand would wrap itself round Jesus's thin wrist. The devil's lips would press against his ear. God would watch and bide his time, and if his Galilean son stood firm, god's cushioned fingers would take him by the elbow and the hand and ease him from the devil's grasp. Why else had Jesus come into the wilderness? To be the chosen one. To be the battleground. To be eased to freedom from the devil's grasp.

So even though Jesus was distressed by Musa's daily visitations, he understood that god was watching him at last. That gave him strength, and helped him to withstand the chilling offers from the promontory and to see the devil's plan more clearly. Musa's offers were too crudely tempting; his summonses for Jesus to vacate the precipice and heal the sick were too bespoke to be remotely innocent. The scriptures said, *The devil comes and offers you your heart's desire, beware; he promises a boat to fishermen, and proffers horses to a man that hopes to ride; he places cushions at your back and brings in figs on silver plates, and wine.* And that had always been Jesus's greatest, maddest hope, his heart's desire, to serve god by driving out illnesses and spirits, to cure and to heal. He did not see himself a hermit, engaging with his god forever in a cave. He did not see himself a scholar, poring over texts. He did not have the learning or the self-regard. He did not see himself a priest. He was too shy.

He wanted most to serve his god in simpler ways which did not require either confidence or reading, ways which could be witnessed by his family and his neighbours. More cowardly ways, perhaps? At best, he'd preach to villagers and children, anyone who would not challenge him and not call out, "Your head's in heaven, Gally. Full of clouds." He'd even be prepared — and glad — to defile himself on those kept out of temples — lepers, menstruating women, prostitutes, the blind, even the uncircumcized — if they would listen to him, if it would cause discomfort to the priest. These were the ones, he thought, that god had created weak and blemished and imperfect by design. These were the chirping innocents that he should rescue from the devil's claw, for he himself was weak and blemished and imperfect by design. These people were his family.

Jesus had always been ashamed of his ambition, but this is what he'd dreamed since he was young. There was a congregation on a hill slope in the Galilee. He was the tallest, and he looked down on their heads. He recognized his brothers' hair, his neighbours' hair, the baker's and the priest's, the leper's, and the prostitute's uncovered hair. But they were tired of listening to sermons. "Come up to me, the sick, the troubled and the blind," he'd say. He'd put his hands on eyes and foreheads, rub out pains, press his fingers into hardened flesh, remove their swellings with a touch, kiss sores. Erase their sins. He'd cure them. They'd be restored, through him, by god. And, yes, he'd find a boat for fishermen, and horses for the men too weak to walk. They'd say — a phrase he loved — "We never knew our Gally after all. He is the bread of our short lives. He is the good shepherd who will lead us out of suffering."

He'd never boasted such a dream to anyone — not to his parents or the priest, not even to his god in prayer, and hardly to himself. This was his smothered heart's desire, unspoken and invisible. Yet here was someone — this resurrected fat man, dangling provisions from the summit of the precipice — who called him by his other name and seemed to see inside his heart. Someone who heard what was not said. Someone who saw what was not on display. No one had ever offered Jesus such perfect blandishments before, or such flattery. Yes, he was tempted to go up and test his healing prayers at the tent, to sacrifice his fast for them. He felt he had the cure in his fingertips. They only had to touch. They trembled at the thought of it. The hands that could remove the knots from wood, release the pigeons pinioned by the twigs, could drive out fevers and disease. He'd be the carpenter of damaged souls. But god was watching him, beyond the devil and the bees, and saying nothing. He gave no sign to Jesus. And no sign was the sign that these appeals to vanity could only be the devil's work. He'd have to learn to block his ears and eyes for fear of joining them, the demons on the rock.

So Jesus closed himself against his tempters. He would not be seduced or fooled by the contents of a leather bag. He half-heard, through his fingertips, Musa calling from the rim, his voice unnatural: "Gally. Gally.

Look outside. There's water. And some food. Dates. Some bread. My wife. Has baked for you . . . Gally, Gally. Speak to us." He did not move. He hardly breathed. He was beyond temptation now. His appetites were dead.

It was hard to concentrate, but he managed to expel Musa from his thoughts and shut their voices out. He set his mind on future, better times: his quarantine had ended; he had proved his worthiness. He saw himself walking through Jerusalem towards the temple, through the trading tables and the booths which filled the outer courts. The merchants and the dealers and the money-changers, the people who wore soft clothes and ate wheat bread and reclined on couches like the Greeks, would all call out to him in their high voices, "Gally, Gally, eat our cakes and drink our wine. Buy pigeons and dates from us." Musa would be there, with leather bags for sale. But Jesus could not be seduced, not by the devil in the scrub, not by the devils crowding at the temple walls. He'd turn their tables over, empty out their bags, drive off their animals. He'd put his foot in Musa's flesh and kick him through the gates.

But first he had the opportunity to kick a bag. It held the devil's water and the devil's bread, the devil's finest dates. How much he'd love to open up the bag and sup on it. How much he'd be relieved to break his fast, and flood the valley of his throat.

He managed to get up on to his feet, although his ankles ached alarmingly and all his bones protested at the effort. He could not swing his foot to kick the bag. He reached his arm out into the early evening light.

There was no sun to warm him; how foolish and how strong he'd been to jettison his clothes. He wrapped his fingers round the plaited rope. He pulled the bag towards the cave, and caught it in both hands. He smelled the bread — the water too — in those few moments that he held the bag. He smelled the blood, the mildew and the carrion that lingered on the leather. He tugged on it. The rope tightened for an instant and came free as Musa or one of his accomplices let go of the far end. He sensed their triumph. He would make it brief. Before the rope could slither from the rim and fall at the entrance to the cave, Jesus had tossed the bag away as if it had claws and teeth, a rabid bat. He hadn't got much strength. He was surprised how heavy it had seemed, but still it cleared the platform of the cave and fell towards the valley, bouncing on the precipice until the water-pouch inside, unseen, split open from the impact of the rocks. The leather bag became too empty and too light to fall much more. It lay — forever; kippered by the sun — between two rocks, too high and too far from the top for any climber to retrieve.

Jesus pressed his fingers tighter in his ears. He was petulant with triumph and alarm, like a boy who'd smashed an egg, frightened of his mother, not the hen. He would not listen to his tempters' shouted words. He hummed to himself so that no more sound or any of the beaten voices from above could penetrate his armour.

CHAPTER
NINETEEN

Night arrived with its sullen wing to double-shade their tents and caves. Jesus slept; he was unconscious for a while, but when he dreamed he dreamed of Musa, no one else. Stroking Musa's eyelids with his thumb. Musa's face marked on the surface of the moon. Musa sitting in the kingdom of the lord, naked and uncircumcized, his great lap open to the angels' gaze. Musa in a market-place, but selling fasts instead of leather bags, with Jesus his first customer.

Musa's salesmanship was irresistible. Of course it was. Jesus could not make the man seem dull, even in his dreams. This devil was not ignorant, a huckster with no subtlety. He was a craftsman worthy of his task. He was a trader and a salesman, after all, and practised in making virtues out of sins. He could sell the mildew and the bruises on his blemished fruit. Their blackened peels are honey-sweet, he'd say. Taste them — pay first — and you will see.

No, for Jesus, the merchant Musa and the devil were the same, in dreams and out. Close cousins anyway, far-travelled, patient, shrewd, unshockable, refined. For every camel-load of merchandise that Musa had exchanged for goods abroad he would have packed a little knowledge in his panniers as well; the whereabouts of some blue, distant town, the predilections of some king, a new philosophy, a freshly coined word, telepathy, the allocation of the stars. He'd have the trick of holding conversations with his customers on subjects as various as that year's lemon crop, the uses of bem and balsam oils, and whether it was proper for a sadducee to eat an egg that had been laid on the sabbath. ("Proper to eat it, wrong to cook it, I would say. Raw eggs are good enough for sadducees.") All his conversations would be sharp. His knowledge was a gleaming weapon, a spear with wings, with which to prick and wound his quarry. Musa would not flee from arguments, or duck his head at words he could not understand. What he didn't know he would invent, and his inventions would be more quenching than the truth. He was a strong adversary for god.

So here in dreams was Musa at his stall, selling fasts to pious Jews, always intending that they should be trapped by their own vanity in some damp cave, on some sheer precipice, with not an ant to keep them company, and only devils' water there to wet their eyes and tongues. Here was Musa calling on the holy wisdoms of Moses, Ezra and Mordecai whose fasts had been sustained divinely. Here was Musa with his hand on Jesus's, the merchant's mouth a short breath from the client's ear, his forked tongue hidden by his swollen cheeks, and whispering, "I challenge you. To battle me. For forty days."

Again, more dreams. He came, this time to Jesus in his cave. He held a carpet viper in one hand, and a desert mouse in the other. "These creatures are your cousins, Gally. They're like you. They go without their food and drink for forty days or more in this same scrub, three months, four months," he said. "If there's no food or drink, they simply switch their bodies off and wait until the rains. That's what you have to do. It's easy. Of course, the pity is that one of them can always break its fast, to eat the other one . . . Guess which. Let's see." He put the viper with the mouse.

Another time the merchant was a priest, his great round head topped off with a linen hat. Bells and pomegranates hung from his blue robe. There were brooches made of sardonyx, a golden purse, a purple cape. His sermon was that fasters who had earned his blessing could expect the greatest of rewards. He could not promise paradise to mice or snakes. But pious Jews? Their prizes were unlimited. With Musa at their side, they would be calm throughout their quarantine and comfortable, he promised them, leaning his weight against the temple door. They would have peace of mind. All the distractions and appetites of public life would be driven off like scrub dogs, and clarity of spirit would come sniffing at their ankles, begging to be lifted up and stroked.

"Towards the end — the last ten days, perhaps — your soul will fly out of your body like a lark," he said. "Believe me, you will pass into the fabric of the sky, until you sit amongst the angels at their table. Keep your elbows in. You'll break your fast with rapture beans and golden goblets filled with nectar. And then they'll call you for your final prize — an audience with god. If you will only place your trust in me."

The final dream. They were in the Galilee. Musa in the market-place, with Jesus and his family, and all the villagers. "Let's have a volunteer, to taste the black skin of my quarantine," he said. "You." He prodded Jesus on the chest, with his imperfect staff. "Try fasting now. Try forty days. You'll find forgiveness if you've upset god. Your oddities . . ." he smiled conspiratorially at all the Galileans, ". . . will be subdued, turned to a profit even. See how deep the nights become, how bright the stars, the longer that you keep away from food and drink. Come, Gally. Bring your brothers, bring your friends. Broken hearts will be repaired. Bald men will grow fine heads of hair . . . Please have your coins ready when you come."

This last nightmare was what Jesus woke up to a dozen times, in the darkness of the middle night. He had expected to dream of chicken and melon, mutton stew, lamb cooked above a vine-wood fire, not Musa preaching fasts. Jesus was at his weakest when he woke. His spirit was destroyed by sleep. He could not recall a single prayer to summon help, or shake away this final dream. His elbows and his knees cracked like seed pods; his bones were noisy ravens laughing at his flesh, tok-tok tok-tok. His body throbbed with cold. These were his moments of defeat. He'd been a fool to throw his clothes away. He'd been a fool to leave the Galilee. He'd been a fool to leap out of his bed to pray. He'd been a very stupid man to invest so much in fasting. His quarantine was little more than bogus goods, false gold, a leaking pot, sold to him by a man who had the devil's tongue. He was not any closer to his god, for all his sacrifice, than he had been when he was six. Surely someone in the Galilee — his priest, a neighbour possibly, someone who knew the hermit scriptures better than himself — could have taken him aside before he left his home and offered some instruction on the torments that he faced if he came to the wilderness alone. Where was the rhapsody? What joy was there in all the suffering? Where was the dignity of death?

No one had said how painful it would be, how first, there would be headaches and bad breath, weakness, fainting; or how the coating on the upper surface of his tongue would thicken day by day; or how his tongue would soon become stuck to the upper part of his mouth, held in place by gluey strings of hunger, so that he would mutter to himself or say his prayers as if his palate had been cleft at birth; or how his gums would bleed and his teeth become as loose as date stones.

No one had warned him how quickly he would lose his will to move about, how even lifting up his arms to wipe away the sweat — so much of that, at first, and then none at all — would become a punishing task; how he'd postpone the effort and let the sweat drip off his brow without regard to cleanliness; how cruelly his body would begin to eat itself as his muscles and his liver and his kidneys fought for fuel like squalid, desert boys battling for a piece of wood; how his legs would swell with pus; how his skin would tear and how the wounds would be too weak to dress themselves with scabs. No

189

one had said, there will be stomach pains and cramps, demanding to be rubbed and soothed like dogs.

He hated dawn. At least at night, he could imagine he was whole. But in the cave's dim light by day, he looked down at his arms and legs and saw how he was turning black in patches where his muscles and his joints were leaking blood. He'd become a leper, a hyena, one of those mottled slaves from the rivers beyond Egypt, flayed brown and pink by some hard master. They wouldn't let him in the temple grounds like that.

Jesus rubbed his joints and warmed his fingers in his mouth. He could reduce these pains. But there were other, shocking pains that could not be rubbed away, the pains of sadness and despair. This was the greatest failing of them all. Someone, surely, could have said, Stay with your parents in the Galilee. For if you go into the wilderness to fast, not just your body but your spirit will, against all faith, begin to bleed. Your spirit will shed its weight as well, its frame will ache, its eyes will dim. You'd be a fool to think your spirit is beyond the reach of thirst and hunger. Nothing is.

They had not even said, Go to the desert if you must, and fast. But do take care. For god is not alone up there, if god is there at all. But there are animals; and the devil is the fiercest of them all.

Perhaps it was a blessing that Jesus's spirit fell apart before his body did, because if it had remained intact as he grew thin and weak on fasting, he might have tried to escape the folly of his unbending quarantine. He might have decided that he ought to take the middle course, the one chosen by the other quarantiners that he'd followed up the scree a few days previously. They were wise and timid, and broke their fasts each day at dusk. He might have climbed the precipice each evening, walked up through the foot-marked pans of soft clay along the valley beds to the perching row of caves, and got in line amongst the poppies for his share of their food. He could have begged for clothes. Or he might at least have seen the sense in this one compromise — by all means to have gone without dry food, but to have kept his throat and body oiled during the forty days with a little water from their cistern, for water is the staff of life and god's great gift to the world.

What vanity to think a total fast can rid a man of sin, or put a man at god's right hand, he might have told himself if his spirit and good sense had not been so subdued. Go from this cave, go home, go now — be penitent, be purified, and sin no more.

It was too late. He had no strength to climb the precipice. Jesus had become a creature of the dark, a fugitive from pleasure, comfort, beauty, light. He sat inside the cave, his hands lapping round his genitals for coolness, or running round the three symbols for the name of god which he had scratched, it seemed a thousand years before, into the rock, or massaging his legs and arms. His face was bleached beneath the dust. His hair was knotted clay. His pupils had grown large and slow, in their attempts to catch and keep the light. He was confused and fumbling. The few sunbeams that came into his cave each morning made him sneeze and itch. My eyes can't take the light, he told himself. That is a sign that I am meant to stay right here.

CHAPTER
TWENTY

The devils on the precipice tempted Jesus three more times. They dropped down leather bags of food and water. But he was stubborn, and frightened enough to resist their gifts. He sent their bags bouncing down the cliff-face, bread for the ravens, water for the lizards, leather for the ants.

Then his tempters must have run out of temptations or of bags, because they did not bother him to break his fast again. They only came on to the promontory each evening, to plague him with their vigil and their verses. He listened but he did not recognize the words they used although his hearing had become thunderous, and all their footfalls were distinct. He heard them sniff; he heard them cough; he heard them draw in breath.

They still called to him, of course, not just the big man but the others too. "Gally, Gally. Gally, Gally," until they tired of it. He learned to recognize the whining miseries of old age, the bitterness of infertility, the swagger of the Greeks. They sometimes begged Jesus to come out of the cave, to talk to them, to prove himself with miracles. But Jesus did not have the strength to show himself, even if he'd wanted to. He'd used up any energy he had dealing with their bags of food.

The little badu, though, did not call out, but in many ways he was the noisiest of them all. He couldn't sit still for a moment. He had to run, or climb along the ledges as madly as a goat, or dislodge stones. He had to crumble earth and throw the pebbles that he found against the precipice. He seemed to be at war with everything. A truly troubled spirit, Jesus thought, on those three or four occasions when the badu came into view, clambering around the tip of the promontory. Here was a demon soul in torment, restless, tiny, dark, uncircumcized. A man entirely lost to god. This is what Jesus would end up like himself if he abandoned his devotions or was defeated for one single moment in his fast. He'd have to spend eternity with stones. He'd shrink and blacken. His foreskin would grow back. He'd have to clamber till the end of time.

Just once his tempters almost trapped him. It was barely dawn on the twenty-second day of quarantine, and Jesus was sleeping. He mistook the scrambling feet which roused him from his dreams to be his own, in headlong flight down banks of scree and bones. "See how our little Gally runs!" When he woke up, the dream persisted. There was shuffling. He thought that there was breathing in his ear. Fright made him strong. He sat up immediately and looked around into the shadows. He found what he was looking for. He didn't care if there were animals. He would have welcomed death if it was death. But it was just the badu standing in the entrance to the cave, an outline, the cloak of Moab purple at his shoulders, and his gifts — some locusts he had trapped, a water-pouch — lying on his hands. His knee was cut

193

from where he'd fallen on the climb, and so he stood unevenly, like a boy. He was less mad and restless than he'd seemed at a distance, less devilish. The locusts and the waterpouch were trembling. The badu was afraid, and so was Jesus. The shadow and the silhouette.

The badu whispered a word, not quite an *ookuroo*, but something soft and boneless. Not a word that Jesus understood. The badu put the locusts on the entrance rock. He touched his heart and then his forehead, to mime that he was coming as a friend. Again a sign that Jesus did not recognize. He held the water-pouch out for Jesus to take, and when the offer was ignored, he tipped some water into his open palms, inviting Jesus to see it, smell it, put his tongue to it. Here was the odour of the Galilee, seeping through the badu's shaking fingers and wasting on the ground.

Jesus concentrated all his power in his voice. He'd practised this — the coming of the devil to his cave. He shouted in the badu's face, "Leave me in peace . . ." But, still, he took a half-step forward as he shouted, just to be a little closer to the badu's hand, and the smell, and the glint of moisture that was left. The badu reached out through the dark, and put his damp fingers on Jesus's face. He wiped the water on his cheeks. Jesus did not pull away. This was too much for him.

"Rub just a little . . . on my lips," he said, although the words were weak and splintered. "Not swallow it." He would have wept at his own weakness, at all the days he'd wasted on his fast, if he had any tears. One drop of water and the devil would rejoice. One drop of water and he'd spend eternity with thorns and flames and rocks.

The badu smiled — invisibly in this half-light — but did not move his hand or press his fingers on to Jesus's lips. He shook his head. He said his word again, and took a half-step backwards out of the cave. His outline thickened with the light, but he seemed small and nervous. He'd not expected Jesus to be naked, or so wild. He offered the water-pouch again, but without looking at Jesus. He closed his eyes and waited, with one hand held out. With the other hand, he twisted his hair as tightly as he could into peaks and knots.

"Who sent you here? To mock me," Jesus said, each word a self-inflicted wound. "I'll not, not drink. But pour your water on my neck and head. I wash my face and eyes in it . . ." Again the badu did not move. He only waited for Jesus to reach across and take the pouch himself. But Jesus held his hands behind his back and muttered prayers. Finally, the badu reopened his eyes, and took another half-step back into the light.

"You mock me, cousin," Jesus said. "You will not even wet my lips."

If the badu had done what he was asked, then Jesus's quarantine might have ended just in time. But the badu was a nervous man, for all his patience. He'd risked his life to climb so far in the darkness. He took more backward steps into the first light of the day and stood outside the entrance to the cave where Jesus's Greek letters promised death to any gentile who tried to come into the inner court. The badu held his hand up and nodded at the remaining dampness on his palm. Again he touched his heart and forehead. He did not speak. He did not smile again. He picked the locusts up and offered them. He held the water-pouch, but did not tip more water out. One leg was flexed. Prepared to run if Jesus tried to grab his arm.

Now that Jesus saw the badu's face, his weakness was replaced by anger, mostly with himself. This was a battle that he would not lose just for a drop of water on his head and neck. He clapped his hands. The bony impact echoed dryly in the cave. It hurt. He clapped his hands again, and shook his head. His neck and shoulders squeaked like a door. His skull had separated from the skin. His hair was weed. He took a step or two towards the badu. They almost touched again, before the badu backed away. "He cannot make me drink, the man," Jesus said. And then his final shout, a piece of yew log cracking in the fire, "Go out from me."

The badu was expressionless, a fish displayed behind the thick glass of a vase. He had not even blinked. His eyes and lashes had not moved, even though he had been shouted at, straight in the face. He simply nodded, turned away without a shrug and let the locusts go, though they were dead. A waste. He could have eaten them himself; a badu delicacy, the desert shrimp. Then he fled, back to the place where he had cut his knee, back to the summit of the precipice, back to his cave. He would not look at Jesus any more, though Jesus called to him while he climbed. He shouted out in Greek and Aramaic, "You have not tempted me. Praise god," and even with some words he knew in Sumar. But no reply. "Coward. Demon. Run to your master like a dog."

Jesus stood outside his cave, elated, naked and transfixed. He almost wept with happiness. So god was taking care of him after all. God was standing guard. Jesus praised the ingenuity of god. He knew another man who hardly blinked. The baker that lived five houses down from their family workshop was as unresponsive as the badu. Small boys would stand behind him at his stall and shout their jokes into his ears. They would insult his bread. But he would not respond.

"O sweet, forgiving god, when I was weak," Jesus said aloud, with no one there to listen to his words. The devil's go-between had come down to his cave to tempt him. But — praise the lord — the devil's go-between was deaf. For everything that god had made was weak and blemished and imperfect by design.

Jesus laughed. How dull and unprepared the devil was.

CHAPTER
TWENTY-ONE

No one need be thirsty in the scrub, unless they choose, said Musa. He and Miri had exhausted all the water in their bags, and so had come up to their cistern at the caves to drink and to refill the empty skins.

Without the open cistern to provide their drink, her husband would have dragged Miri from her loom, just when the purple-orange birth-mat was almost complete. She only had to loosen the warp, a little at a time, and then her mat could be cut off the loom and the four hundred ends tied. Tying these umbilicals was the guarantee that her pregnancy would be successful. But Musa only cared for mats that he could sell. He would not have put up with thirst rather than separate Miri from a mat which would produce no profit. He would have sent her out to hunt for water.

There was, she'd already noticed, little sign of any water in the scrub, apart from the soft clay in the flood beds of the valley below the caves. She'd not persuade her husband to drink clay. There were no converging gazelle tracks, or stones piled up in columns to mark where someone else had found a well or spring, or any tell-tale, spongy pit of greenery. She would have had to uproot salt bushes for the meagre store of water in their roots, or dig out tamarisks which always had their little fingers planted in a patch of damp. But, thank heavens for the cistern at the caves. Digging into that had been a bit of luck, Miri thought, though she would rather it were filled with Musa than with water.

She did not resent the brief break from the birth-mat to go up to the caves. She'd have a chance to talk to Marta, and she might succeed in walking the pain out of her thighs, and exercising her back and neck. She could not tell if it was the weaving or her pregnancy that made her ache so badly. But she was most aware of her growing bulk around the waist when she sat cross-legged at the loom. The baby neatly filled the space between her legs. Her clothes were tight and she was hot, even at night. Her breasts were hurting, and there was an amber discharge from her nipples to mark the coming of her milk. She had nosebleeds, and sudden cramps in her legs and feet which even crampbark could not relieve.

Yet still she'd concentrated on her loom, and the retreating trellis of colours. She'd sat on the woven fabric, helping to maintain the loom in tension, and she'd found comfort in the intimacy of weaving, her pregnant body on the birth-mat wool. She'd lost herself in it. She'd shut out Musa and the discomforts of her life. She felt somehow that finishing the mat would free her of the man. Perhaps she'd fly away on it, her baby sitting neatly in her lap.

Miri was content, when they had clambered up the slope below the caves, to sit and rest for a while before she filled the water-bags. It was mid-afternoon, but there'd been very little sun to keep her and her husband in the tent. It was not hot enough to sleep. The salt sea valley was still sharp with light, but in the hills solid clouds were stacked like unworked slate, as sturdy as the land itself.

Despite the heavy coolness of the afternoon, Musa was too short of breath to go back to the tent straight away, although he had appropriated Shim's walking staff to help him get about and he had Miri to carry all the water for him. Besides, he had an unperfected plan which required that he should stay exactly where he was as long as possible, at least until he saw a way of getting what he wanted and deserved. It was a question, not of wickedness but pride, he told himself. He had to turn a profit at the end of this forced stay in the scrub. He couldn't go down to Jericho with no successes to boast about. No merchant would. A merchant always wants a victory. Musa had had no luck down on the precipice. Perhaps he'd have a little luck up here. Bad luck for someone else.

He felt that he'd been split in two by his short stay in the scrub. Those twins again. It was the weeping, lesser twin who went in search of luck down at the promontory. The twin who prayed. The twin who hoped to feel the healer's touch again. It was the trading potentate, the fist, the appetite, who came up to the caves. Each step that Musa took towards the cistern, put Jesus at a greater, safer distance. The landlord left his superstitions in the tent. He took his irreligion to the perching valley in the hills. He was ambitious. He would make his mark. He would surprise them all.

So, he sat down in the shade of rocks, next to the lower cave where Marta slept, and demanded hospitality. He did not care that his tenants were fasting, concentrating on their prayers, and — by this thirtieth day of quarantine — short-tempered and depressed. He had Miri clap her hands and call out, "Gather, gather," as she'd done on that earlier occasion when Musa had first come up to the caves.

The badu did not answer Musa's call and show himself, but Aphas and Marta were more obedient; Aphas because he always hoped that Musa would seduce the healer to come up to their caves, and Marta because the sound of Miri's voice was irresistible. Finally, even Shim responded and came down to his landlord as slowly as he could to find a spot, a little distance from the rest, and safely out of Musa's reach, where he could show how calm he was, and unperturbed.

"What do you have? I'm tired," said Musa. They brought their landlord dry dates to eat — the same dates that he'd sold to them a day or two before — and the stripped-meat remains of a slipper deer which the badu had brought back the previous evening. Musa was not satisfied with that. He had a nose for something sweeter than a deer. "What else?" He noticed Aphas would not look him in the eye.

"What have you got you shouldn't have?" he asked the old man. Just a hunch. But, if the hunch paid off, he knew it would seem frightening and magical that he could read their minds. Aphas blushed. He stammered even. "We've got a little honey, if you want." And so, reluctantly, they offered him some of the dripping honeycomb which they were keeping for themselves, wrapped in some damp cloth. It gave them what little energy they had and should have lasted till the end of quarantine.

Musa ate his honeyed meat and dates. He held his hand out while Marta poured a little water from a bag on to his greasy, sticky fingers.

"Where did you find the meat and honeycomb?" he asked. He was feeling dangerous and mischievous, and excited, too — because the nearness of the woman's lap, the slightly rancid taste of meat, had given him the idea which would perfect his plan. He belched. He rubbed his stomach. Just practising.

"The little badu got them," Aphas said. "Somewhere around." He waved a hand about.

"Somewhere around? Not on my land, I hope. I told you once. This isn't common land. Anything you see is mine. What should I do? Put wooden gates on those . . ." he pointed at their rows of caves, ". . . if I can't trust my guests. Give me the comb, what's left of it. Miri, bring it here! I am not pleased. You're dining on my honey, now. And stealing meat."

"It was the badu," Aphas said again. "Not one of us."

"Might have found it anywhere," suggested Marta, speaking to herself a shade too loudly. She half-suspected from what she'd heard from Miri that Musa's claims to any of this land were bogus.

"What, is the woman speaking now? Let's hear. What have you said?"

"They might be bees from anywhere . . ."

"What anywhere?" asked Musa. He turned to Marta, cocked his head, narrowed his eyes. What kind of woman argued with a man? This kind; square-faced and

202

large; broad-backed. "Beyond my land there is my cousin's land. And then my uncles' land is after that, and then my land begins again. That's further than a bee can fly. That's further than any one of you can run before you're caught. Let's not fall out." He spoke the last line with his sweetest voice. He turned to Aphas again. He had to hide his smiles. "Where did your neighbour find the nest? Near here?"

"We didn't see. We saw, but . . ."

"What did you see?" He had the afternoon to waste. He'd bully them.

"We saw him, well, he got a length of stick . . ."

"You say he went to fish for bees?"

". . . and he took a bit of bone he found and hollowed out the stick . . ."

Musa allowed the man to chatter, only interrupting now and then, a herdboy idly tweaking an old goat's rope. This billy posed no threat to him. Musa could afford to let him talk. The talking was an opportunity for Musa to perfect his plans, to come up with some way of sending these men on errands in the night while he could stay behind to occupy their caves. So it was only with half an ear that Musa listened to Aphas while he described with the wonder of a townsman how the badu had plugged one end of the hollowed stick with a piece of rotting apricot . . .

"What apricot? Where have you stolen apricots?"

"We bought the fruit from you."

"Well, then. They were good apricots, and cheap. Too good to put in sticks. Go on, then. Speak. I didn't say that you should stop."

The badu, Aphas continued, had pushed the plugged end of his hollowed stick into the ground outside his cave and then backed into the shadows, on his haunches, to wait for bees. It wasn't long before a bee had landed on the stem, and crawled into the hollowed stick in search of fruit. It flew away. It came back with companions from its nest, and soon there were a hundred bees transporting dabs of apricot.

"The badu put his thumb down on the open end. Like that," said Aphas. He slapped his own thumb on a rock, though not as dramatically as he had hoped. "He'd trapped ten bees inside the stick. What did he do?"

"He got ten stings?"

". . . he let one out to fly away. He followed it, down there. Until he couldn't see it any more, or hear its buzz. What did he do? The same again. He let another one get out, and followed that. We saw them go. That's all we saw. They went behind the rocks into the thorns. It's clever though. A third bee, and a fourth, and then a fifth, and getting closer all the time. He'd got ten bees to run behind, you see? When they go free they always fly back to the queen inside her honeycomb."

"*My* honeycomb," said Musa.

"It's just a trick for getting to the nest," concluded Aphas. "He only had to make some smoke to keep the bees away and help himself. He came back with the honey. He doesn't speak. He didn't say whose land it was."

"My land. My bees."

Shim laughed. He was not dozing after all. "Now there's a parable for all of us to contemplate," he said, encouraged by Musa's evident good humour.

Musa had been vexed enough by Aphas and his lengthy lecture on the badu ways of finding honey, yet had resisted the temptation to silence the man. But no intervention from the blond was tolerable.

"What parable?" he asked.

"A parable of spiritual endeavour. A quest, like ours, for enlightenment . . ." said Shim.

"Enlightenment, enlightenment, not honey? Which would you rather have with dates?" Musa turned his head away. Shim's interruption should have ended there. But he was already in full flight.

"The bees, let's say, are prayers, or even days of fasting in the wilderness. You let one go, you follow it, it's gone. But still there is no prospect of enlightenment or sign of god. You are still lost. You have to persevere. It takes you forty bees, let's say, before . . ."

". . . before, let's say, your landlord's sick and tired of listening, and bored, and turns you out into the desert without a water-bag."

"I heard a story once, about a water-seller who . . ." said Aphas.

"Be quiet." Musa lifted up a warning finger. "Now I will talk." He was the story-teller, no one else. Enough of parables and chatter. He wanted their attention back on him, and quickly. He did not want to lose control, not for a moment longer. He'd have to charm his victims first — despite his impulse to do otherwise — and then he'd put them in their places for the night. He knew exactly what to do.

"Why should I want a water-bag?" persisted Shim, as quietly as he dared. "There is no need for anyone to be thirsty in the scrub, unless they choose. You've said as much yourself. I think those were your words . . ." He hadn't been as amusing or as brave during the quarantine before. But no one laughed.

"Go, then," said Musa, scarcely audible. "Leave my cistern. Walk out there and take your chances like a fox. Pray for water to appear. Rely on god. Let's see how well you live." Musa made as if to rise. "Up, up," he called to Miri, and began to shift his weight into his shoulders. He gripped the curly staff. This was not charming in the least. "Let's see how well you do out there, tonight," he said again.

"I do not think, I do . . . not think . . . I know. . ." Shim laughed thinly. He'd gone too far. Some deference to Musa was required. "I only ask. What can you tell us, then? What should a thirsty man . . . what should he do?" He sat as tamely as he could, hands limply in his lap, the model pupil with his sage.

"Those were my words. No need for any thirst, as I have said and I will say a hundred times again," Musa began, after he had called for Marta to bring water, had wet his lips and face and hair, and studied all the folds and pinches in the cloth at her waist. "There's always water to be had, if you know where. Do you know where? The principle's the same as finding honey with a stick. But not the parable. Not the parable that he has given us." He waved the staff at Shim. "My parable is this, that someone with a nose for trade like me can always sniff out what he wants. Honey, water, gold . . ." He sniffed dramatically, and Marta almost thought he'd winked at her. "My turn to talk."

206

He told them how he'd crossed a desert once where nothing grew, a desert — "let's say" — forty days from side to side. Five camels, and four cousins, and himself. They'd taken sixty goats, salted mutton, indigo and horns to trade with black men on the river with three banks. The journey had been easy and all their goods were quickly sold. They had obtained a hundred monkeys in exchange which they could sell in Nabatee where monkey flesh was thought to be . . . he winked again; he did not say the word . . . an aphrodisiac.

"Alas, we had been fools. Don't anybody nod. We didn't know how thirsty a hundred monkeys could be," he said. "Or how much noise they'd make. A hundred hairy Shims. Clacker-chack-chat all day."

At first they meant to put the monkeys on leashes and let them walk behind the camels. But the monkeys were riotous. They didn't want to walk. They tugged on the leashes. A hundred monkeys, with their heels dug into sand, are stronger than three camels. So Musa and his cousins had to bunch the monkeys up like chickens and tie them by their legs to the leathers on the flanks of two of the camels. Musa rode the third; his cousins could walk. They were small enough, and fit enough, and more obedient than monkeys.

They loaded the other two camels with bullock-skins filled with water, and set off through the fringes of the desert early in the morning while the air was cool. The monkeys didn't seem uncomfortable. Hanging upside down in bunches was customary for them. They screamed and gibbered without cease. At first, it was amusing. Musa and his cousins screamed and gibbered, too. But after a few days the noise became a torture.

207

They made slow progress. The desert proved itself to be as fickle as a carpet, smooth and welcoming if stroked with the pile, but tough to drag the fingers through against the lay of the wool. Their little caravan had stroked the pile on its journey out. Now it was travelling against the nap of the wools. The sun was at their backs, and baking hot. The monkeys gibbered, screamed as ceaselessly as crickets, even when the camels snapped and spat at them. They only quietened when his cousins gave them water. His cousins gave them water all the time.

After fifteen days, said Musa, they realized that they were lost: "No prospect of enlightenment, no sign of any god." That had never happened to their caravan before, although they'd crossed a hundred deserts. One of his cousins, called Habak the Hawk because of his long nose, normally could be blindfolded and only had to sniff a palmful of soil to recognize the smell of every place they'd ever visited. He put this desert dust and powdered rock against his nose, but could not put a name to where they were or point towards their destination. They span him round to sniff the air; he couldn't say if he was standing on his head or feet. They looked for signs of any caravans. But there had been high winds, and even the tracks that they had made themselves on the journey out had been swept away, together with the smell. They persevered, hoping to encounter other travellers, or find horizons broken up by trees, or recognize some star beyond the dust-filled night, or see a bird.

After twenty days they found their own tracks again. But no goat tracks, just four men walking and five camels, and the channels made by monkeys trailing their long fingers in the sand. They'd travelled in a five-day circle to this place, and now their bullock-skins were running out. The monkeys, with hardly any water left to keep them quiet, coughed and cackled through the night. It didn't bother them that their heads were full of blood.

Musa paused to pull his own empty water-bags across, and hold them up, an illustration for his listeners. This is what a shortage of water looks like; this is thirst; this is what I had in mind for Shim. He wasn't sure quite where his tale was leading him. He had no end for it, not yet. There was no point to it, except to charm. But Aphas and Marta didn't seem to care. They nodded to the story-teller to urge him on. This was better than any parable. It didn't matter that it had no point, except to make them wonder at the world. Even Shim was listening, despite his tightly fastened lips and eyes.

"We had to save the monkeys *and* ourselves, though there was not enough water there for both of us," continued Musa, glad to see how loose of posture and how opened-eyed the woman had become. "What would you do? Don't say. You'd throw the monkeys on the sand; you'd club them all to death, and drink the water all yourselves. Admit it now. Of course you would. But then you are not merchants. And you do not understand how trading is the truest test of man. It shows his strength, his worth, his piety. To buy and sell is just as spiritual as prayer or going without food. Will any of you say it's not?" He looked at Shim. "A merchant's never-ending quest is not for things that you can't touch or buy, like Shim's enlightenment — what use is that? — but for something. . ." He had to stop to recall the exact words he'd heard his eldest uncle use a hundred times. ". . . but for something new and real and grand. And valuable, of course. To make the world a richer place. We're gods, we're little gods. We're *big*. And so . . ." He looked at all the faces there, except Miri's, obviously, and would not look away until he'd won a smile and nod from each of them. ". . . we could not go back from the desert to our uncles with nothing to show for our long efforts, with nothing to sell except the bloody remnants of the monkeys. Who'll buy those? A merchant never goes with empty panniers. That shows a loss of faith." He paused. He smiled, a real and joyous smile. "What will you have to sell when you go home? What will you show your uncles after forty days of quarantine?" He held his hand up. They should not reply.

Musa told how he and his cousins had persevered against the desert's grain. They'd travelled forward, day by day, in hope of finding wells or springs or dry river-beds where they might dig for water. They blindfolded their cousin Habak, to concentrate his sense of smell. They put him on his hands and knees to sniff the sand in search of moisture, but all he smelled was barrenness and heat. They hunted without luck for any evidence of life but they found nothing apart from themselves. They dreamed of finding tamarisks with lakes of water at their roots, and honeydew along their stems, but there was nothing to be found, excepting thirst.

"Still our monkeys laughed," said Musa. "They were glad to see us lost. They liked to watch us frying in the sand. It suited them. They didn't want to go to Nabatee and end up in a pot. Who would? They'd rather starve. Never trust a monkey on a camel's back. That's good advice . . . Never trust a thirsty woman or a dog." He laughed, but turned the laugh into a sudden cry of pain. He held his chest, and winced. A little indigestion, possibly. "Perhaps, I ought to rest a while," he said. He touched his brow. "I'm hot." He closed his eyes.

"You're teasing us," said Aphas. "I hope you're teasing us. What happens to the monkeys now? Of course, do rest if you're unwell. We wouldn't want you to be unwell . . ."

"Ah, so our neighbour would trade the ending of the storyteller for the ending of his story," said Musa, breathing heavily. "The monkeys matter more than me . . . ? I would have hoped a sick man such as you would have more feeling for a fellow invalid."

"No, no, do rest . . ."

"I will not rest. There is some respite to my pain, thank god. Bring water then. Put that good shawl the woman has around my shoulders. I will continue while I can." The shawl was warm and sweet, and smelled a little gingery from Marta's balm.

The time had come, Musa said after he had drunk the water and clutched his chest a few more times, when he and his caravan had journeyed through the desert to death's door. Drink something, anything, or die, that was the choice. They'd have to take a knife to Musa's camel. He'd have to walk like his cousins, ankle-deep in sand.

They'd cut into the camel's hump and stomach. They'd have to drink her waters, blood and milk, and let the monkeys find what sustenance they could by dining on her entrails and her fat. The monkeys would have to swallow camel upside down.

"But no one makes me walk," said Musa, rubbing his side. "A clever merchant never walks. I closed my eyes. I put my head to work. I thought, let's kill a couple of the monkeys. Let's take our meat and drink from them. The meat's already nicely hung, it should taste good. But think of it. What did I say about the monkey meat? Why do they savour it in Nabatee? It makes a man thirsty for his wife. What use would that be for the five of us, with nothing there to comfort us but sand? It is a sin for a man to waste his seed with camels. Our sons would have two toes.

"And so I didn't take a monkey by the throat and use my knife on it. I cut one monkey free. I held its tail. I whispered in its ear, I said, Find water. You're a bee. I didn't have to put it in a hollow stick or block its backside with an apricot. You should have seen it run. It knew its only chance of getting away, back to its river with three banks, was first to find some water and then be off. My quickest cousin, Raham, followed it into the dunes until he lost it. Monkeys move like rats. So does my cousin Raham. But the monkey soon went out of sight. It didn't buzz. We couldn't follow that. But we could track its little steps in the sand, its tail, its swinging hands, until we found it once again, exhausted by the running and the sun. Half dead. No water yet. We tied it up, we hung it by its ankles with its brothers and its sisters. Then we let another monkey go . . . I whispered in its ear, Enjoy your run, you monkey boy . . ."

It took them fourteen monkeys and two days, Musa said, but finally they saw a line of rocks and thorn which led down to a dry valley bed and there they found their fourteenth monkey sitting in an open cistern underneath a slab of stone, bathing like an empress in a bowl. "We helped ourselves. We didn't have to smoke out bees. We washed. We drank up to our brims. We refilled our bullock-skins. And then we let the camels in. Sweet water, with a touch of ginger to its taste."

Now they left the desert in the past, and followed down the valley, taking their directions from the gullies cut by the last downpour of rain a year or so before, until they came to leafy trees and habitations and to fields which had, Musa said, "a wispy, adolescent beard of grass". They got to Nabatee in time to make a profit, with only twenty monkeys perished on the way, and Musa hadn't walked a step. "My story ends with me a little richer than I was." He looked at Shim: "Your learned commentary, please. Don't disappoint us now." He took a breath and held it in his lungs, so that his face began to redden. Now was the time to take them by surprise.

"This is a story," Shim said, with care, "that might serve for us all. The first thirteen monkeys that you followed did not reach the water that you sought. It was only that you persevered until the fourteenth. It's perseverance you are teaching us. For that my neighbours will be grateful . . . I am sure . . ."

He would have said a little more, attempted to improve his standing, if Musa had not cried out suddenly, and slapped his hands across his stomach. "This pain . . . is more than I can tolerate," he said. He closed his eyes and blew out air. He put his hand into his hair. "I'm burning hot. My head."

"Shall I bring more water?" Aphas said.

"No, no. Just let me rest."

Musa opened half an eye, and looked around. Shim, he noticed, was almost smiling. Marta had stood up and looked alarmed. His wife had put her hand up to her face. He could not see her mouth. She'd be concerned, he thought, that the devil had come back to him and that she'd soon be widowed by a second onslaught of the fever. On a rock, beyond the furthest of the caves, he saw the badu balancing on one leg like an egret, one foot resting on his other knee.

"No, no," Musa said again. "I must lie down. It's here." He pointed to his side — a sharp pain in his liver — and ran his hands across his abdomen — an area of general suffering.

"Something you've eaten," said Aphas helpfully, although he could not imagine that anybody's liver pains were worse than his. He'd defer to Shim for cleverness and to Musa for a blinding tongue, but he'd counted general suffering to be his own reserve.

"That meat," said Musa, in his most boyish voice, "it was bad. Your honey hid the taste." He'd let his tenants think they'd poisoned him. "I'm hot." And then, once Miri had come up to fan him with her scarf, "I'm cold. This is bad . . . They steal my meat, and now they poison me." Musa would have doubled up with pain if he could. He was too big to bend. Instead he rolled over on his side, and spread out in the dust, a wounded animal, its great head cushioned only by some stones. He'd seen Aphas acting out his cancer in the last thirty days, and had not been impressed. Musa could do better. Winces and deep breathing weren't enough. He experimented with some uncontrolled spasms in his leg. He clutched his ear. He looked as frightened and as baffled as he could. This was not low cunning. Musa did not like to be accused of that. His cunning was the highest kind; it was his version of a miracle.

The wind had lifted. The afternoon was cold and coming to an end. The clouds had brought the darkness early. He had no time to waste. "I need to sleep," he said.

The women lifted up a leg apiece, while Aphas, Shim and the badu dragged their landlord by his shoulders to the nearest empty cave — the one a few steps along from Marta's which opened on to the sloping terrace, screened only by a few salt bushes and the coppery debris of the cliff. They laid him on the soil with only Marta's shawl as his cot-clothes. They put his head on it. He put his nose in it. He liked the warmth of Marta and her smell.

His wife and his tenants stood in the entrance of the cave, blocking out the light, whispering. What should they do with him? Not one of them had said, "Be well again," or stroked his brow. Everybody knew of people who had died as suddenly as this — the same unheralded pain, the cry, the fingers stretched across the chest, the grey-red face, the final, chortling breath. The world might lose some stories if Musa died, but not much else worth keeping. The prospect of his death was tolerable. His death was overdue. Miri did not even dare to pray.

Her prayers had let her down before. Would there be a second chance of rolling Musa down the slope into the cistern she had dug for him? Why waste good water on the man? They'd only have to block his cave with stones to make a sepulchre and mark the stones with chalk to warn future quarantiners and any passing Jews that there was a corrupting body inside.

"Miri, Miri, come to me," he said at last, his voice more vulnerable than she had ever heard it before, his face invisible. He made her kneel and put her ear against his lips. His breath was warm and dry. No eggy smells, this time. "Go to the tent for me, take care of everything," he said. "I cannot walk. I must sleep here. Bring back a flask of date spirit in the morning as soon as it's light. Bring rugs and blankets, some pillows for my head. Collect some herbs. Bake something sweet for me tonight. The honey's there. And don't forget to fill the water-bags. Tell him to come." He pointed at Aphas.

Aphas knelt as best he could, and strained to listen to his landlord's slowly fading words. "Go with my Miri, uncle. Keep her safe, for there are brigands in these hills. And wolves, bad wolves. A woman should not be alone out here. Call him and her." Now Shim and Marta were summoned. She knelt a little distance from Musa's side, her head cocked to hear what he wanted from her. Shim, though, was reluctant to kneel down at all. He worried for his ankles and his little toe, despite his landlord's sudden, devastating illness. But Musa found the strength to raise his voice: "I beg you, one of you, it doesn't matter which . . . Stay in your cave tonight, and bring me water if I call. Say prayers for me if I should die.

Take care of Miri and the goats . . ." He struggled for some breath. "The other one of you. This is my final wish. The Gally saved my life before. Go down to him while there is any light. Stand on our rock where we have stood so many times. Call out until your voice has gone. Stay through the night and pray to him. Say that I'll die unless he comes. Have pity on a man . . . Which one of you will go?"

He meant, of course, which one of you will stay. He knew it would be Marta, naturally. An unattended woman could not stand out on a rock, past midnight, praying to a madman in a cave. There was a risk, of course, that Shim would be the one to stay behind. Then Musa would go to his cave at night and smash his yellow head in with a rock. A secondary pleasure.

Everybody gladly did as they were told. Aphas and Shim would rather go down to the tent and to the promontory than stay with Musa. Let him die or let him recover on his own. They did not want to witness either. Aphas thought how comfortable he'd be, sleeping on rugs for a change. Miri thought of the hours she could spend, in candlelight, tying knots on to her mat. Shim had reclaimed his curly staff, almost as soon as Musa had fallen to the ground. He liked the idea of a private vigil on the promontory, wrapped in his thickest cloak, alone at last with Musa's very stupid boy — although, of course, he'd not call out too loudly to the Galilean or press too hard for him to come and minister to Musa. He had no faith in shepherd boys. He did not want a miracle.

They hurried off, the three of them. They ran away.

217

Marta shrugged. She didn't really care that she was left behind. Another night of quarantine, so what? She was the least resentful of them all. Musa's stories softened her. She couldn't really fear a man who was so captivating, and so sick, and who had fathered Miri's child. If only Thaniel had been able to tell a tale like that. If only he were not so dull. Perhaps she would be pregnant, too.

Musa kept away from Marta. He played with time and let the woman go about her evening tasks. He heard her footsteps, smelled her fire, heard her coughing in the smoke. He did not bother her. He was at peace. The cave was warm enough. Its floor was soft. He slept. He'd wait till night. They were alone at last, or only separated by the earth between their caves.

There was the badu left, of course. An easy person to forget. After everyone else had received their whispered instructions from Musa, he had come and knelt inside the cave. He'd felt his landlord's forehead and shaken his head as if to say, This illness is bad. You stand no chance; or, This is Nothing. I'm not fooled. Get up and go back to your tent. He'd pressed his cheeks, his hair into Musa's face. Musa could have bitten him. He could have smashed his hennaed head in with a rock. Instead, he whispered in his ear, "Enjoy your run, you monkey boy . . . Keep out of sight." But really, Musa didn't care about a madman such as him. He was too small to intervene between such large adversaries.

218

CHAPTER
TWENTY-TWO

It would have been the perfect night for Musa's death, if he'd been truly ill or if some god, fooled by the noise that Musa made, had decided that the time had come to put an end to him. The sky was mourners' black. No stars. Nor hardly any moon. What little light there was was muffled in the stacks of mist, which made the outline of the hills seem less solid even than the clouds. A passing world, but heavens everlasting. The earth was insubstantial and the sky was hard.

On such a night, death could have crept in unobserved, rubbed its fingers over Musa's eyes and passed his heavy soul up into the heavens without betraying its stern work by casting any shadows in the scrub. If he'd cried out, "It touches me," in those few moments when the vapours of his life were pressed out of his flesh and mixed in with the clouds, no one would have come to cling on to his chubby toes and plead, "This man is merchandise that can't be touched. We will not let you take this man from us."

The badu was awake all night, it's true, but he would not come to Musa's aid. He would not and he could not hear the vapours and the flesh divide. Marta was only dozing, possibly, but she was meek and sensible enough

219

to stay inside her own cave for the night, whatever noises she could hear. Musa might call for help from his small family, as he had done before, "Miri, Miri. Come to me, quick, and save me from . . ." A dying man could reasonably expect his wife to battle for his life. But Miri was too far away to care that he was calling. She and the old man, Aphas, were sleeping better than they'd slept for many days, out of hearing, in the tent, and for the moment unconcerned about her husband's fate, except in dreams.

Only Shim, far out on the promontory, cross-legged, transcended by the darkness and his own alarm, was sifting every sound he heard. A tumbling stone. The dry bronchitis of a stirring wind. A roosting bird. He was the only one of them to hear the nudging and the cussing of the clouds as death and its grey carriage went voyaging across the night. If he prayed at all at hearing it, he only prayed that death would stop at Musa's cave and not descend on Shim. Let Musa die, he thought. His time is overdue. The world will be a better place if Musa's life is short. But I have value in the world, and work to do, and there are still ten days of quarantine to serve. My time's not come.

Yet Shim would not deceive himself for long. His view was Greek, of course. Death wouldn't intervene to make the world a better place. He'd be a fool to think it would. Death is a servant sent to the market with a list, and far too dull to have discretions of its own. And death is economical, as well. It only barters for the unprotected and the weak, because they're cheap and easy to obtain. Death wouldn't tire itself with Musa, not yet. He was too young and strong and irredeemable for death. He was too large. He would refuse to die, however ill he'd seemed, however tightly he had held his sides and writhed in pain. There was not much chance that Musa would be dead by the morning. He'd be alive. Shim knew it in his bones, though he hoped otherwise. What if that illness was a sham, a trick, to carry out some deathly, stern work of his own?

No, death would not grapple with Musa when there were easy pickings such as Aphas, old and cancerous, to choose instead. Or Miri, even, weakened by her child. So many pregnant women died before their time. Death liked the price of them. They were a bargain, at two lives in one. Or Shim himself. He was not well prepared to struggle for his soul. He felt so weak and undefended in the night; no roof, no courage for protection. Death could easily help itself to him, drop its talons on his shoulders like an owl and lift him from the rocks. Or else, more likely, death would come out to the promontory not as an owl but in Musa's shape to seize him by his ankles and bring its fifty fists down on his head. Why else had Musa sent him there to pass the night alone, so cleverly, except to separate him from the rest and murder him? No one would know if he were dead. Musa would only have to roll the body off the precipice — no need for volunteers to drag it to the edge — and go back to the cave to resume his illness. He could tell his neighbours that Shim had had enough of fasting and had fled. Or Shim had tumbled in the dark. Or Shim had achieved such deep tranquillity that he'd transformed himself into a stone.

So, for the first part of the night, Shim cowered on the promontory, expecting Musa to arrive and making shapes of Musa from the darkness. Musa, silent. Musa, huge. Musa, running on his toes, with flames and serpents at his fingertips. Death with Musa riding on its back. Musa, black and swift, invisible. Shim had never known a night so dark and still and full of possibilities. But he was not terrified for long. He heard the cussing and the nudging of the clouds diminish. His fear diminished, too. The sky grew quieter for a while. Resting, and digesting. If death had come, Shim thought, then it had passed him by. But he was sure that someone else had died, close by. He smelt it in the air. What would he find when he went back to join his neighbours in the morning? Was Musa safe? Were Marta and the badu spared? Had death sniffed round the tent where Aphas and Miri were sleeping, and taken both their lives or one?

It was almost midnight when the lightning came to pierce the clouds and let the avalanche of thunder-claps come tumbling to the earth. The sky was only threatening. A mummer's show of strength. It meant no harm. The rain and the scrub had reached an understanding when the world was made to let each other live their lives as much as possible in peace. The clouds came down to sniff the hills, to scratch their bellies on the thorns and rest their weight on this warm land before the weary battles of the night. They could not help spilling just a drop or two, enough to make the tent reverberate and Shim to wonder whether he should

222

flee back to his cave at once or — better — join the others in the tent, if any of them had survived.

But these clouds were only passing through. They would mostly take their waters north across Sawiya and Jerusalem into Samaria, and to the Galilee. They'd rather wet the leaves of oaks and terebinths than waste themselves on thorns; they'd rather wash the dust off myrtles, brooms and asphodels. Before dawn the first raindrops would kick up Galilean soil on to beans and onion sets in deep-ploughed fields, and splash the red-black earth from summer barley roots. Jesus's brothers would bring the chickens in and lie awake while the rain beat down on their flat roofs and broke up the lime marl which they had laid across the planks and joists and reeds, to keep their rooms rainproof. Someone would have to use the cylinder of stone when it was light to roll the marl back into place. Not me, they thought. It's not my turn. Not me.

But in the scrub, the native marl stayed almost dry. The clouds and lightning moved away, banging on their shields. The sky grew soft with moonlight once again, and then sharp with stars. And with the stars, the wind came in, glad to range around the empty forum of the sky; a gladiator, looking for a fight. It was an angry wind. See me, it cried. I've chased the clouds away. The thunder and the lightning have run off. I've stripped the night of any warmth it had. There's nothing I can't do to you.

This wind had no agreement with the scrub. They were old enemies. The scrub exposed its rocks and ridges to blunt and bruise the wind. And in return, the

223

wind picked up the dust and thorns and threw the loose stuff of the scrub about, and tore the dead wood from the trees like some mad boy. But on this night the wind was not prepared to settle for dead wood. It pitched itself against the scrub. The brittle trees could not withstand the wind at all. A tree can only bend so much, and then it snaps or comes up with its roots.

Shim would have stayed much longer on the promontory had it not been for the wind. There was enough moonlight now to give him the courage to remain outside all night. He'd like to prove himself against the darkness. He'd like to be a colleague of the stars. And then — if anybody looked across at dawn — they'd see him as a tranquil silhouette, sat on his rock against the rising purples of the day, half flesh, half stone. A noble sight — more noble, surely, than the Gally, hiding in his cave. Then Shim would walk up to the tent, the low sun at his back, the shadows of his body and his staff cast out in front of him like cloaks thrown down by worshippers to make a path. He would take his time. His steps would be reflective. His face would not betray how long the night had been, how close he'd come to death. My husband's dead, the wife would say, with any luck. Or, Aphas passed away. Or, there's been an accident; the badu fell and killed himself. A lion came. There'd be a funeral, and Shim would be the one — who else? — to lead the rituals and then to recommit his neighbours to their last ten days of quarantine. They'd all defer to Shim until the end.

Except there was a cruel, defiant wind, and it was cold. Shim could not stay a moment more. It was not safe or sensible. He had not come on to the promontory because he'd wanted to, he reminded himself. He had been sent. He had been tricked. "Call out until your voice has gone," Musa had said. "Stay through the night and pray to the Gally. He saved my life before. Say that I'll die unless he comes. This is my final wish." Then die, thought Shim. That is *my* final wish. He would not pray as he'd been asked. Who'd know? Instead, he only whispered at the wind, as it attacked the precipice, "Gally. Fat Musa says he's dying. Says you've got to come and save his life, up at the caves. Have pity on the man, he says. There now. That's it. I've done. Go back to sleep."

Shim wrapped his cloak around himself and left a little after midnight, when the wind began to loosen stones and earth around the promontory, and sent them sliding down the slope into the silence of a fall. He was surprised how hard it was to walk. The wind picked on his knees, and lifted up the cloak around his head. It bruised his cheeks and ears.

It was not easy climbing in the dark, but at least it was obvious at first what route he had to take. Each of his steps should go a little higher than the last. He fell forward and felt his way with his hands. But once he'd reached the flat top of the precipice, he lost all sense of where he was. The air was even more blustery than on the cliff, and even though the night had sharpened he could not see the outline of the hills. His eyes were watery and almost closed against the wind. He squatted on the ground, and felt about him with his staff. The storm was strong enough to blow him down to Jericho.

He tried to remember which direction it had been coming from while he was sitting on his rock. It was, he thought, blowing roughly in line with the precipice, hugging the cracks and rifts and stretch-marks of the valley sides, as if the valley had been shaped itself by wind. So, if he kept the gusts blowing on his left cheek, then he was bound to walk inland, away from the cliff edge. He felt his way like some blind beggar with his feet and staff. His hair was tugging at his head. His face was struck by bits of leaf and thorn, and stung by dust. His clothes and straps reached out towards the waters of the north.

He might not have found the tent at all, if he hadn't stopped to shelter, curled up in his cloak, behind a rock. He'd spend the rest of the night right there, he thought. It was not cold enough to freeze. There was no rain. The rock provided some protection. He ran his staff along its base and into any crevices he found. He might not be the only creature which had taken refuge from the wind. He hugged himself. He was surprised how much he missed his cave; his neighbours even.

It was not long before he heard the cries beyond the wind, a woman's voice, a man's, six goats', the buffeting of cloth. He gladly left his rock and battled with the wind towards the sounds that could be mistaken for the vast percussion of the storm-pressed, canvas billows of a ship. He could almost taste the salt, and hear the panic of the conscripts on the oars. And there, at last, was Miri clinging to her flattened tent, a little fisherwoman hanging on to sails with broken rigging, amongst the snapped and wayward masts and poles. Her house of hair, so flexible of build and lifestyle, had bent before the wind too much.

Aphas, a shadow, darker than the night, was too slow and weak to grip the tent cloth firmly enough. He ran around at first, grabbing everything that moved, a length of rope, a tumbling loom, a bolt of cloth, some clothes, a round of bread. But when he made a pile of them, they only rolled away before he had a chance to find a rock to weigh them down. He did not try again. He was too old to set himself against the drumming antics of this wind. He found some shelter amongst some rocks. He didn't care what happened. He'd rather die than spend a night like this.

Shim had to hurry now. It didn't matter if his steps were not reflective, or if his face betrayed how long the night had been. He was no tranquil silhouette. He was at best a moving shape, two bending legs, a flagging cloak, but one that ran to Miri's aid and helped to pull the untamed tent cloth in, and tugged the ropes and tent poles out of the flying darkness of the night. At last they made a pile of goat-hair cloth, the four sides of the tent, the roof, the coloured curtain that had divided Musa from his wife. They lay on it, spread-eagled, deafened by the flapping edges of the cloth. What could they do? They waited for the light to drive away the wind.

A metal pot set off across the scrub, between the maddened goats, its flight powered by a fist of wind. It was a tuneless, leaden bell which tolled itself and found new notes on every rock it struck.

CHAPTER
TWENTY-THREE

The Gally knew what wind this was. This was the wind
on which to fly away. Its gusts and blusters came
looking for him in the cave, bursting in like rowdy boys
to shake him from unconsciousness. Get up, get up, it's
time to go.

He had prepared for them. His fast had made him
ready. Perhaps he'd served his thirty days just to be
equipped for the wind. Quarantine had been the perfect
preparation for his death. His body was quiescent and
reduced; dry, sapless, transparent almost, ready to
detach itself from life without complaint. A wind this
strong could pluck him like a leaf, and sweep him
upwards to the palaces and gardens that angels tended in
the stars. It was a wind of mercy, then, for all its bluster,
sent by a pliant god who was prepared to bend the rules.
His god, praise god, had not insisted on the forty days.
He had not left Jesus in his coma, wasting and unclean,
until the final moment of his quarantine. He'd taken pity
on his Galilean son. Come now.

It seemed to Jesus, when he woke and put his hands
out to the wind, that he was already dead and living it.
Those family faces which he had summoned as his allies
and his witnesses, that woody workshop in the Galilee,

the fields, the boys, the shady corners in the temple yard, were only feeble memories. Another person's life. A story told by someone else. Those pigeons trapped amongst the vegetables would not be freed by Jesus any more. There was no future there for him. No fleshy future anyway. He had surrendered food for dreams. He'd traded in his flesh for everlasting holiness. What would his parents and his neighbours say if they could see him now? They'd say he was a very stupid boy.

But still, of course, he found the strength to drag himself — as good as saved, as good as dead — out of the cave, on to the entrance rock. He clung to it, his body naked to the wind. Already bones had pierced his skin. His chest had folded in on him. Sores on his legs and mouth no longer even tried to heal. His teeth and gums stuck out like balconies across his face. He could not shift the pain behind his eyes, though he was almost blind. He did not feel the cold. In fact, he hardly registered the wind now that he was wrapped in it. He could not separate the wind from all the rushing in his ears. He was as numb as wood. They could have driven nails into his feet. He'd not have felt a thing. His heart was too weak now to send his blood as far as that. His heart had decomposed. "Make sacrifices to god, and then prepare yourself for the winds of judgement," the scriptures warned. He was prepared. He was the sacrifice.

There was a time of clarity, before his body parted from his soul. There always is. It always comes too late. That's what makes this moment of departure large and borderless. He summoned up the words for his last prayers. Some Aramaic words, some Greek, some *ookuroos*, some tok-tok-tok. His prayers were answered in a way. There was a voice, borne on the wind, blown in across the cliffs, a voice not Jewish and not Greek. Jesus's bones were shaken by the voice. It teased him for a moment with a little hope, even though there was no hope. It raised him from the precipice and placed him in the scrub. If there were any beasts around, then they grew mild. The voice took charge of him. It walked him to the row of distant caves. It led him to the remnants of the flattened tent. It took him to the swelling liver and to the troubled womb. It took him to the badu's ears. It carried out its ministries on Shim. It worked its miracles. It said, "Fat Musa's dying now. You have to come and save his life. Have pity on the man. There now. That's it. That's all there is and ever was. Go back to sleep."

He was asleep. He slept in the Galilee, Jerusalem, in Caesarea, Greece and Rome. He slept in lands where orange was the only colour, where all the lakes were full of gold, where every donkey had two tails, where there were lines of strangers waiting to be saved. He placed his fingers on their heads and said, "So, here, be well again." A common greeting from the Galilee.

The wind nudged round him, searching for a hold. He lifted slightly, felt his body parting from the rock. The earth had lost its pull on him. He was all surface, no inside. His leaf had fallen finally. He was a dry, discarded page of scripture now. The wind embraced him, rubbed the words off him. It made him blank. It made him ghostlier than air. Not yet, not me, he might have cried, if he'd had any voice. What trick was there, that he could use, to bring companions to his side? What lie, what cowardice, what treachery, would put him back inside his Galilean cot?

This was his final blasphemy. He begged the devil to fly up and save him from the wind. He'd almost welcome the devil more than god. For the devil can be traded with, and exorcized. But god is ruthless and unstable. No one can cast out god. It was too late. Jesus was already standing at the threshold to the trembling world which he had sought, where he would spend his forty everlasting days. So this was death. So this was pain made powerless. So this was fruit turned back into its seed.

Jesus was a voyager, at last, between the heavens and the earth. There was a light, deep in the middle of the night. He tried to swim to it. He tried to fly. He held his hands up to the light. His hands were bluey-white like glass. The light passed through. The mountain shivered from afar. He felt the cold of nothing there. He heard the cold of no one there. No god, no gardens, just the wind.

CHAPTER
TWENTY-FOUR

Musa slept like a donkey. He slept like a dead donkey. If someone had beaten him with a stick, he wouldn't have woken up. It was a pity no one came with sticks.

The wind disturbed him finally, though not when it blew. Such winds could not disturb his sleep. But when the storm had passed, there was a heavy calm which prodded him awake. His cave had proven warm and comfortable, despite the weather, and so he felt well rested and alert. He knew exactly where he was and why he'd come, despite the utter darkness. There were no moments of confusion. He'd slept with an erection, ready for his visit to the other cave, so even before he'd opened his eyes the pulsing in his lap reminded him of his great plan. He rubbed his testicles. She'd not escape. She'd not run off. He'd have her trapped inside her cave, as soon as there was any light.

Musa pressed his face into her shawl. There's still a trace of her, he thought. A trace of spice. Enough to make him salivate. He pulled his own clothes up and untied his undergarments so that he might rub his genitals with her shawl. "Give the dog a bit of cloth to smell," that was his policy, "and it will sniff the owner out." And then? And then he'd put his body in the entrance to her cave. She'd be just visible to him. It didn't matter if she screamed. It mattered if she didn't scream. She'd cower in the shadows or she'd run at him. Perhaps she'd have a stick and try to beat him off. He'd hold her by her ankles or her wrists. He'd press his nails into her flesh. He'd take her lip between his teeth. A woman would not want to tear her lips. She'd stay as still as possible, on tiptoes, with her lip caught in his mouth, her body arched around his stomach. Now he could put his hands exactly where he wanted.

He'd have her naked, with just two tugs, two rips across her back. Her clothes would hang from her, like sample cloths. He'd tie the shawl around her waist and have her sit on him, the flesh and fabric settling and lifting on his thighs, her mouth on his, their ample breasts pressed flat against each other like leavened cakes of bread. If she tried to pull away, the little bag of money on its drawstring round her neck would swing between them like an incense pot. Now Musa had a happy image of himself. He'd seize her by her drawstring and pull her breasts and lips back on to his. That's what he'd do, one of the many things he'd do, when he had trapped her in the cave.

Musa pushed the shawl away from his genitals and let the cold air calm him down. He dared not touch himself again, not yet. He had already come too close to ejaculating. That would be expenditure without returns. How many times he had had sex with women just like this, alone, his penis in his hand, recalling some short encounter from that day. If only he could possess these half-glimpsed women in the flesh, every one of them. If only he could rope them up in bunches and hang them by their ankles from his camel sides, like monkeys. He'd go each night to pick a plump one from the bunch. He was deserving of them all. If they aroused him, then they should satisfy him too. Women that he'd only glimpsed for moments in a market crowd. Women married to his cousins, caught out half dressed at their ablutions. Older women, careless with their clothes. Girls too young to wear a shawl, too young to care if Musa saw their legs. Women who had argued with him at his stall, their faces fiery and their shoulders square. Women seen with sickles in their fields as Musa and his camels journeyed by; he'd call to them, and they would stand up, perhaps, arch and stretch their aching backs, and wave at him, shake all the chaff and dust from off their clothes.

How easy it had been to dip his hands into their remembered lives at night. To rove about them with his fingertips. To have these strangers do exactly as he said in his imaginings. There'd been no bruises and no screams from them, except, of course, on those occasions when he summoned little Miri to his bed to stand in for the woman that he'd picked that day. "Wave at me, Miri. Do it, do it. Stand there. Arch your back. That's right. Be quiet! Pull up your tunic. Stretch." Be someone else, besides my wife. Be anybody else. Be everyone.

Now Musa's heart was beating far too fast for comfort. His breath was laboured, but, at least, he would not have to waste himself into his hands or on his wife that night. There was a chance — a certainty — that all these beating, breathless moments in his past could, by

234

some miracle, be brought to life. He'd help himself, through Marta, to all the women he had ever seen, to all the chances he had ever missed. He would express himself on her, like he'd expressed his anger on the little jenny he had killed. He'd put his pestle to good use again. He'd kick the woman's shanks. She'd go down on her knees. He'd like to see the stubborn creature's head fall loose. He'd like to see her tumble to the ground. She'd close her eyes when he pushed into her. He saw her face, he planned how it would be, and it was plump and beautiful and bruised. Her fabrics were all silks, and all her silks were torn. Do what you want to me, he'd make her say. You are the landlord. This is rent.

Musa lifted his head up off the ground, rolled on to his side, and shifted his weight on to his knees. There was no one to pull him to his feet. But he was nimble for a change. He felt so young and well, and aided by strong demons who helped him stand. He had waited thirty days for this, and he would take his time.

It was still too dark outside the cave for him to see the damage of the night, how the wind had ripped the branches from the trees, exposed the roots of plants and left a unifying cloak of dust across the scrub. But there was light enough for him to make his way, her shawl around his shoulders, between his own cave and his neighbour's. He looked around, and listened carefully. No sound, except for his own panting. No sign of anyone about. The badu always made a noise if he was moving. He must be sleeping, then. Musa edged along the sloping ground. No poppies had survived the night. He watched his step. He did not want to send a stone rattling down the hillside, and wake her up and rouse the badu. He had to be as sudden as he could. He had to take her by surprise. His clothes were loosened, and his testicles furrowed and retracted in the cold, like shrinking slugs with salt put on their backs.

This was not wickedness, he told himself. This was his duty and his right. Marta wanted him. Why else would someone such as her, sophisticated, wealthy, well-born, well-built, waste so many days with Miri, except to use his wife as an excuse to spend a little time with him, the story-teller and the merchant king? Why else had she such tempting breasts, such thighs, if not to have them touched? Why else had she come to the caves at all except to go back to her husband pregnant? He'd overheard her say as much herself. That's what she'd prayed for on the promontory. She wanted to return to Sawiya, transformed by miracles, made fertile by her quarantine. He would oblige. He'd do what the little Gally had refused to do. He'd throw his seed on to her fallow ground.

Musa had an image of her from the day before, sitting on the rocks while he invented and recounted his adventures without water in the desert. She had not stared at Miri but at him. Her lips had parted when he spoke. One leg had fallen loosely to the side, beneath her clothes. She was loose-limbed for him. Her eyes were wide and fixed on his mouth. Her face and skin were full and clear. She'd smiled at him. She'd given him her shawl as a favour and a sign. This was an invitation to her cave. This was her fault.

She'd thank him, afterwards. He'd see to that. He'd not be satisfied until she'd said how glad she was he'd come. "A miracle. You are not barren now," he'd say when he had finished with her. "That husband of yours is the only one to blame. He's not a man. He isn't any use. But see how big my Miri is becoming. See how big the barren women are whenever I come to their market-places. I send them home with something in their bags, and they've not parted with a single coin. They've made a profit out of me. Their trees are heavy with my fruit. You've never seen such vines as theirs. That is the magic of my trade. My caravans supply fertility. What good is fasting, then? What good are prayers? What good's obedience to all the laws, when Musa takes you as his bride?"

"Up, up!" he'd say. He'd make her pull him to his feet.

Marta had not slept much during the wind, of course. She was less self-possessed than Musa. Storms never brought good luck or gentle dreams to her. And even after the storm she was too uneasy and uncomfortable to sleep. She was still awake when Musa crept up outside and stood waiting for some better light to act as his accomplice. Now that the wind had gone, each tiny sound he made was amplified inside her cave. She heard her landlord's breathing, and she heard the scuffle of his feet. But Marta was not frightened by the sounds at first. She did not imagine for a moment that Musa was outside. She'd seen how ill he was the evening before. How hot and heavy he had been, how weak his speech. She'd have to go when it was light to take him water, to check if he were dead, but she was in no hurry for the dawn to come. She entertained herself by thinking what the sounds might mean.

At worst the scufflings in the scrub, she thought, would be the badu, tugging at his hair and turning over rocks with his toes. He never seemed to sleep. He often prowled around at night and made strange, liquid noises, like a hyena with its snout inside a deer. The more she listened, though, the more she wondered if these sounds were human at all. A man's disturbances would be more weighty. These were too light and birdlike to be threatening. An owl. Gazelles, perhaps? It was — at best, the very best — that little, straw-boned sister from the tent, with untied hair, and a peeping, rodent face. Her Miri, then — come up to the scarp with rugs and pillows and "something sweet" as she'd been instructed by her husband, only to find him dead inside his cave? She was ashamed, but Marta wished it could be so. Then she and Miri could be sisters till the end of time. She could be an aunt to Miri's child. They'd go back to Sawiya, arm in arm, the widow and the barren wife. That would be worth a thousand days of quarantine.

Marta listened carefully, but she could not really fool herself that this was Miri waiting in the dark. She'd not make that mistake again. Yes, surely these were the same sounds that had frightened her before, on her first day. The raucous snails, the lizards and the flies, the worms, the millipedes, the whip bugs and the slugs had gone into the cistern for their drink. It was the fourth day of creation yet again, and the water teemed with life. Once more, she listened, held her breath. But, no, she hadn't got the answer yet. The sounds were too dry and close to be the cistern. The sounds were unfamiliar as well, except for one which finally she recognized, the flux and reflux of a breath too regular to be an animal's. It was the sound of someone inhaling and exhaling through his nose.

It was not long before what little light there'd been outside had disappeared. The someone who'd been breathing blocked the entrance to her cave and was standing there, as dark and still as some large stone. Marta prayed. She had to be an optimist. She had to think it was the healer. She'd half-expected he would come. Their meeting was ordained. Perhaps there'd be a miracle. That's what she'd prayed for, after all. That is what she'd dreamed. That was why she'd spent so many evenings, when it would have been much easier to stay with Miri at the loom, waiting on the promontory and watching for a sign of life outside his cave. It had to be the Gally, then, who blocked her light. Who else? There wasn't anybody else. Please god there wasn't anybody else.

She heard his tongue. She heard his lips. She heard the salt-bush rustling and then her own name, whispered by a man. She even welcomed it. "Marta, I have come for you." She did not want to recognize the voice at first. It was so soft, and too distorted by the echo in the cave. It still might be the Galilean voice. How could she be certain anyway? She'd never heard him speak. She'd never even seen his face. She'd only caught the almost-sight of him, the shy and nearly shadow on the precipice. She'd only ever seen his humming rocks. She held her breath. She waited for the shadow to approach. There was still room for hope.

"Come in," she said, and prayed, All thanks to god, and let it be the Gally. Let him have climbed the precipice to minister to me. "Marta, I've come for you," he'd said. He knew her name. The first of many miracles. He'd swell into the holy king and reach into her cave. He'd cup her face inside his giant palm, "Be well . . .", and he would build his kingdom in her empty spaces.

Again he said her name. And now she knew his voice was far too high and comical for one so pitying and strong. She watched the shadow, and, yes, it swelled and reached into her cave as she had dreamed. It came into her empty spaces. This was no boyish skin and bones. This man was large, and getting larger too. He held her wrists. He cupped her head inside his giant palms.

What was her latest article of faith? If anything could happen, then it would.

CHAPTER
TWENTY-FIVE

Musa picked his way through the debris of the night, below the caves. The storm had lifted stones to show their hidden faces. It had made firewood from bushes, and pulled up roots and soil. Lice and termites tumbled in the daylight where the earth was scarred, busy with repairs. The birds were feeding everywhere. Their nests and eggs had been destroyed, but they could fret on insects until their stomachs burst. What footmarks there had been on the scrubby slope, to show the comings and the goings of the quarantiners, had been removed by the wind. A layer of dust and grit was spread across the ground, like seeds and flour sprinkled on a loaf. This was the way the world had been before mankind, the childhood of the earth when it was innocent and undisturbed. This was the way the world would be when all mankind had gone, when the cleansing wind of prophecy had swept all sins and virtues from the earth and the wilderness was strewn with fallen and abandoned faiths.

Musa's footprints were the morning's first. Those were the ones that normally belonged to the burglar, the adulterer, the son who'd run away at night, the village sneak, the chicken thief. But Musa did not feel ashamed. He felt about as guilty as a boy with flour on his hands as the only proof that he had stolen bread. That is to say, he knew he had done wrong but he was glad of it. The bread had tasted good. His shame was thin and white. He'd blow it from his fingers with a single puff.

He'd left the woman with some bruises on her arms, it's true, some broken skin, some little aches and pains that would not show although they might take time to mend. The inside of her lip was cut. Her anus had been torn. But he had let her keep her money-bag. He was no thief. She'd been a disappointment to him, actually. She'd screamed. She had insulted him. She'd struck his face a dozen times with her soft hands. She'd spat. She'd even tried to hit him with a stone. Her anger and her awkwardness had made it difficult for him; he'd had to concentrate on quelling her instead of satisfying himself. He'd had to be alert and always remember to keep the tightest grip on her — her hair, her ears, her arms, her throat, her drawstring — or else she would escape from him. She could jump up and run, but he could not.

She'd only quietened when he'd stunned her with his fists. But he had not enjoyed her stunned and unresponsive. He hadn't wanted sex alone, with no participant except himself. That had never been the plan. He had ejaculated twice — the first time far too quickly within moments of his arrival in the cave, and the second time without much feeling. He would have liked more time with her to attempt a third and more considered consummation. But, try as he might, he could not ready himself for her. Unconscious women were not attractive in his view. They could not display their fear. And so he'd covered up her body with her shawl — no one could say he was entirely inconsiderate — and had stepped out into the dawn a slightly disappointed man.

But still he could congratulate himself. At least he'd made a trading profit on the night. There'd be no cost because she'd not breathe a word to anyone. If he'd had any doubt of that he would have snapped her neck at once and blamed her death on the badu, or some brigand in the hills, or on the wind. He knew the punishments for forcing Jewish women to submit to passions such as his were harsh, especially when gentiles were involved. If Marta reported Musa to the Jewish courts and was believed, they'd circulate his name to every dusty corner of the land. They'd track him down if he ever came within a dozen days of Sawiya, and then they'd carry out the letter of the law. They'd cover him in tar and burn him, waist-deep in a pile of dung. They'd thrust a lighted torch into his mouth. They'd bury him in stones. He'd taken quite a chance to sleep with her. He had been brave.

But Marta would not take a chance. Musa knew she would be sensible, not brave. She wouldn't want to speak his name to anyone. "What were you doing there in any case, alone?" they'd say. "Why did you tell the man, 'Come in'?" No, Marta would be silent. She'd want to bury the experience at once. When fear and shame are comrades, tongues lie still. Besides, he'd threatened her. One word of this outside the cave, he'd said, and I'll call all my cousins here to visit you. They'll do the same as me. I'll come back to visit you myself. There's nowhere you can hide.

Yet Musa felt exposed somehow. He was revealed—
to Marta at least — for what he was, cheap goods, bad
stock. No merchant ever stays around to answer for the
blemishes and flaws on the merchandise he's sold. That
is the time to pack his bags and go. So Musa could not
wait until the end of quarantine, to endure her fear and
sullen glances for ten more days, although that prospect
was not daunting. He would not wait until the end. The
scrub could not enrich him any more. Already he was
making plans. He'd conquered Marta. Now he set his
heart on Jericho.

He was relieved to reach the pans of soft clay in the
valley below the caves, and turn towards the tent. It was
satisfying to have put a short distance between Marta
and himself, and the walking on the flatter surface would
be, he hoped, less cruel on his ankles. The clay had been
renewed and freshened in the night by the few drops of
rain. The wind had ironed it flat, then rippled it. It was a
tidal estuary of mud, bubbling with pockets of trapped
air, and it was cold around his toes. Already Musa was
tired. He had no staff. He had no wife to take his arm and
help him with his balance. His knees and hips were
aching badly. The wet clay was harder on him than the
slope. But he could hardly sit in it and rest. He took it
slowly though.

Musa found no pleasure in the footprints that he left,
or the suckered protests that his sandals made in the mud
as he buried them and lifted them. His tracks were deep
and obvious. He would have preferred to have left no
marks at all, no debts. Caravanners like to come and go,

according to the verse, And let the dust that they have raised, Fill in the footprints they have made.

It was not long before Musa spotted movement at the far end of the pans. The sun was in his eyes but he was sure that there was someone coming up towards him, a someone who was light enough to walk across the mud without their sandals sticking. It might be the badu, or the blond returned from his hopeless vigil on the promontory. Musa would demand some help with walking. It might even be his wife, collecting herbs or bringing up a flask and blankets to her ailing husband at first light as she'd been told. About time too. Musa stopped, rubbed his side, practised breathing awkwardly. He had been ill, he must remember that. He was recovered but still weak, he'd say. Another miracle.

But it was Jesus walking in the mud, bare-footed, naked, thin and brittle as a thorn. So, then, Shim's bogus, midnight mission had been fruitful after all. His vigil on the promontory at Musa's behest — "Say that I'll die unless he comes" — had worked where all the other days of prayers and exhortations had failed. Musa chuckled to himself. He was rewarded for his tricks, no matter what he did. His little Gally had appeared at last. He'd come up from his cave to cure Musa for a second time. This second miracle would be an easy one. He'd only have to exorcize the demons from Musa's hip and knee, and scrape away a little mud. He'd only have to wipe away a lie.

Musa did not take another step. He waited while the man approached, as thinly as an egret, his body wasted to the bone, his too large hands and feet, his swollen joints. Only his genitals seemed unaffected by the fast. This was nothing. Musa was not shocked. He'd seen worse sights before than naked mystics. In his travels, he'd seen recluses who'd made themselves as yellow and transparent as amber by their deprivations. He'd seen the hermits of Khaloun who fed on insects, nothing else. Their skins were hard and cracked like cockroaches. He'd seen worse ulcers, looser teeth, more hollow eyes. But he had never seen a man appear so weightless and invincible as Gally seemed to be.

Musa did not know what he should do. Salute the man when he arrived like an old friend? Fall down on his knees, or run, though both were difficult for someone of his size and in mud that deep? Pretend to be still ill and in need of healing? Could he fool Jesus with his tricks? Musa compromised. He took one step backwards, held his side and winced, and almost crouched, not quite a deferential bow, not quite a posture of defence, not quite an ambush. He was stooped too low to see the Gally now. He waited for the figure to come closer, oddly fearful of it but triumphant, too. Another victory. Here was the one who'd tipped the water on to Musa's lips and cheeks. Here was the face that he'd last seen a whisper from his nose, inside the tent. The peasant's and the robber's face. The healer's face. From that distance in the open scrub, it had not seemed so young as it had been when they first met. The hair was pale. The body was the colour of the land behind.

What should Musa say to greet his Gally? It was embarrassing. He could hardly call out, "Good morning, cousin. Know my face?" as if they were chattering acquaintances from some market-place. Or, "I'm the one that comes for you each day. At last we meet again . . ." or, "Speak to me, then. We were good cousins thirty days ago. This *is* my land." Such pleasantries were not appropriate for one so holy and so thin. But Musa need not have worried what to say. His Gally would not cross the mud to stroke his eyelids with his thumb or talk to him or pass his judgement on the landlord's weaknesses. When Musa stood and looked again, the man was at a greater distance and almost indistinguishable from the shadows and the bushes. He had taken a lower path, through a sloping basin of thorn and rock, and was walking away from Musa with the confidence of someone who was full of god at last.

Musa watched — relieved, rebuffed — as Jesus set off up the scarp, his body bones combining with the scrub rocks and the sunlight to make a hard-edged pattern which pulsed and slanted all at once. Musa put his hands up to his mouth. "What do you want?" he called. The Gally did not seem to hear. He was too far away. He pulsed and slanted, disappeared, became a man again a few steps higher up the slope, was lost between the landscape and the sun. Who was he looking for, if not the merchant king? Had he come for the water in the cistern? Or was he heading for the woman in the cave?

The air became much colder than it ought to have been. Musa barely dared to breathe. He could have sworn the man was glowing blue and yellow, like a coal.

CHAPTER
TWENTY-SIX

It was Aphas who saw Musa first, a little after dawn, coming slowly through the rocks towards the flattened tent, wearing his boots of mud, his hair heavy with sweat. He did not seem so big somehow, as if a single night of quarantine up at the caves had been enough to shorten and to narrow him. Even the goats could tell he had improved. They did not scatter when he walked amongst them as they usually did. He did not try to kick their legs.

"Your man is back," said Aphas, "Look." Mira looked, and so did Shim. They did not run to greet him, glad that he'd survived another illness and was well enough to walk. Their day-dreams perished at the sight of him. They stayed on the panels of the tent as if they thought the wind could strike up again at any moment, and waited for him to rage at what had happened to his home. Miri knew what he would do and say. He'd twist her wrist: "What use are you? Look what you've done in just one night." He would not be ashamed to slap her ears, even with Shim and Aphas looking on. He'd slap their ears as well, if he had half a chance.

But no, he merely shook his head and rolled the broken tent poles with his foot.

"You'll have to make another one," he said, "when we get down to Jericho." He looked at Miri, sitting amongst the few possessions she had rescued from the wind, the finished birth-mat on her lap, untied, her broken loom in pieces at her feet, her face and hair made ashen by the dust. "You'll have to get another loom."

"How is your stomach, then?" she said, still nervous of the man. "We prayed for you, I promise. We sang for you all night . . ."

"Your prayers were answered. See? I'm well. The wind has blown all the pain away. My wind in here . . ." he rubbed his stomach, ". . . became the wind outside. See what it's done." He shrugged again, and spread his hands above the tent, a stoic almost. "This is the price we pay."

What should they make of Musa now? To those survivors at the tent, he seemed transformed. They all had been transformed by the bombast of the winds, of course. There's nothing more dispiriting than clinging to a flattened tent at dawn with nothing looming up to help beyond the scrub except more scrub. They had been circled seven times in the night. The wind had sounded seven fanfares on its horn. And their skin city had been levelled to the ground. There are no kinder winds than that. There isn't one that comes along and puts up tents. But Musa, they supposed, had more reason to be dispirited than any of them, if he was human. Even though he'd missed their dramas with the tent. He had been badly ill, and must be more humbled and exhausted by his struggles. The idea that the midnight wind had originated in Musa's stomach did not seem far-fetched, to Aphas at least. His stomach *was* large enough to lodge a storm. And demons could take many shapes. A demon driven out of Musa's gut where it was warm and comfortable might want to take revenge on Musa's tent. That much was logical. He sympathized with that. What had his landlord said, those many days ago? "I only have to belch for there to be a storm." Perhaps he'd belched so great a storm that all his rage was spent against the scrub, and he was left as harmless and as fragile as a blown egg. An empty shell. Certainly, none of them had ever known the man so quiet. They had not thought that he could be pensive or melancholy. It hardly suited him. His heavy jaw seemed heavier. He'd lost the teasing challenge in his eyes. He was distracted and reduced. Perhaps, his second meeting with mortality had made a better, lesser man of him.

Even so, Shim and Aphas kept their distance, and even Miri — unwidowed for a second time — was slow to offer Musa her assistance, or to run around and find his food and drink amongst the scattered trappings. At last he said, "Bring me the flask." Perhaps date spirit would restore him, and give him courage. For reasons he could not understand, his passing encounter with the Gally had been frightening.

"I don't know where it's gone," said Miri.

"Hunt for it, then."

Miri had still not found the flask amongst the salvaged remains of their property when there was a warbling noise, and the badu came running up, covered in dust and scratches. He was talking for a change, but not a

250

language anybody knew. He seemed unusually excited, his tongue too small for what he had to say. He's seen the Gally, Musa thought. Or else he's seen me coming out of Marta's cave. He's seen her bruises. It's just as well that he can't talk. But the badu was not pointing to the valley of the caves. He was pointing to the precipice. He caught hold of Shim's wrist and tugged.

"What is it, now? Let go."

He pulled Aphas to his feet, and tugged him for a few paces towards the promontory. He did the same to Shim. And when Shim shook him off, the badu got hold of the curly staff and handed it to Musa. Again he pointed to the precipice, and mimed a prayer. He waved his hand towards the precipice, walked off a dozen paces, beckoned them to follow him across the scrub.

"He wants us to walk," suggested Shim.

"What for?" said Musa. "I'll not walk another step today."

"Something to do with the Galilean boy."

"The Galilean boy has gone already. I saw him walking. This morning."

"*Who* did you see?"

"The Gally. Walking."

"Walking where?" asked Aphas, terrified of what he might have missed during his night-long absence from his cave. "Have you been healed by him? What did he say? Where is he now?"

Musa shrugged. He shook his head. "Nothing . . ."

"You saw him, though?"

"I saw him, yes. He shows himself to me. He's there, somewhere. Up at the caves. Unless he's gone into the hills."

"We didn't see him pass," said Shim. "We didn't hear him walking. And we've been here all night."

Musa wouldn't argue with Shim. He only said, "He's silent when he moves . . ."

The badu gave up on the men. But Miri was easier to drag along the ground, and more easily persuaded by the badu's grimaces and cries.

"Go with him, then," said Musa. "See what the noise is all about. Leave me in peace to think. Yes, go. See if my flask has blown over there."

It wasn't long before she had returned from her first visit to the promontory, leaving the badu on the cliffs. "You'd better come and see," she said. "There's someone dead." Musa's mouth was hanging open. He looked stunned. He's been caught out telling lies, thought Miri. She was pleased. *He shows himself to me*, indeed. *I saw him walking, earlier this morning*. How had her husband hoped to benefit from telling lies like that?

At first they could not see the body lying on the rock outside the cave. The dust had made the landscape all the same colour; the shapes were indistinguishable. But they could see the ravens picking at some carrion, and hear the tok-tok of their beaks. The body was beneath the birds.

"That's him," said Musa, clasping his hands tightly to stop them trembling. He felt as if his head was full of bees.

"Who was walking? You said. Up at the caves," asked Aphas.

Musa stuck his chin out and shrugged. "That was him, too," he said tentatively. "I must have seen the ghost pass out of him. Unless I dreamed it. Might have dreamed it. You know I've not been well." He tried to recollect the figure, gliding on the mud. Had he really seen a living face? Had he seen anyone at all, or was his conscience playing tricks on him? His memory was far too faint and imprecise to be entirely sure. Even if he shut his eyes he could only picture Gally spread out on the rocks with ravens on his face. And if he opened them and looked across the precipice towards the cave, the picture was the same. Whatever Musa had seen that morning, one thing was certain now; the Gally was beyond help.

They waited on the promontory and watched the badu climb down to the Gally's cave with ropes and cloths to save the body from the birds. The badu did not seem afraid of death or ravens. They stood their ground, with bloody beaks, and stabbed at the badu's arms. But he swept them off and picked the corpse up in his arms as if it were no heavier than a stook of reeds — indeed, it was no heavier than reeds — and wrapped it in the torn tent curtain which had once divided Miri from her husband. The Gally's naked feet protruded from the cloth, like some small boy playing hide-and-seek behind a tapestry.

The badu tied the wrapped body with rope, secured an extra line to it and climbed once more up to Shim at the rim of the precipice above the cave. They pulled the body up, past the overhanging rock, the canker thorn, the crumbling contours of the cliff. The ravens made their last assault on Jesus's protruding, swinging feet, but nothing could prevent the burial of Jesus now.

"No need to dig a grave," said Musa, coming up with Aphas and his wife to join the other two. "We have a grave. My little donkey's grave. It must be meant for him . . . It was always meant for him."

"You mean we should use the cistern?" said Shim.

"It was a grave before it was a cistern."

"What will we drink?"

Musa shrugged. He didn't care what anybody drank. He wouldn't stay another day and so he didn't need to know about their thirst.

"You can't bury him in the water that we drink," persisted Shim.

"Whose land is this? Go somewhere else for water. Go down to Jericho and drink your fill. There's an empty cave below that you can have for free, if you're not frightened of those birds. Climb down. Do what you want. But this man has a grave already dug for him."

Shim and the badu carried Jesus to the tent and rested there while Miri gathered extra water-skins to fill before they used the cistern. She found some food for them to eat as well, and some blanket cloths. Everyone would have to spend the night in caves. The tent was useless now.

They took the body through the pans of mud and up the scarp, with Musa, Miri and Aphas following as mourners. They should have put a flower on the Gally's lips, but there were none left standing. They had to make do with some blackened poppy petals. And then they put the body in the same cave that Musa had used the night before, for safe keeping, until everything was ready for his burial. They blocked off the entrance with uprooted thorns, and lit a fire close by to keep the flies away. The wood was damp; its smoke was black, then purple-grey, the proper colour for a funeral.

"Where's Marta?" Miri asked.

CHAPTER
TWENTY-SEVEN

"You'd better make a sacrifice to speed the Gally on his way," said Musa.

Shim and Aphas nodded warily. Their landlord was being uncharacteristically comradely with them; anything to hold their attention and keep their minds off his wife. They could hear Miri searching in the rock falls beyond the caves, calling "Marta, Marta," with rising desperation in her cries. But Musa raised his own voice to drown hers out. He did not want the men to help Miri. If one of them found Marta alive, sobbing and bruised, what might he ask her? What might she reply?

It would suit Musa if he never saw the woman again. He was angry with her. She had not been sensible. If she'd had any brains she would have packed her few belongings and set off home already, saving trouble and embarrassment for everyone. But Miri had searched inside the cave and Marta's clothes were still there. A woman would not leave without her spare clothes. So she was either hiding in the scrub, or something bad had happened to her. Something fatal, Musa hoped. She brought these problems on herself. If she were dead, they'd have to hold a double burial, the Gally and the woman in one grave. She could be a handmaiden for

Jesus for eternity. An honour, actually. Too good for her. But if she were still alive, then the very sight of her would spoil the Gally's funeral. Musa wanted to despatch the healer with proper, blameless piety. He did not want his little sins to stand as mourners at his side.

"You cannot send him to his maker without a sacrifice," said Musa, breaking his own silence. "Come on, come on. What will you do for him?"

"What kind of sacrifice?" asked Shim. Was this to be a sacrifice of principle or dignity or money? He was running short, although he still had some coins hidden in his cloak, and didn't want to part with any.

"What do these people sacrifice? Their daughters, probably. Some animal, then. We have to spill a little blood for the man, to wet our funeral prayers. That's how it's done in the Galilee. They take an ox and slit its throat."

"Regrettably, I cannot lead you to an ox," said Shim, much relieved. "I haven't noticed any oxen hereabouts . . ."

"There are your goats," said Aphas helpfully. "Kill one. It would be generous."

"Wasteful, too," said Musa. "And only generous for me. What would be your part in it?" He would not agree to sacrificing merchandise, not even for the Gally. Goats provided milk and meat and fuel and skin. Killing one without a proper purpose would be a four-fold waste. "Send him," he lifted his chin towards the badu. "He's the hunter, isn't he? He's already poached enough birds and deer from off my land. Send him to catch something for us. I think I can afford him that."

Musa threw a stone at the badu to draw his attention. "Explain what we want," he said to Aphas. "He's used to you." He watched the old man mime the catching and the slaughter of an animal. The badu did not seem to understand. He grinned and shook his head, until Musa took his ornamental knife out of its cloth and made a motion with its blade across his throat, followed by the hand-sign for a prayer. Then the badu nodded. "See, he's not as stupid as he looks," said Musa. "How could he be?"

The badu hurried off towards the valley. He'd almost understood. He was to catch a bird for Jesus. The smallest funeral offering. He had mistaken Musa's praying hand-sign to be a bird, the fingers pressed together like closed wings, the thumbs protruding like a little head. The badu knew exactly what to do. Catching birds was easy. He'd been doing it for years.

He ran down to the tent and hunted through the goatskins until he found Miri's cooking chest. He popped a little cube of hard salt between his lips, and unravelled a fraying length of green cotton thread from one of Musa's ruined samples. He wrapped the thread around his finger and tiptoed amongst the goats, which had been let loose to graze on the tattered fabrics and any food that they could find. To anyone that watched it would seem that he was whispering in their ears, more evidence of lunacy. A madman speaking to the goats. What did he want with them? To tether them with his thin thread? To strangle one of the goats for Jesus, perhaps?

258

The badu searched the goats until he found one with a blood-filled tick in the skin folds of an ear. Easy to see, but not so easy to get out. Some smoke, blown from a burning stick, would usually make a tick detach itself. But the badu hadn't any smoke. Instead he took the now softened cube of salt out of his mouth. He crumbled it into the goat's ear and rubbed it into the skin. Salt was better than smoke for catching ticks. A goat with a burning ear would not stay still. The tick, however, hated salt. It contracted, darkened, and fell into the badu's palm. That was the easy part.

The hard part was to tie the thread around the tick's abdomen without popping its blood sac, and without the tick attaching itself to the badu's finger. But he was practised. He had harnessed hundreds of ticks since he was small. He could have pulled a chariot with them.

The badu took the fastened tick into the nearest stand of thorns. What little rain there'd been in the night had tempted last year's seeds to hazard their first green shoots. Insects, tempted by the moisture and the exposed sap of wind-snapped branches, competed for a meal. So did the birds. Finches, wheatears, warblers had come from nowhere to gorge themselves. And there were circling hawks, of course, waiting for the plumpest opportunity.

The badu put his tick on an exposed flat rock amongst the bushes, a little grape of blood, and weighed the thread down with a stone, a finger-length from the tick. It could not wiggle away, out of the unforgiving light. It couldn't even fall very far, but it had just freedom enough to advertise itself with its struggles. It didn't like the thread around its abdomen; it didn't like the sun. The badu backed away, downwind, running the remainder of the thread through his fingers, until he found a hiding place behind a bush where he could not be seen but from where the twisting tick was visible. Now he would fish himself a bird.

He was an expert at keeping still, though anyone who'd seen him in the past thirty days, running in the rocks, tugging his hair and hands unceasingly, would have been amazed that one so plagued by movement and loose limbs could be so quiet and patient when it suited him. Perhaps the truth was this: he was a madman only when observed, the cussed opposite of those who conspired to be rational in company and cultivate their manias alone. The badu, without any witnesses to click their tongues at him and shake their heads, appeared entirely sane. He crouched beneath a thorn bush in the scrub, a blood tick offered on a thread to passing birds. And he was happy, too. He had his plans. He'd do his duty to the Gally who had died, and then he'd make a rich man of himself.

It wasn't long before a banded wheatear came, a male, on its way north to breed. For all its mating splendour, its damask eye plumes and its black flights, it was tired from its long journey, and glad to have such easy and nourishing prey. The trick, it knew, was not to peck the tick. The bulb of blood would burst. Instead, the wheatear turned its head and took the tick whole. It lifted up its head to let the feast fall into its crop.

The trick for the badu was to wait. If he pulled on the thread too soon, before the wheatear's throat had ended its spasm of swallowing, the tick would pop out of its mouth again, without the blood. If he pulled on the thread too late, the wheatear's flight might be strong enough to snap the cotton. The badu waited until the wheatear spread its wings, two beats, and then he jerked the thread. The wheatear tumbled in the air, and fell on to its back. The badu was already there. The bird was his. Not quite the perfect sacrifice, of course. Not quite as generous as a goat, not quite as heavy as an ox. But better than no sacrifice at all.

The badu only broke one wing so that the wheatear could not fly away. He held it, quivering, in both hands. It didn't peck at him for long. Only its trembling chest showed that it was still alive. He snapped the thread off at its beak and carried the bird to the men, waiting at the grave. They were disappointed. They had hoped that he would catch a little deer at least.

"If that's the best that this mean land will offer us, then damn it and so be it," Musa said. "We'll make do."

"This is, undoubtedly, the meanest place I've ever seen," said Shim, with feeling, kicking at the stones and waving his hands around at all the unrewarding wilderness, the unremitting sun, the unrelenting landlord. He was already persuading himself that it was time to leave.

It was not fair of them to blame the scrub for being stingy with everything except for space and light and stone. Even if it had not displayed much magnanimity towards the men, it had, at least, been generous to Miri. It had not maddened her or lamed her, yet. It had not made her ill or thin. In fact, she was the only one of them to put on any weight during the thirty days. It had allowed her to complete her birth-mat; there'd been delights in that, despite the wools. And, in the night, it had even conspired with the wind to free her from the family tent. An act of charity.

But Miri was exceptional. She had bewitched the scrub on her first day. They were equals in their plainness and their endurance. Usually it was a less forgiving, more dogmatic host, despising doubt and mocking faith at once, and favouring the predatory, whatever their beliefs. It was even-handed in its cruelties. It did not normally discriminate between the donkey and the mule. It did not prefer the vulture to the crow. It did not favour hennaed hair over blond. It did not hang its trees with food or fill its hollows up with drink to make life easy for its guests. The scrub required its passengers to take care of themselves or go without. The scrub was economical, as well, like some old man, and boundless in its barrenness and poverty. Its air was thin; its earth was pale; its weeds were frayed; its moods were fractious and despairing.

But there was also something rich, at times, about the scrub, despite itself. Something sustaining, unselfish, fertile even. Perhaps this was because it made no claims. It did not promise anything, except, maybe, to replicate through its array of absences the body's inner solitude and to free its tenants and its guests from their addictions and their vanities. The empty lands — these very caves, these paths, these desert pavements made of rock, these pebbled flats, these badlands, and these unwatered river beds — were siblings to the empty spaces in the heart.

Why else would scrubs have any holy visitors at all? Ten thousand quarantiners had come to these parched hills and passed their days, some delirious with illness; others feverish with god, and guilt and lunacy, unravelled from themselves by visions of a better and eternal world; the rest made mad by fasting. Yet, at the end of their forty days, the scrub sent all of them away enriched and dryly irrigated. Even Aphas. Even Shim.

But the chosen one or two, the very few, were rewarded for their quarantines with sacred revelations. The scrub allowed them up its steep and narrow tracks, and through the softened silhouettes of hills, to their attending gods. And there it stretched its grey horizons to reveal what far-off armies were approaching with their spangling phalanxes of spears, what distant kings and preachers came with gifts and prophecies, how slow and never-ceasing was the world. And there it gave its voyagers their glimpse of paradise.

Jesus had achieved these sacred fields and seen horizons on horizons without end. He was still there.

And Musa, too. Yes, even Musa — especially Musa — had had his glimpse of paradise and felt the fingers of his preacher king. He would not go back with nothing to declare. The scrub would not return him empty-handed to his market-places. What greater generosity than that?

CHAPTER
TWENTY-EIGHT

Miri was not interested in visions or prophecies, or in a god. She'd never called on him for help, not even in the fist of the storm when her mother's loom was breaking into pieces. But she was praying now for Marta. She ran from cave to cave, and then from bush to bush, in a panic, yelling for the woman, anticipating all the joys of finding her, yet fearful that Marta was already dead. She'd seen the death or something just as bad in Musa's eyes.

It was a barking fox that finally led her to Marta's hiding place. Something tasty must have tempted it to show itself in daylight. Some easy carrion. Miri feared the worst. But it was only following the spots of watery blood which Marta had spat out as she ran for safety in the rocks when she'd seen Musa and the line of mourners climbing to the caves.

Miri pulled her, trembling and limping, into the sunlight. Her clothes were torn. Her wrists were bruised. Her lower lip was split and swollen on one side, still bleeding. She had to brush away the flies. That was an injury that Miri recognized. She'd had a mouth like that herself. She still had the scar. Musa liked to grip her lips between his teeth.

"What happened to you?"

Marta hadn't got the courage to speak.

"It's Musa, isn't it?"

She shook her head.

"Who then? There's no one else . . . I know it's him. It's him!" Miri punched her hands together. "That man's made fools of everyone. Again! He wasn't even ill. All lies. He'll bring the heavens down on all of us . . ."

"No . . . I fell."

"Musa must have pushed you then. Look what he's done."

"It was the wind . . ."

"The wind? How could the wind do that to you?"

"Threw stones and bits of stick at me. I fell . . ."

"It's him."

"No. Don't make me say."

"Listen, Marta. Give me your hand. Just say you didn't fall. Be brave. Tell me. I know my husband, what he can do. He leaves his thumbprint everywhere."

"He doesn't know I'm here? Don't let him come."

"It's over now. He's finished with you now. Just tell me what the demon's done."

"Can't tell. There's nothing left to tell . . ." She was sobbing, pushing Miri away yet still holding tightly to her wrists. Her face was dry. No tears. "Don't make me say."

Miri put a finger on the uninjured side of Marta's mouth. Miri's cheeks were wet with tears. "Don't say. I know what he can do. You haven't got to say. Don't say."

"What can I do?"

"You can't stay here. You have to come back to the caves . . ."

"I can't."

"You must. You're safer there. There's five of us, and only him. I'll take good care of you. He'll stay away, I know. What can he do to you with us around? He's frightened of you now."

"I'm scared . . . to go."

"Come on. I need your help. The Gally's dead. You saw the body they were carrying?"

Now Marta could not stop the tears. "The Gally's dead?"

"We've got to bury him. Come on. Be brave."

Marta did as she was told. She followed Miri. Held on to her arm. Entwined her fingers into hers until they reached the caves. She'd find an opportunity to tell her sister what the wind had really done.

Musa did not even look at them. He sat in conversation with the men, facing across the valley, with no expression on his face, his fat neck creased, a stack of twenty grimaces. He called to Miri only once, without turning to face her. "We're waiting."

"What for?"

"For you to get the Gally ready for the burial."

Preparing bodies was women's work, in his opinion. The men could sit and pray, while Miri and Marta — glad to be busy and out of sight — gathered the leaves and bark of trees to make their shrouding ointments. They picked morning star and hyssop, dill pods, and the yellow spices from solanum stems to perfume the body.

Then they pulled back the smouldering fire and thorns, lit cups of candle-fat, and took refuge inside the smoky cave with Jesus.

They stood hand in hand in the ducking candlelight and the plumes of clearing smoke looking at the wrapped body, uncertain where to start. Only his hands and feet were visible, and so they cleaned them first with water taken from his grave. His skin was cold and dry. Despite the broken nails, the blisters and the sores, his hands and feet were still beautiful, as polished and unyielding as sculpted wood. The fast had thinned and lengthened his toes and fingers, so that the bones and joints were round and ripe like nuts in pods. The women unwrapped him from his curtain, removed the poppy petals from his eyes, and stood back to let the candles light his face. Marta gasped. She touched the Gally's cheeks and lips, and shook her head. She was almost smiling, for the first time that day.

"What's wrong?" said Miri. "Are you all right? Sit down. I'll do it by myself."

"No, let me help. I want to help." Marta touched his cheeks again. "I'm not afraid of him. He's only skin and bone."

The women covered Jesus's face with a cloth, to protect his mouth against the devil and to protect themselves from the dangers of looking a dead man in the eye for too long. That was the superstition, "Dead eyes looking, Bad luck cooking." But neither of them felt ill at ease with Jesus. Nor did they feel much reverence for him. His body was too damaged and degraded. Only his feet and hands had caused any wonder. The rest had been more cruelly treated by the fast and was not beautiful. But touching him was not distasteful. It felt more like a blessing than a chore. They'd have good luck, not bad. Miri and Marta did not talk while they were preparing Jesus. Their task was far too solemn and distressing. He was so young and disfigured. But they were glad they could at least share and halve the task with each other. They washed his body, wiped away the dried blood, the film of dust and ash, and cleaned his eyes and mouth and loins. They shut his eyes and pulled his lips over his teeth as best they could. His gums were so badly swollen that his mouth would not close. His grin was wide and mirthless. They anointed him with the herbs and ointments they'd collected, and burnt the seeds for incense in the candle cups. Finally they bandaged his feet and hands, and wrapped him in the curtain once again. They'd done as much as any woman could. Now it was men's work to carry him down to the cistern, and bury him. No woman should come near the grave. Miri and Marta stayed inside the cave, watching candle flames while Jesus was interred.

"What was the matter, when you saw his body?" Miri asked. "You gasped. You seemed surprised by him."

"I knew his face," Marta said. "Dear lord, how well I knew his face. That's how I always knew his face would be."

"How could you know his face? You never saw him. You always said he wouldn't come out of his cave."

"I know his face from dreams. If it was dreaming."

"You dreamed his face?"

"A hundred times. Even this morning. Outside the cave . . ."

"He was dead this morning! You've seen yourself how dead he was."

"I watched somebody walking up. I hid. I thought it was your . . . Don't make me even say his name. You know. Then I saw *him*. I knew it had to be the Gally. The same dead face. Just skin and bones. He was as near to me as you are now. I could have touched him. But he touched me. He touched my cuts and bruises. And then he kissed my feet."

Miri laughed. "That only happens in a woman's dreams."

"He touched my stomach afterwards, like a priest. He said, This is a son for Thaniel. How could he know my husband's name? He said he'd given me a child, with just his fingertips."

"That's something else that only happens in a woman's dreams."

Outside, there was no wailing at the funeral or any ululations to alarm the women. The men did not tear their clothes, or chastise themselves, although chastisement was deserved. But each of them, including Shim, touched the Gally's bandaged foot, which still protruded from its curtain shroud. They prayed for further miracles. They had to treat his death not as a setback but as an opportunity, a chance to be restored by the blessing of his spirit passing through them on its voyage to his god. Musa prayed the hardest of them all.

A touch, a touch, the merest touch, to save him from the world.

The grave had been ankle-deep in water, but the badu, always happy to amuse himself with stones, had lined the bottom so that the bed was hard but dry. They lifted Jesus — all four men as bearers, a limb apiece — and lowered him into the grave, face down. They could presume he was a bachelor, without offspring. He seemed as weightless as a child. What married man or father would leave his family to starve himself to death like this? They sacrificed the wheatear with Musa's ornamented knife. Its blood pumped on the curtain shroud. Musa dropped its body at the healer's feet. They filled the grave with earth and stone, hardly speaking to each other, and not looking in the grave until the body was entirely covered. Even Musa kicked a little earth into the grave and sighed as often as he could.

"This death is hard for me," he said, not entirely without truth. "I was the only one who really knew the man."

They marked his grave with forty stones. It seemed appropriate. Their mourning ought to last for three days at the least, they knew. No one should walk or make a fire or cook. They should not wash or shave. They should wear dirty clothes, if they were truly dutiful. But they were not his family and need not spare three days for mourning. His was a stranger's death despite their vigils at the precipice and all the hopes they'd spent on him. If they were at all despondent, it was because his death showed how much they'd failed themselves. This was only the thirty-first of their forty days, but it would be their last. How could they boast of that, down in the valleys, in the towns? The healer was a disappointment. He'd betrayed them all by dying. Their water cistern had been sacrificed. The tent was flattened. So were they. They'd leave at dawn and put an end to quarantine. There was no choice. The wind had blown all the spirit out of them. The scrub was telling these six trespassers to go.

CHAPTER
TWENTY-NINE

The badu disappeared that night. So did the goats. When everybody came down from the caves at dawn to salvage what they could from the tent for their descent to the valley, the only sign of any animals was dung. Musa checked his store of treasures with which he planned to re-assert himself in the summer markets to the north. He opened up the saddle-pack with shaking hands. He half expected to find the badu had replaced his treasures with a rock, but everything was there, untouched. The twist of Berber cloth containing jewellery, some coins and a little gold; the seven perfume bottles.

"Some thief!" said Musa.

But still the landlord and his tenants were surprised by the badu. He wasn't quite as mad as they had thought. He hadn't had to hand over his silver bracelets to Musa on the last day, as Musa had intended. He hadn't paid a coin for his food or rent or water. He hadn't even worked for them, by portering his landlord's goods down to the road for Jericho as he had promised. And now he had six goats to milk or eat or sell. A decent profit on his thirty days of idleness.

Musa cursed the hundred corners of the sky, and prayed that every demon of the scrub would lie in wait for the little thief with snares and thorns and traps, that he would fall into some pit and starve. But no one really thought the badu would come to any harm. They'd seen him clamber on the precipice. The deepest pit could not imprison him. They'd seen him come back to the caves with deer, and wheatear, and with honeycombs. He couldn't starve. Besides, he had six goats as his companions. It was almost pleasing, to think of them, the hennaed badu and the swart-haired goats, their bleating conversation and their dainty steps, making their escape across the scrub. Aphas and Marta, Miri even, wished the badu well. He'd bettered Musa. They'd dreamed of doing something similar themselves.

But it was Shim who seemed most angry and betrayed. Had he perhaps become fond of the badu, or was it simply that he felt a little safer with him in their company? What could the old man or the women do to intervene, if Musa caught him by his ankle again and decided to pluck his toes of his foot like unripe berries? They were too weak and frightened of the man to do anything but watch. The badu, though, had seemed disturbed and kind enough to give some help, and now he'd disappeared. Shim called for him, just in case, but he didn't answer or appear. Shim even went down to the promontory to see if the badu was sitting there, or climbing on the precipice, but there was no sign of any living thing. Even the Gally's cave seemed untouched. It seemed unreachable, in fact. No one with any sense would try to climb down to it without a ladder and some rope. "A stupid boy, a very stupid boy," he thought, to soften the defeat of not remaining on his own up at the caves until the end of quarantine. He ought to stay behind, but the truth of Musa's challenge from two days before was ringing in his head: "Take your chances like a fox. Pray for water to appear. Let's see how you live without a water-bag." The Gally hadn't lasted very long without a water-bag.

No, Shim would not waste another day on this mad enterprise. He'd take no risks. He'd stay as quiet as possible. He'd do as he was told for a change. And by the evening he would be released from his landlord and the scrub for ever. He was not happy when Musa asked to borrow his curling staff for the long walk across the plateau and the descent down to the valley road, but it was a sacrifice that Shim would make without a protest. A man of education and enlightenment should not attach himself too madly to a mere possession. Tranquillity and self-respect were more important than a length of wood. He'd not relinquish those to Musa. But let him have the wood.

Musa sent the two men ahead. They had been given heavy loads. Their progress would be slow. In addition to his own possessions — his rush bed-mat, his cloak, his water-bag — Shim had to carry two saddle-packs of Musa's goods, strapped across his back, a rug and bedding on his shoulders and a half-full woven sack of grain in his hands. Aphas, in deference to his age and illness, only had two bags of utensils to transport. Bulky but not weighty. The women would have to carry what was left. Some clothes and wools, dried fruit and another woven bag of odds-and-ends for Marta. The heavy water-bags and two camel panniers for Miri, draped round her neck on ropes, with the still-unknotted birth-mat between the ropes and her skin to prevent chafing.

Musa would not carry anything himself, except the staff. That was his golden rule for travelling, to have his hands free in readiness for trade and conversation. A merchant must not seem to be a camel. He had to come and go without encumbrance. He wanted, if he had the chance, to make his peace with Marta. That was really why he'd sent the men ahead, to give him time alone with her. Yesterday seemed such an age away. He'd buried what he'd done to her along with Jesus. The wake was over. They should begin anew. But Marta stuck closely to his wife, like some shy girl. If he came close to her, then she moved away. She would not even look at him, he'd noticed, or answer him with anything beyond a whisper, passed through Miri.

Musa understood her awkwardness, of course. A woman guilty of adultery, willingly or not, would be embarrassed for herself, or fearful that her husband might find out and have her stoned. But he would tell her that she had nothing to be frightened of. What happens between people in the privacy of night is hidden even from the scrutiny of god. For god must sleep. And men and women ought to make the most of it. He'd give her one of the little phials of perfume, well, half a phial, if she'd only lift her head and look at him. That should be enough to make amends.

What should he do about the tent? It would not satisfy him to leave the wreckage there, as Miri suggested, and allow their misfortunes with the wind to benefit some undeserving traveller or provide free shelter for the badu, should he still be in the scrub. So Musa had the women pile up the poles and walls of the tent, and throw on anything that would burn — the bits of damaged cloth, torn curtains and rush beds, the pieces of the broken loom, even uprooted bushes.

"Go on ahead," he said to Miri. Marta turned away. "And wait for me when you get to the top of the scree." He was a small, spoilt boy who wanted to light a fire and enjoy the damage and the flames all by himself.

Musa took his flintstones from their pouch and struck a spark on to a little pile of kindling. There was, thankfully, no wind. The flame seemed eager to oblige. He added twigs, and soon had sufficient heat and flame to make himself a brand of sticks and cloth.

The bushes were the first to flare. Blue flames, and then grey smoke as what little sap there was inside the stems bubbled out of the wood. The loom and tent poles soon joined in, but were made from harder woods and burned more slowly and with whiter smoke. Then the goat-hair tent sides gave in to the heat. They did not burn. There were no flames from them. They blackened, reddened, glowed and fell apart. They smelled like sacrificial meat. Their smoke was yellower and more determined than the thorns'. It hung above the ground like a sulphur mist at first, but finally was lifted up in narrow braids into the cooler air above.

There was no one to help Musa now. His uncles and his cousins were as insubstantial as the smoke. His two porters were out of sight. The women were too far away to call. The silence in the scrub was so deeply brewed that Musa did not know if he should cry out loud for joy or for help. He left the fire to itself and set off, across the scrub, and through the wind-blown remnants of his life. There was a copper pot he recognized. Some cloth. A scarf. He walked as quickly as he could to seek the company of women.

And there his fever devil stayed, below the caves, its feet in flames, its body shrouded in the yellow smoke. It curled above the salty scrub, shivering and abandoned, insubstantial and attached to no one, biding its time.

CHAPTER
THIRTY

Marta and Miri had not stopped to watch the smoke. They were too busy walking. They hardly talked. The path was difficult and narrow, and kept them apart for much of the time. Even when they reached the wider tracks worn by the many caravans which came across these hills to Jericho they did not walk side by side. Marta led the way, nervously avoiding any vegetation and rocky ground where there might be snakes or scorpions, but she hurried nevertheless, hastened by a mixture of fear and excitement. Ahead was better than behind.

Miri needed space around her to cope with the panniers and water-bags which she was carrying. The birth-mat, wrapped round her shoulders to stop the ropes from cutting into her, soaked up the sun and soon was wet and heavy with her sweat. She was a bit annoyed with Marta. She had expected her to take her time, to stay as close as possible, so that they could at least stretch out to touch each other once in a while or exchange a word or two on their last day together. Miri knew that she and Marta would have to go their separate ways as soon as they had reached the trading road. Sawiya was a village near Jerusalem, towards the west.

The summer markets where her husband would want to go were beyond Jericho, far to the north. But Miri's friend was rushing ahead far too quickly and was impatient if Miri walked too slowly or started to chatter.

It was easy for Marta to hurry, thought Miri. She only had one bag to carry and some clothes. Her load was relatively light for such a tall and wide-boned woman. And she was not six months pregnant with a child. Her hips and back were not oppressing her. "Slow down, slow down," she said a few times to herself. But not too loudly. She was increasingly annoyed and tired, but beyond all that she understood why Marta seemed so selfish and distracted. She had been raped. She was weighed down with twenty panniers of fear. The fattest man in Judea was sitting on her back. Of course she'd want to break away from him.

Miri could have stopped and rested had she wanted to. She could have found some block of shade and waited for her husband. Then she could have walked at his slow pace and made Marta wait alone for them at the summit of the landfall where the scrub collapsed into a steep ravine of scree. But Miri wanted time alone with Marta. She wanted to recapture, if it were possible, the cheerful times when they had worked together on the loom. The landfall was the final opportunity for them to finish what they'd started. While her slow husband laboured like a swaying cart across the scrub, she and Marta could sit cross-legged, facing each other, with the purple and orange birth-mat stretched between them. They'd spread the still untied ends across their laps. They'd bunch the warps in fours and each complete the birth-mat with a hundred knots. They'd finalize their bold, unlikely friendship by tying it into the bold, unlikely wools.

So Miri did her best to keep her friend within sight. It didn't matter that her arms felt stretched and that her shoulders ached almost beyond endurance so long as she could still see Marta walking ahead of her. By early afternoon they had crossed the plateau and were waiting side by side, at last, at the summit of the landfall as Musa had instructed. Below them, Shim and Aphas had already begun the descent. They could see Shim's blond head and hear the tumbling scree as he slid through the stones. Aphas was a little way behind, using all the larger rocks to steady himself but moving quickly for a man who'd been so faltering and ill. They were not carrying their loads.

"Look there," said Marta, pointing to a ledge of rocks a few steps from the summit of the scree. There were Musa's saddle-packs, the rugs and bedding, the sack of grain, the two bags of utensils. The men had simply dumped them there and fled.

Miri dropped her bags and panniers where she stood and stretched her arms and shoulders to relieve the pain, and drank a little water from the bag. It was too warm to be refreshing. Now she had an extra worry. Her husband would be furious when he discovered how his porters had betrayed him. Who'd pay for that? Who'd have to add the saddle-packs, the rugs and bedding, the sack of grain, the two bags of utensils to her load? His wife, of course. But she kept her worries hidden. She couldn't bring herself to speak to Marta yet. She did roll out the birth-mat, though. She sat with one end on her lap, as she had planned, and began to bunch and tie the threads. She'd see if Marta volunteered to help without asking. She'd not forgive her otherwise. But Marta did not volunteer to help. She stood and looked out across the valley to the peaks of Moab. Her lip, in profile, was still fat and misshapen. Her hands were trembling.

"Come on," said Miri. "Sit down with me. Let's finish this. Before he comes."

They had not finished it when Musa finally came into view. He waved Shim's staff at them from the sloping plateau which led down to the landfall, and called, "Wait there." He was tired of his own company. He hadn't spent so much time alone and without assistance for years. The journey so far had been unnerving and exhausting. His ankles ached. His chest was tight. He had to pause after every few steps to catch his breath. He'd not been born for walking. Just one more day, and he'd be back with camels where he belonged. Only the landfall stood between him and the markets of Jericho.

It would be difficult to go down the landfall. He knew how treacherous the scree could be for anyone as large as him. He had already pictured how stones would fall out beneath his feet and slide away, how larger rocks would tumble at him from above. He'd need the women to take him by the elbows and help him down. Marta would refuse, of course. She would not want to touch him.

"I need more help than you," he'd say to Miri. He'd lift his chins at Marta. "She has to help as well. Come here."

"I won't."

He pictured ways of making her.

But when he was just a few hundred paces from the women, so close that he could see the colours of the mat, Marta suddenly stood up, wrapped her fingers round Miri's wrist and pulled her to her feet.

"We have to go," she said. "Don't look at him. Bring that." She pushed the mat into Miri's hands. "We'll finish it another day. Get water."

Miri grabbed one of the water-bags — not a moment of bewilderment or hesitation — and began to gather the other panniers and her own belongings.

"Leave those." Marta pushed the panniers away, and added Musa's clothes and wools, the sack of dried fruit and the woven bag of odds-and-ends to the pile. They'd have to leave it all behind. She pulled the other water-bag to the edge of the descent and threw it down as far as she could on to the rocks. "Let's see how he manages," she said.

With only the smaller water-bag and the birth-mat to carry, the women were able to move quickly. They did not have the time to laugh or cry, or answer any of Musa's threats and promises. He was too close and dangerous. He was throwing stones at them. They would not stop their hurtling descent until their landlord and their husband and the father of their child was out of hearing and out of sight. They were light-limbed like adolescent girls. They had no need of anybody now. They had no need of miracles.

Marta and Miri hurried on in silence down the landfall, concentrating on the loose rock and the uncertain footing. The scree grew softer as the temperatures increased, closer to the valley floor. The earth was gypsum, spiced with salt. It smelt of eggs. But by the middle of the afternoon — already covered in a yellow film of salt — they'd reached more gently sloping and more sweetly smelling ground, a landscape of soft chalk which a child could pull apart in its hands as easily as breaking bread. The land was more reliable, at last, and they could walk side by side down towards the trading road, where travellers and caravans and soldiers were going to and coming from the gated cities of Judea. They walked amongst the donkeys and the men, and only then could exchange their tears and smiles.

"Where can we go?" said Miri.

"To Sawiya."

"What will you say to them?"

"I'll say you are a widow, abandoned in the wilderness. I'll say your husband was a merchant who died of fever. I'll say the wind took all your things away and that it was my duty to offer help to you, because you're pregnant and you have no one."

"It's almost true.

"It's true."

"How will I live?"

"You'll weave. I'll be the baby's aunt."

Marta's lip was still a little sore, her body ached, but she felt untroubled for the first time in ten years. All the bad things in her life had been abandoned at the top of the landfall. The vultures picked them clean. Was she a foolish optimist, made rash and heady by their escape from Musa? Most probably. But, for the moment, she was sure her fortunes had reversed. She'd started running down the scree and everything had changed. Everything outside of her. Everything within. She felt she was not barren any more. She'd heard it said that women knew instinctively when they were pregnant, almost from the moment of conception. They didn't have to wait for periods or pains. Their faces tingled, as if their cheeks had been touched by angels.

With Miri at her side, Marta felt as if she'd already plucked a star out of the sky. One more would not be difficult. Perhaps another star was already brightening inside of her. It didn't matter whose it was, if it was Musa's or the scrub's or even granted to her in a dream, by the Gally with his single touch. Her husband, Thaniel, wouldn't know or care so long as she grew fat. He'd said that she should go away and pray for miracles. She'd been obedient. He had commanded that she should give birth. And now he could rejoice with her.

It was bad luck to look behind. They concentrated only on the way ahead. Even when they saw the thin, blond head of Shim in front of them, and spotted Aphas walking with a new authority beside him, seeming younger than he had and vigorous, they did not call out a greeting. They kept themselves entirely to themselves, as they had planned to do. Two women with the fleshly scriptures of at least one pregnancy imprinted on to them. Two women blessed with god and child. They walked until the evening closed in. It did not matter where they spent the night. They were back in the world of the sane and would be safe. Only their faces ached, from smiling.

In the morning, they would carry on along the valley towards Jericho and then take the hilly route through Almog. Green hills. In two days they would reach the approaches to Jerusalem and skirt around the city, through the mud-faced houses on the mud-faced hills, towards Sawiya. They'd join Marta's neighbours, raising voices, raising sheep, competing for the shade beneath the fig trees in their yards, fighting for their places by the fire. The uneventful world of villages.

They'd be in Sawiya before the end of quarantine. Quite soon, they'd share a table in a room, colourless except for candle flame and the orange and the purple of their mat. They would be dining well on fish. It would be still, the stillness of the small and tired. If there was something in the world that was bigger, stronger than their table-top, they would not care. It had not spoken to them yet. They were not listening. They were contented with their grainy universe of candlelight and wood and wool.

CHAPTER
THIRTY-ONE

Musa did not waste his energy. He could not vent his anger on the scree. He rested for a while to catch his breath, then gathered his possessions in a pile, the goods abandoned by the men, the goods abandoned by the woman and his wife, the wools, the bedding, all the fabrics of their life. He could not leave them on display for anyone to help themselves. He'd rather have another fire. But there were huge rocks a little lower down the landfall where he could hide his merchandise. He didn't have to carry anything. He only had to let it slip and roll, and then push the goods into a crevice. When he left, he'd block it off with stones. He could come back, or send someone, to claim his property at any time, so long as the scree did not give way and claim his treasures for itself.

The water-bag which Marta had thrown down the scree was too far out to reach, beyond his climbing skills. He had no water, then. He'd be a fool to try to carry on in the heat of the afternoon. The sun would finish him. Certainly he could not attempt to give chase to the women. Instead, he sat beneath the crevice of the rock with his possessions at his back, hiding in the shade. When the sun went down, he wrapped himself in bedding clothes and sat, cursing his misfortune, not getting any sleep. He'd never known a longer night.

In the morning, as soon as there was any light, but before the sun had any strength to it, Musa forced himself to stand and resume his descent to the valley. He only carried the blond man's staff. He hid the perfume bottles, the gold, the coins and the jewellery in his underclothes. He pushed the ornamented knife into his sash. He was surprised how even-tempered he was feeling. He'd been restored by a night of cursing. Now he only saw one challenge in his life. If he could safely get down to the bottom of the landfall, then what could stop him getting into Jericho, and who could stop him there from trading up his bad luck into good? Who'd dare?

His wife and child were far ahead. He couldn't catch them now. He wouldn't try. He was divorced from her. He'd look for someone else to pull him to his feet and wash his back in Jericho. Some woman with a little flesh. The very thought of it relieved him of his anger. He made slow progress down the scree, leaning on his staff for ten steps at a time, and then resting until he grew too stiff to rest. He stopped before midday and once again took refuge in the shade. This time he slept, his head on shale. It left its imprint on his face. There were a few thin clouds that day to screen the sun, so Musa could continue his descent in the afternoon without the opposition of the heat. He finally reached the trading route late in the day, and took his place amongst the stragglers who would have to fight for places at the single inn on the approaches to the town.

Musa was alarmingly tired, and even a little lame. He walked more slowly than the other travellers, all younger, smaller men, loaded down with bags or dragging their possessions on wooden sleds. But one or two dropped back to talk to him. One offered him some water from his bag. Who could he be, this grand, impressive man, with his covering of dust and scratches, his wondrous curling staff, his ornamented knife, and nothing on his back to mark him out as a trader or a proper traveller? He looked like some king-prophet come down from the hills, like Moses, with his prescriptions for the world.

They were amazed at all the stories he could tell. He'd come from forty days of quarantine up in the wilderness. He hadn't drunk or eaten anything. He'd gone up thin and come back fat, thanks to god's good offices. He'd shared his cave with angels and messiahs; he'd met a healer and a man who could make bread from stones. His staff had come to him one night, a dangerous snake which wrapped itself around his arm and turned to wood. They could hold it, for a coin. One touch of his staff would protect them against all snakes. He had, he said, some phials of holy medicine. A sniff of each, and all their illnesses would be cured and all their troubles would be halved. He would not charge them very much, as they were friends and comrades on the road. "Come to me at the inn tonight," he said. "And you will see."

One of the travellers gave Musa food to eat. Another let him ride inside his donkey cart. He sat on bales of scrub hay, his fat legs hanging off the back. What little sun there was came from the summit of the precipice.

Musa looked up to the scree, shading his eyes against the light, and checked the spot where he had left his wordly goods. He was alarmed for an instant. There was somebody climbing down towards his hiding place, half hidden in the shade. A man or woman? Musa was not sure. Whoever it was did not stop to search amongst the rocks, but hurried down across a patch of silvery shale. Now Musa had a clearer view; a thin and halting figure tacking the scree, almost a mirage — ankleless, no arms — in the lifting light.

Musa shouted to his new companions. "Look there," he said. "That's one I mentioned to you. The healer. Risen from the grave." But they were not sure that they could make out anyone. The shapes they saw could be mistaken for disturbances of wind, and shadows shaking in the breeze. But Musa was now almost certain what he was looking at. It was his little Gally, coming down from death and god to start his ministry. He recognized the weight and step of him.

Musa wondered if he ought to ask the cart-owner to leave him at the roadside to wait for Gally. But Musa was afraid of being wrong. What if he waited and the man did not appear? What if he waited and the man was some thin figure with another face? What if the man were what they said, a shadow shaking in the breeze? Musa pushed the very thought away. He would not wait, he persuaded himself, because it was not sensible to wait. There were practicalities to bear in mind. The cart was not the choice of emperors but it was comfortable enough, and preferable to walking. The Galilean might be a healer and the lord of miracles, but he was not a cart. No, Musa had to persevere. He'd go ahead until he reached the inn, and then he could pay for two places for the night, if there were any places left. One for himself and one for Gally. "Show me how to turn stones into bread," he'd say, "and we'll go into business. I'll make you richer than Tiberius." They'd make a deal, and shake some empty cups on it.

And if he did not come into the inn? Then Musa would not be disappointed. Life was long. He could expect to meet the man in Jericho, among the palms, beneath the henna blossoms. Or in Jerusalem. Or Rome. Or in the land behind the middleman, the hill behind the hills, the village that you reached when all the villages had ended, where blue was silver and the air was heavier than smoke.

In the meantime, this would be his merchandise, something finer and less burdensome than even colour, sound or smell. No need for camel panniers or porters or cousins. He'd trade the word. There was a man who had defeated death with just his fingertips. "I am the living proof." He'd travel to the markets of the world. He'd preach the good news. That would be easy. Musa had the skills. He had been blessed with this one gift. He could tell tales. "He came into my tent," he'd say. "He touched me here, and here. 'Be well,' he told me. And I am well. And I have never been so well. Step forward. Touch me. Feel how well I am."

Musa looked towards the distant scree again. He told himself this was no merchant fantasy. His Gally was no longer thin and watery, diluted by the mirage heat, distorted by the ripples in the air. He made his slow, painstaking way, naked and barefooted, down the scree, his feet blood-red from wounds, and as he came closer to the valley floor his outline hardened and his body put on flesh.

Musa raised an arm in greeting, but there was no response.

The Gally's eyesight was still weak, he'd say. The man would have seen the rocks at his feet, perhaps. But not the distant valley or the hills. And so he could not spot his landlord riding there. Nor could he contemplate the endless movements on the trading road, the floods, the rifts, the troops, the ever-caravans, the evening peace that's brokered not by a god but by the rocks and clays themselves, *shalom, salaam*, the one-time, all-time truces of the land.